THE BYRNE BROTHERS

SILENT VOWS

JILL RAMSOWER

Silent Vows is a work of fiction. Names, characters, places, and incidents are the products of the author's imagination or are used fictitiously. Any resemblance to actual events, locales, or persons, living or dead, is entirely coincidental.

Edited by Editing4Indies

❀ Created with Vellum

Books by Jill Ramsower

The Byrne Brothers Series

Silent Vows

Secret Sin (Novella)

Corrupted Union

Ruthless Salvation

Vicious Seduction

The Five Families Series

Forever Lies

Never Truth

Blood Always

Where Loyalties Lie

Impossible Odds

Absolute Silence

Perfect Enemies

The Savage Pride Duet

Savage Pride

Silent Prejudice

The Of Myth & Man Series

Curse & Craving

Venom & Vice

Blood & Breath

Siege & Seduction

SILENT VOWS

JILL RAMSOWER

Noemi

ONE

Some events in life are so transformative, they can leave a person speechless. When my father had my mother killed six months ago, words completely escaped me. Nothing I could say would help me understand or keep me from being in danger, so I chose not to say anything at all.

For the past six months, I hadn't spoken a single word.

Not to my brother or my best friend. Not even alone in the dark.

I hadn't made a sound since I'd woken up in the hospital after the car wreck that had taken my mother's life. At first, I was in a state of shock while processing what had happened and trying to comprehend the magnitude of my loss—my mother and father gone in the blink of an eye.

Dad might not have been in that car, but he was dead to me all the same.

He'd orchestrated the accident that had stolen the best part of my world from me. My mother. My heart. Without her, a gaping hole had been carved from my soul.

In the midst of my crippling sorrow, fear and fury simmered to life beneath my surface. All of it was directed at one man. The same man who should have been my solace and sanctuary. I became so furious with my father that I feared what I might say. That he'd hear the accusation and frustration coating my words and figure out I knew the truth.

So I didn't dare open my mouth.

The bruising across my neck from the seat belt and doctors speculating about possible trauma gave me the perfect excuse. My father was only too happy to accept my silence. He had whisked me back home to a life I no longer recognized. A life under virtual lock and key.

Days turned into weeks turned into months.

The one time each day I could be alone beyond the walls of my father's home was during my morning coffee run. Each morning, I was allowed to go get coffee—with supervision, of course. Umberto, the goon assigned to keep tabs on me, had quit following me inside after the first couple of months on my daily errand. He stood outside on his phone while I sat at a table with my breakfast and contemplated how to escape the clutches of a mafia life I now hated.

I would have run away if things had been that simple, but they never were. The issue was my younger brother. I couldn't leave him behind, but getting him to come with me would be a challenge. He idolized my father. Always had. Even if Dad allowed us to be alone together unobserved, convincing Sante would be a monumental task. The dilemma plagued me every single day. I'd been biding my time for the right opportunity, but after six months of constant supervision, I was growing more worried by the day that my chance would never come.

"Hey, Noemi. The usual?" The kind older gentleman behind the counter waved when I entered. The morning crew at the coffee shop all knew me by name, though I never talked to them. I'd only had to write out the explanation for my silence once, which was a relief. They'd been very understanding and did all the talking for me.

I smiled and nodded. After paying at the counter, I took a seat as far from the door as I could get and took out my current read. My phone was monitored, so I rarely used it, even to quell boredom. I'd never been a big reader before, but lately, it had become my favorite escape. I was only a few pages into a chapter when a masculine voice spoke behind me.

"You shouldn't keep such an obvious routine. Hasn't anyone ever told you that?"

I couldn't see him but knew the comment was directed at me. While the nature of his observation should have alarmed me, it was the seductive way his deep voice feathered across the back of my neck that made my spine stiffen.

Slowly, I turned to peer at the man who sat behind me and tried to remember how to breathe when my gaze collided with the bluest eyes I'd ever seen. A deep blue so radiant it hypnotized like those fish down at the bottom of the ocean that dangled brilliant lights to distract their prey before swallowing them whole. Even the shadow cast by his prominent brow couldn't dull the richness of color.

A full twenty seconds passed before the meaning behind his words slashed through my stupor and yanked me back to rational thought.

How did he know I kept a routine?

I most certainly would have noticed if this man was a regular in the café. Even without his mesmerizing eyes, he wasn't the sort you could forget. Cloaked in an air of power and privilege, his presence demanded attention and respect. Maybe even fear. It was carved in the angular cut of his jaw and the commanding way he carried himself. He was a beautiful predator, and he'd been watching me. Why? For how long? And how had I never noticed?

Unnerved, I turned back around and decided to ignore him, unsure what else to do.

"But then again, maybe not so predictable."

My eyes snagged on the page. I should have known a man like him wouldn't accept rejection.

"Seems like every book I ever see in a woman's hands is a romance, setting unrealistic expectations of some perfect fairy-tale life in their heads. But that's not what you're reading, is it?"

My book was about murder. A mystery novel to help keep my mind occupied rather than dwelling on my problems. I liked romance as much as the next girl but needed something darker and more compelling. Something more relatable to the state of my life.

Unsure what else to do, I took out the notepad I kept with me at all times. I planned to jot a note explaining that I couldn't speak in the hopes that it would end our encounter, but other words materialize at my fingertips.

Is it so unrealistic to expect men to be decent human beings?

I couldn't believe I was engaging him, even as I shoved the pad toward him.

The confusion I expected him to show at my lack of verbal response never registered. Instead, I was met with a wolfish smirk.

"It's unrealistic to expect decency out of anyone, man or woman. In my experience, we're not so different from our prehistoric ancestors as we'd like to believe."

I raised a brow and scribbled my response.

Speak for yourself.

I couldn't help myself. Something about him tipped the scales of my control after months of perfect restraint.

Shadow dimmed the turquoise slivers in his eyes. "Believe me, I am. There is absolutely nothing civilized about me."

Shocked by the intensity of his response, I stared as he rose from his seat. Expecting him to leave, I was surprised yet again when he went to the counter to retrieve my coffee and bagel. I'd been so consumed with our exchange that I hadn't heard the barista call my name.

The stranger placed my food in front of me, lifting his thumb to his perfect lips and sucking at a dab of cream cheese while his cobalt stare pinned me to my seat.

"Enjoy your breakfast," he murmured before casually prowling away.

I was left utterly flabbergasted after one of the strangest encounters of my life. Aside from the odd topic of our brief conversation, he never batted an eye at my lack of verbal communication. As if he'd already known. But how? Did he know who I was?

I was suddenly kicking myself for not asking his name. My eyes returned to his retreating form as he passed through the café door, then reappeared outside the shop window. In an instant, Umberto was toe-to-toe with the man, challenging him with the same energy as an angry rhino.

Had Umberto seen the man talking to me? No, because if he had, he would have come in and confronted the man immediately. If not that, why was he so angry? My jailor had been distracted, and I'm sure that added to his irritability, but it was still unusual for him to be so confrontational.

My entire body tensed as I watched the two square off. Umberto was huge, but the stranger didn't seem remotely bothered. If I'd had to guess, I would have said defending himself against angry goons was an everyday occurrence. He was the picture of cool indifference, which only seemed to enrage Umberto even further.

My father's watchdog sneered as he spoke, lifting his hand to point a finger into the man's chest. Before he could make contact, and seemingly out of nowhere, the man's fists whipped out in a series of punches so vicious and lightning fast that Umberto dropped like a leaden weight to the ground. He didn't even get in a single strike.

The stranger spit onto his unconscious opponent, then instantly resumed an air of serene passivity as though the last ten seconds had never happened. He smoothed back his black wavy hair with a steady hand, turned, and pinned me with a breathtaking stare before disappearing down the sidewalk.

As if I needed another reason to hate the Mafia life I'd been born into.

Ruthless ambition and callous irreverence to anyone in their paths were innate qualities of all made men. I didn't know who the stranger was, but he was just as bad as the rest of them. Maybe worse.

There is absolutely nothing civilized about me.

I shivered at his remembered words, then hurried outside to check on my hapless bodyguard. Umberto was out cold on the New York City sidewalk. For the first time in six months, I had a rare opportunity to slip away and disappear into the city. I could run. Go to my cousin's and tell her everything.

And what about Sante? Where would that leave him?

Alone. Abandoned. I couldn't do it. There was no point in pretending running without him was even an option.

Taking a deep breath, I squatted down and patted Umberto's cheek, shaking him until he roused with a series of muttered curses.

"Fuckin' pikey. The fuck he go?" He glared up and down the street.

I ignored his question and helped him to his feet. He wiped at his bloody nose with the back of his sleeve, and I left him to gather my things back inside the shop. I abandoned my uneaten food and ignored the curious stares of everyone in the café. I hadn't been the only one to watch the scene unfold.

"Let's get the fuck out of here," he grumbled as soon as I returned outside. His voice was muffled, and I absently wondered if his nose had been broken. Not that it mattered to me. As one of my father's lackeys, he probably deserved far worse.

I followed him to the car, curious about the mysterious stranger and mildly disappointed that I'd been robbed of my coffee routine. At least the morning hadn't been boring, that was for certain.

"Jesus, Berto," my brother blurted when we returned home. "What the hell happened to you?" Sante looked me over to ensure I was unharmed before returning his attention to my bloody guard.

Umberto just grunted and stomped off toward the bathroom.

I took out my pad and explained.

Just a little altercation on the street.

Sante shook his head. "That guy never could back down. Such a hothead."

I smirked, finding it amusing that he thought himself so much more mature. At the ripe old age of seventeen, he was hardly the epitome of logic and sound decisions. In fact, since our mother had died, his volatile teen emotions had been even more prevalent. I hated to witness the changes in him—partially because he'd always been so sweet before but also because his struggles had magnified his desire to follow in my father's Mafia footsteps. He saw the power and prestige while being blinded to the uglier aspects of the job.

The Mafia twisted men into monsters. It drained all their humanity and left their souls hopelessly disfigured. I couldn't think of anything more horrendous than Sante being made. But he idolized our father and the Mafia. He didn't want to hear what I had to say. I would have told him the truth about what had happened right away if I thought he would believe me. If I thought it would save him.

I wanted to help my little brother, but I'd have to find another way. I hadn't made much progress solving that particular problem, but at least I'd convinced him not to drop out of school. I had argued via scribbled notes that Mom would have been heartbroken if he had left before graduating. He had reluctantly agreed to attend his senior year in another month when school started. It was a small win but a victory, nonetheless. And until I won the war, I would continue to fight my silent battle against my father's influence. It was what my mother would have wanted—what she would have done if he hadn't killed her.

Giving Sante a sad smile, I pointed up to indicate I was headed to my room and retreated upstairs. Once alone, I flopped onto my bed, lifting my hand to look at the book I was still holding. I studied a small tear in the hardback's jacket cover, though my mind was busy envisioning a pair of captivating blue eyes.

It was so typical that a man like him would scoff at the idea of romance. He probably doubted the existence of anything he hadn't experienced himself—like empathy and compassion. Such a bleak, narrow-minded view of the world. If it hadn't been for a spark of heat I sensed beneath his icy blue stare, I would have sworn the man was hopelessly detached from humanity.

A knock sounded at my door, startling me from my thoughts and causing me to drop my book. My father, Fausto Mancini, the most powerful capo in the Moretti family, stood in my doorway. For years, he was more of a name than an actual presence in my life. Mom and Sante and even our cook were more of a part of my life than he ever was. His absence left me struggling with feelings of abandonment and hurt when I was younger. Now that I'd had six months of his tyrannical attention, I thanked God that my father had ignored my existence for as long as he had.

"I have to be out of town for the next two days. I don't want to hear that you've stepped one toe out of line." His corrosive voice hung in the air around me like a noxious gas, poisoning my insides.

I hadn't had a day of reprieve from his sinister presence since I left the hospital. The thought of two days away from him made my heart flutter with anticipation.

He must have sensed my response because the corners of his eyes tightened. "Don't try me, Noemi. Bad things happen to people who defy me." He stepped closer into my room. "I think you know that, don't you?" He studied me, and I tried to regulate my breathing, though my lungs seized at his insinuation. It was the first time he'd ever indicated he suspected that I knew the truth. Why now? Because he was leaving town and wanted to ensure I behaved?

"I've seen the way you look at me," he continued. "You don't have to say a word for me to read your thoughts." His deep mahogany eyes dropped to his hands as he casually assessed the state of his manicured fingers. "Two days. I'll be watching." He gave me one last glare before walking away.

His not-so-veiled threat was unnecessary because he was right. I knew exactly what he'd done, and I was plenty terrified of him already. If he thought there was any chance I'd tell someone what he'd done, he'd kill me in a heartbeat.

I couldn't fathom what my mother had ever seen in him. Had he always been so heartless? Was it possible for someone to start out as sweet as my brother and be transformed into something so cruel?

My stomach clenched tight at the possibility.

It would break my heart to sit by and watch Sante morph into something unrecognizable.

They aren't all so bad as Dad.

True. Uncle Gino was decent enough. He seemed to care about Aunt Etta, Mom's twin sister. But if he was faced with choosing his wife or his ambitions, which would come out on top? I wasn't sure, and that spoke volumes. The answer was no clearer for any of the family men I'd grown up knowing. Sure, they were friendly enough at gatherings, but they could also be frighteningly cold.

I wasn't willing to bet my life on the outcome of that question. I wanted no part of the mafia world.

I didn't have my own money or an obvious way out, but I wouldn't give up. An opportunity would present itself, and I'd be ready when it did.

One Week Earlier

"YOU KNOW WE WON'T QUIT UNTIL EVERY LAST ONE OF THEM stops breathing." I held tightly to Aunt Fiona as the last of the family filtered to their cars after saying their final goodbyes to Uncle Brody. Only the immediate Byrne family remained, which was still about three dozen of us. Hundreds had turned out for the funeral. Even my grandparents had been driven the hour outside the city for their son's burial, though they rarely left their house anymore.

My uncle's widow shook with muffled sobs. It made me want to light the entire city on fire.

The Albanians had put five rounds into Brody's chest

outside one of our clubs. We'd immediately gone after them and struck back, taking down a half dozen of their men, but those fuckers were like cockroaches. We hadn't seen the last of them.

"Come on, Ma. Let's get you home." Oran, the eldest of Fiona and Brody's kids, took his mother into his side and gave me a grim nod of thanks before leading her to their car.

As I watched them walk away, my uncle Jimmy came to stand at my side. While the three Byrne brothers and my father had jointly brought our organization back from obscurity, Jimmy was the unspoken leader. He was also my godfather and the man I aspired to be. I respected and loved my dad, but Jimmy had an untouchable quality to him. The world quieted in his presence. As a kid, I studied everything about him. Now that I was grown, I spent every day striving to earn his respect.

"This never would have happened fifty years ago." He clapped a hand on my shoulder. "Back in the day, when the Irish owned Hell's Kitchen, no one would dare fuck with us."

"I wasn't around then, but I've seen what you've been able to create in the last ten years alone. We're close to regaining the power Paddy and the others knew back then, thanks to you."

"We're getting there, but the other organizations still think we're weak. That's the only reason they came after us. They'd never dare move on the Italians or Russians." Jimmy began to slowly stroll toward the street with me beside him. "What does that say about us? It says they think we're vulnerable. A target." He paused and stood silent for several beats. When he spoke again, his voice was the low rumble of distant thunder. "Things have to change."

I met his steely gray stare with unwavering confidence. "You tell me what's needed, and I'll do it."

Chin lowering a fraction in approval, he continued walking. "Tell me, how did your dinner go with the Italians? I never got the chance to ask with everything that's happened."

The same night my uncle was gunned down, I'd been off at Jimmy's request to meet my birth mother for the first time. Not only was she fucking Italian but she was also a goddamn Genovese—wife of the Lucciano family consigliere, Edoardo Genovese. I'd been having dinner like the fucking Brady Bunch while Uncle Brody was bleeding out on the sidewalk. I was pissed I hadn't been there to help him, but Uncle Jimmy had been insistent about me going to meet my birth mother. I had no interest in bonding with the woman who had given me away. But from the minute the adoption agency had contacted us to say that Mia Genovese was interested in meeting her son, Jimmy swore it was fate. The start of a new era in which the Irish and Italians were allied.

I was skeptical.

But as I'd said, I trusted Jimmy and was prepared to do what he asked of me.

"It went as well as could be expected. Edoardo Genovese knew from my choice of restaurants that I was connected to you, and he still showed up." The dinner hadn't been as terribly awkward as I'd envisioned. I still didn't plan on extensive bonding with my birth mother's family, though my half sisters were surprisingly entertaining.

"I'd say that's a good sign."

"Sign of what exactly?" I asked, a niggling sense of unease tensing my shoulders.

Jimmy stopped again, this time pinning me with his impenetrable stare. "I know how you feel about your past, Conner. It's understandable. But you're rooted in our family now. Ties with the Italians won't change that."

Logically, I knew he was right. But aside from being adopted, I wasn't even a Byrne in name. My adopted mother was the only sister of the Byrne brothers. Her married name was Reid, which only served to separate me further in my mind's eye. I doubted the others would have agreed if I'd voiced my feelings, but their thoughts on the subject didn't change the way I felt. I had already spent my life defending my right to sit alongside my cousins. Highlighting my newly discovered Italian heritage only made things worse.

"I hear what you're telling me. Doesn't mean I want to hang out with them."

His features hardened. "It might be time you work on your perspective, son. We've been handed a golden opportunity. A way to ally ourselves with the most powerful families in the city. Think of what that would mean for us."

This time, I was the one to stop and stare. "What exactly are you getting at?"

His chin lifted and chest expanded before he spoke the words that would change my life forever.

"A marriage. The Italians and Irish bonded by holy matrimony."

I might as well have been sucker punched in the gut. His statement winded me, tilting the world on its axis.

"You want … me … to *marry* … an Italian?" I asked, struggling to even say the words.

"I know it's not ideal, Conner, but I can't think of any other circumstances that would present this unique opportunity. An alliance like that could cinch our place in this city and be crucial to our survival. Think about it. What happens if the other bottom feeders see what the Albanians have been able to do and decide they want to come after us? We don't have the resources to fight them all off, but with the Italians at our side…" He didn't have to continue for me to know how vastly different our circumstances would be. While we were one family, the Italians had the power to join their five ruling families against any common enemy. It made them nearly unstoppable.

An alliance like that would be monumental for us, and I was an essential component. It should have made me enormously proud, but I couldn't stop the whispers in the back of my mind that my Irish family was just trying to get rid of me. Not fully one or the other, I didn't fit in anywhere.

Stop your fucking whining and grow up. Who cares if you like the idea?

What Jimmy said was true, and I knew it. This could be huge, and I should be honored to help my family in any way I could. Debating about my feelings was pointless anyway because when it came down to it, I knew I'd do whatever Uncle Jimmy asked of me.

"Tell me what you want me to do."

Three days later, we sat down to lunch with Edoardo Genovese and his brother Enzo, who was the boss of the Lucciano family and the head of the Italian Commission. Jimmy had spoken to them after the funeral, and to my astonishment, they'd agreed to consider our proposal. I hadn't expected much to come of his idea. What incentive could the Italians possibly have to enter such an arrangement? Yet they got back to us a day later and asked for a meeting. I was still struggling to grasp the implications.

"Gentlemen," Jimmy greeted when they joined us. "We're honored to have you at our table. I wasn't sure how our proposal would be received, so today is a very pleasant surprise. Edoardo, I know you've met my nephew, Conner, but I'm not sure Enzo has been introduced."

I stood and shook hands with both Genovese men. "It's a pleasure."

Enzo nodded. "You've given my sister-in-law such peace by agreeing to meet with her. I know it couldn't have been easy for you. I won't forget what you've done for her. As for lunch today, we're always pleased to sit down with honorable men such as yourselves."

"You're willing to meet with us," Jimmy pointed out somewhat coyly. "But does that mean you're actually entertaining the arrangement I've proposed?"

Enzo held back his response until after the server had taken our orders. We'd chosen an independent restaurant in neutral territory to ensure we were all on equal footing, but that meant being cautious about what was said near outsiders.

"We are, in fact, very interested in your proposal. We've done our best to keep it quiet, so you may or may not have heard, but the Sonora Cartel has recently given us trouble in the city."

Jimmy and I exchanged a surprised glance. We'd heard nothing about the cartels advancing into the East Coast but could only imagine the chaos that might ignite.

Enzo continued. "We dealt with the gentlemen giving us the most problems, but there is no guarantee that whoever comes to power next won't continue the charge into our city. Edoardo and I have talked it over and decided a broader network of associates could only benefit us. In addition"—his gaze locked with mine—"we want Conner to know that he has family on both sides of this table."

Well, I'll be damned.

I hadn't expected that. Italians were notorious for their strict delineation between Italians and outsiders. I was illegitimate with no clue who my father was and raised among the Irish, so the last thing I had expected was for the Genoveses to call me one of their own. My birth mother wanting to meet me was entirely different from these men accepting me into the family.

"You do me a great honor," I forced past my shock.

Enzo smiled. "Well, then. If we're all agreed, let's talk particulars. "I've spoken to the other bosses and compiled a short list of possible matches for you to consider. We only included women of respectable rank and suitable situation." He gestured to his brother, who extracted several sheets of paper from a leather portfolio and handed them to me.

My stomach clenched as reality set in that this outlandish idea was actually moving forward. A part of me had been certain nothing would come of our lunch, so I hadn't worried about the outcome. My gut churned as I scanned through grainy color photographs printed on standard printer paper. Next to each was a list of background and basic information. I felt like I was picking out a used car, not a bride.

Was I actually considering this? Would I bind myself to some Italian Mafia princess I'd never even met?

Jesus Christ.

I scanned each page with unseeing eyes, too busy keeping myself calm to register the faces before me until the very last page. I paused to take in the striking image of a young woman peering over her shoulder at the camera. All the women had been attractive, but something about this one captured my attention. I couldn't say exactly why. It was an intangible quality. The piercing way she looked at the camera as though she could see right through it.

"You'll want to take that last one out of contention," Edoardo offered. "She never should have been in the pile."

"She in a relationship or something?" I asked.

"No, she was in a car accident six months ago. Her mother was killed in the wreck, and Noemi's vocal cords were damaged. She's mute and, from what I hear, pretty traumatized. No clue why her father nominated her. She's hardly been seen outside of her house since it happened."

Mute. Now *that* was even more intriguing. The sheet

listed her age at twenty, a full eight years younger than me—a sizable gap but not insurmountable.

"She scarred or have other physical damage?"

"Not that I know of," Edoardo mused.

Just how traumatized was this girl? I wasn't interested in taking on drama, but the prospect of a silent wife bore merit. I could lead my life as I wanted without nagging or disruption and allow her to do the same. For the first time since Jimmy had uttered the word alliance, I began to see hope.

"I want to know more," I murmured, eyes still glued to the page.

"Is that really what you want?" Enzo asked in a wary tone.

I lay down the pages and leveled him with an even stare. "I won't know until I meet her, but she's a beautiful woman, and something tells me we might work well together. If her father has consented, and she's volunteered herself, I see no problem pursuing the match."

"Very well." Enzo dropped his chin in a subtle bow. "I'll have more information to you by the end of the day."

I took my freshly filled wineglass in hand and held it aloft. "To a lasting alliance, gentlemen, and a new era of prosperity."

And to Noemi Mancini, prepare yourself. Life as you know it is about to change.

Present

He took Sante with him when he left town. A part of me had hoped he wouldn't, and I'd have a chance to talk to Sante alone and finally start the process of escaping with my brother. Dad would never have made things so easy for me. It had been idiotic to even entertain the scenario.

Instead, I used my father's two-day absence to enjoy a rare reprieve from his watchful eye. Umberto was still a stone's throw away, but that wasn't the same as having the man himself breathing down my neck. I watched movies, listened to music, and daydreamed about getting on a boat with Sante and watching the New York skyline disappear in the distance.

Escaping would have been ideal, but two days alone was a close second.

The end of my respite came in the form of a text from my father informing me not to be late for dinner. I wasn't sure why he felt the need to remind me. Ever since Mom's death, he'd insisted we eat together each evening at seven sharp. I hadn't been late once.

Just another flex to remind me of the power he holds over me.

I heaved a heavy sigh and tossed my phone onto the bed.

You've got this, Em. The more obedient you are, the more he'll trust you, and the easier it will be to get far away from here.

Two hours later, I emerged from my room and plodded downstairs. I smiled at Sante when I saw him seated at the table along with our father, who launched to his feet at the sight of me.

"What the hell are you wearing?" He sneered. "You look like a fucking urchin. Go put on something respectable."

The second he stood, fear cleaved my feet to the ground, holding me motionless. I glanced down at the stretchy pencil skirt and oversized cotton blouse I'd put on for dinner. The look was casual but far from hobo. Dad had never cared in the slightest what I'd worn to dinner, so I had no idea what had gotten into him.

When I lifted my gaze, Sante peered at me apologetically but kept his lips sealed.

"Sante, go check in with Umberto and make sure he keeps a cool head tonight." His voice dropped to a menacing growl as he crept around the table toward me.

I fought back waves of betrayal as I watched Sante disappear down the hall.

Then it was just my dad and me. Alone.

I wasn't sure what was going on, but alarm bells were

screaming inside my head. A cold, sticky dread clogged my veins and sent my pulse racing.

"There's been an offer for your hand. An important alliance."

For my hand? As in … marriage? What the hell is he talking about?

He continued to push closer until he had my back pressed against the wall. "You will not fuck this up for me." His hand cupped my throat, his thumb coarsely drifting back and forth over my windpipe. "You *will* agree to this union, but I want you to understand that your departure from this house does not keep you from my reach. If you spread a single word about whatever it is you think you know, there won't be a rock you can hide under where I won't find you." His hand tightened—not hard enough to bruise, just enough to crystalize my blood into ice at the threat of my thinning airway.

I kept as still as possible, pleading with my body to cooperate.

"I'll know it was you. You don't have to speak to be a rat," he growled.

My nostrils flared as spots dotted the edge of my vision. I finally caved and grasped his wrist, unable to overcome the clawing desperation.

His beady black eyes bore deep into my soul a second longer before he finally released me, though he remained rooted to the spot, a malignant invasion of my space. "His name is Conner Reid. He's Irish, and he'll be here any minute. Now go up and put on something presentable before you embarrass me."

I nodded, slipping along the wall and away from my father before rushing back to the safety of my bedroom.

Holy shit, what just happened?

My legs shook more with each step I took.

Closing my bedroom door, I leaned against it and tried to

slow my racing heart before it exploded from my chest. I had to think clearly. Dad had agreed to marry me off to someone as part of an alliance. I was going to be married.

Holy shit!

The guy's name was Conner Reid. The name was vaguely familiar. I'd never concerned myself with my father's dealings, but it was impossible to ignore bits and pieces.

Think, Em. Think!

This Reid guy had asked to marry me as a part of an alliance. He's Irish, so the Italians want to form an alliance with the Irish. But why me? Of all the other Italian women available, how the hell had my name even come up?

The desperation in my father's eyes flashed in my mind.

Of course, this was his fault. Having his daughter at the heart of a critical alliance would be huge for him, and he wouldn't think twice about selling me off like cattle. So what did that mean for me? Instead of escaping the mafia, I would be permanently married to the Irish mob. Not the fate I'd wanted, but it would get me away from my father. It was a possible solution, at least, in the short term. Though, once I was out of the house, I wasn't sure how much access I'd get to Sante. And if this guy was just as bad as my father, maybe I'd end up worse than I'd started.

Panic coated my palms in sweat and sent my heart rate clamoring.

I couldn't tell if this was the chance I'd been hoping for or a total disaster. My thoughts were all over the place, my emotions a mess. Salty despair pooled on my lashes, and each breath I took grew more shallow and stilted.

I had to calm down.

Dad would be furious if I went to dinner blotchy and red-eyed. I forced my lungs to take in a long, deep breath, then slowly released it.

See what you can learn while you get changed. Try not to overreact.

I nodded to myself and grabbed my phone from the bed. Dad monitored the device, but I needed to know what I was getting myself into, and there was one sure way to find out. Pippa was my cousin and best friend. She was also a horrific gossip and busybody. I adored her and missed her dearly. My father had kept us apart, and I'd been forced to play the grieving daughter card to explain my absence. Pip had been understanding, though I could sense her patience was coming to an end.

She would have answers for me, and I didn't think my father would care if I asked about the Irishman. In the past, he'd never paid me any mind at all. The only thing he cared about now was that I kept my mouth shut about my mother's *accident*.

Me: Who is Conner Reid?

Pippa: Hello, random.

Me: Don't have time. I need details, now!

Pippa: Shit, now you got me worried. I think he's one of the Irish thugs—runs a gambling club, I think. Let me check. Brb

I threw the phone on my bed and rummaged through my closet.

What was I supposed to wear to meet my potential fiancé? Did I want to look good or scare him away? What would my father do if I chose the latter?

A chill skated down my spine and settled into a solid arctic mass in my gut.

I definitely didn't want to find out the answer to that question. Anything sexy was off the table. I was already being pimped out; I didn't want to look any cheaper than I already felt. Options limited, I chose a forest green sheath dress that bordered on professional, then freshened up my hair and makeup just in time for my phone to ding.

Pippa: Remember a while back when a man was found in East Harlem burned alive?

Me: Yeah?

Pippa: Rumor was Reid was behind it. Thought I remembered the name. Why the hell are you asking?

Oh shit.

Newscasters had called it the most grizzly murder in decades. No one had ever been charged with the crime, but it had been all over the television for weeks. I had still been reeling over my own mother's death and hadn't paid much attention to what had happened. Now, I wished I had.

Me: He may be my new fiancé.

I knew she would be rabid for more details, but I didn't have time. The doorbell had already chimed in the distance.

Time to see what my fate held in store.

I took yet another deep breath and forced back a rancid bouquet of nausea from blossoming in my stomach. My heels clicking on the wood floors announced my approach. When I rounded the corner, all three men stood. My father. My brother. And the man from the coffee shop two days earlier.

My lungs seized, frozen with shock, and my legs refused to budge an inch.

Suddenly, the puzzle pieces began to slide into place.

That was how he'd known who I was. Why he didn't question my silence, and why Umberto had been furious to see him. The man was a deadly rival. A beautiful monster slated to be my new husband.

Dad began to give introductions, spurring me back into motion, but my ears were ringing too loudly to make out his words. I walked mechanically to the chair beside Conner, which he helped me into before seating himself. I stared straight ahead, unable to meet his eyes. Those mesmerizing cobalt eyes that had ensnared me the second I walked into the room.

This was the man I was going to marry.

The man who had beat Umberto into a bloody pulp in a few swift strikes. The man whose dominating persona had clung to me long after he'd left the room and who'd admitted outright that he wasn't remotely civilized.

What a beautiful disaster.

Him. My life. Our impending marriage.

I couldn't bear to think about any of it. Fortunately, my brain didn't seem to function around him anyway. His presence filled the room, pressing on the walls and chasing out the air, making it hard to breathe.

I'd never been more glad that no words were expected of me.

"It's a pleasure to meet you, Noemi. Can I get you some wine?" Conner asked coolly, as though this were his house, and I was the guest. I imagined he was at home anywhere he deigned to be because he deemed it so. His presence was so commanding that I wasn't sure the winds of a hurricane would dare stir a hair on his head for fear of his wrath.

I nodded.

My gaze snagged on the black ink staining the back of his left hand. I hadn't noticed it at the coffee shop. A rose. It extended up beneath the cuff of his expensive suit, and I couldn't help but wonder how much of the body beneath was similarly marked.

I sipped from my wine, suddenly parched.

Conner and my father launched into an easy conversation, leaving me to my thoughts. The difficulty of including me in a conversation made it understandable, especially considering men like these rarely included women in their affairs anyway.

I wondered, if this man knew I didn't speak, why had he

chosen me? Or was that the whole point? He liked the idea of a silent wife. Was I about to fall into the hands of a man even more oppressive than my father? What would happen if he found out after our marriage that I could speak? Would I have to stay silent forever to keep myself safe?

My heart leaped into an Olympic sprint, making my head spin.

Conner was speaking to my father, but I could only hear the hypnotic undertones of his deep voice because my ears were ringing so loudly. Then a firm hand slowly clamped down over my bouncing knee, forcing my body to stillness. My father couldn't see what was happening beneath the table, and Conner continued to speak as though the rough skin of his palm wasn't holding me captive, but every fiber of my being was focused on the place where our bodies touched.

Slowly, ever so slowly, his thumb traced back and forth over my knee.

Was he … comforting me? Not exactly. From him, the gesture felt more like he was commanding me to calm—a somewhat authoritarian gesture—but it worked, nonetheless.

My pulse eased back to a normal rate, erasing the threat of cardiac arrest. Finally, I took in a long, steady breath, filling my lungs with much-needed oxygen.

Then just as casually as it had appeared, his hand was gone—as though this type of communication was normal between us. As though I hadn't just met the man ten minutes before. I got the sense that time and space meant nothing to Conner Reid. He made the rules in his world, and the rest of us were meant to adjust accordingly.

Conner was just as imposing as my father, maybe even more so. What did that mean for me? A life of terror and pain? I wasn't so certain of that. For some inexplicable reason, his brand of domination didn't strike fear in me the same way my father did. Was I simply the hopeless romantic he'd accused me of being and letting his beauty blind me to the truth?

The uncertainty of my situation terrified me, but as for Conner, I wasn't so sure how I felt. He affected me profoundly—that I couldn't deny. So much so that it was hard to pinpoint exactly how I felt about him.

But he was my new fiancé, so I was bound to find out soon enough.

SHE WAS DIFFERENT AROUND HER FATHER THAN SHE'D BEEN AT the coffee shop. Or was she just acting different now that she knew who I was? It was impossible to say, but the change in her was obvious.

A week ago, she'd been bolder, even in her silence. I'd half expected a shell of a girl, fragile and grieving, when I first met her. Noemi wasn't remotely broken. I wasn't even sure how she'd been deemed traumatized, to begin with. It had only taken one brief interaction for me to know the loss she'd suffered wouldn't be a problem.

More than that, I'd felt an instant draw to know more about her. My curiosity was so great that it unnerved me.

After our brief exchange, a craving for more gnawed at my insides. It was so unsettling that I'd lost my temper with that asshole bodyguard of hers. I never should have hit the guy, but I was so on edge that I lashed out. Served him right for getting in my face.

I'd been a little worried afterward that my actions might cause her father to withdraw his consent, but that wasn't the case. I'd called Jimmy the minute I was back in my car and told him to move forward with the arrangements. By the end of the day, he'd confirmed that the deal was done.

From that moment on, I wondered what her reaction would be when she learned my identity. I knew she'd be surprised, but I hadn't expected her to be so shaken. Was it the shock of seeing me again that got to her or her father's presence that caused the tension?

Considering the fucking Italians and their tendency to be overprotective with their daughters, daddy issues shouldn't have come as a shock. Hell, maybe that was the reason she'd agreed to the marriage. A chance to get out from under his thumb.

I liked the idea of her silence, but seeing her stiff and unsettled grated on me. I found myself hoping she'd return to her feistier self once we were alone again. I shouldn't have. The whole point in choosing her had been to minimize the disruption to my life. That and her beauty. I'd have been lying if I said her stunning looks hadn't played a role in my choice. When she walked into the dining room in that dress hugging her sleek curves, something deep inside me stirred awake. Something primal and raw.

Her eyes were mossy green, and they sparked even more radiantly next to the green fabric of her dress. Her brown hair was straight and thick, falling just past her shoulders, and her sultry lips were a fucking wet dream.

On second thought, if I had a daughter like that under my roof, I might keep her under lock and key, too.

My hand had rested on her knee for no more than twenty seconds, yet I could still feel the silky texture of her skin against my fingers all through dinner. Twice, I'd had to grip my napkin to keep my fingers from wandering back to her for more.

Feeling her still beneath my touch would have been a hell of a lot more enjoyable than the mindless chatter I had to endure with her father. The asshole never once engaged her in the conversation, though he didn't seem to have the same reservations about involving his son. Like I gave fuck all about the kid's senior year of high school. The man was a total fuckwit if he thought I was there for him. But this wasn't my first rodeo. Seated at his table, I was bound to follow his lead. If he didn't address her, neither would I.

At least, that had been my plan.

By the end of our meal, it was clear Fausto had no intention of involving his daughter in our conversation. Fuck that. I wasn't leaving his house without talking to Noemi. She was going to be my wife, for Christ's sake. I wanted her quiet, not invisible.

"It's been an honor, Fausto. You have a beautiful home, and your cook is phenomenal."

The man dropped his chin and waved his hand with a flourish. "We're going to be family soon. You're always welcome at my table."

"Thank you. And I would stay longer, but I'm afraid I have some business needing my attention. Before I go, would it be possible to have a private word with Noemi?" I kept my eyes trained on Fausto, curious what his reaction would be.

"Of course." He smiled thinly. "Sante and I will give you two a moment alone." His eyes briefly flashed toward his daughter before he followed his son from the room. Was it a warning? Did he think I was going to fuck her on his dining room table? Crazy fucking Italians.

I pushed my chair back at an angle until I was facing Noemi.

Finally, we were alone.

My heart beat as fast and frail as the wings of a butterfly.

Conner was staring at me. Studying. Waiting. I needed to push back my chair and meet his gaze like a normal, rational human being, but my body wouldn't cooperate. I wasn't sure what this man wanted from me, and I was scared to find out.

"You must not be a romantic holdout if you've agreed to this." His comment struck a nerve, spearing through my hazy state of shock.

I took the notepad that had remained untouched throughout dinner and scribbled my response. Sometimes I used my phone to type out messages, but I preferred a notepad. It was the same when I read books. I liked the feel of paper in my fingers rather than a device.

Pushing back my chair, I held out my message and finally faced him.

I wasn't told about the arrangement until you arrived.

His stoic mask slipped for a second. "Is that right? Yet you sat through dinner without complaint." Two pools of turbulent azure studied me with a scrutiny that made me squirm in my seat.

Turning the page, I scribbled again.

What choice did I have?

I didn't know what I was thinking, being so honest. If he told my father I was challenging the engagement, I would be in so much trouble. I needed to be more cautious, but he seemed to draw out my brash side. Made me reckless and emotional.

Conner shrugged, drawing my attention to how well his suit fit his broad shoulders. He was athletically built and tall. When he'd first helped me to my chair, he'd towered easily a foot over me. At five-two, that wasn't unusual for me, but somehow his intimidating presence magnified his height even more.

"And if I said you have a choice right now? You could say the word, and I'd call the whole thing off." His response stunned me. I hadn't expected him to give me an out, but I wasn't sure how genuine it was. His words said one thing, while the flash of anger in his eyes said another. For a man who normally exuded effortless calm, I got the sense he was pissed.

Why had his offer to back out made him so upset? And why had my first reaction been to argue? Did I *want* to marry this man? I couldn't possibly know the answer to that. I didn't know him well enough to form an opinion except to know he was a criminal. A man forged in the same fires as my father. I hadn't wanted that for myself, but this might be the escape from my father that I'd been praying for.

I was so damn confused. I didn't know what to think, so I didn't. I went with my gut and slowly shook my head side to side.

"No? Are you telling me you're willing to go through with it?"

I nodded, my stare unwavering.

I wasn't sure if he was even aware, but his entire body relaxed a fraction. He was pleased. My heart did a funny dance at the realization.

"Here's what I propose, then. Neither of us expected to be in this position, but there's no reason we can't make the best of it. A sort of professional arrangement. Our families get their alliance. You'll have status and security while keeping the interruptions to my life at a minimum."

A professional arrangement? What did that even mean? How would I feel about a marriage in name alone? Would he expect sex? Children? Just how *professional* would the marriage be?

He must have seen the wariness in my eyes because his own darkened. "I'm not planning to fuck you against your will, Noemi. I don't need to coerce sex from a woman when plenty of others give it freely."

I flinched at the lash from his comment. He hadn't spoken harshly, but the reality of what he suggested was repulsive enough that I couldn't help my visceral reaction. I hated the idea of a loveless marriage. A husband who slept with everyone but me. Would I be given the same freedom? Maybe if we stayed apart and I had my own relationships, it wouldn't be so hard to tolerate.

I peered deep into his eyes and tried to guess his response to my next question before I hesitantly held up the notepad.

What if I wanted a lover?

I knew how these Mafia men worked, whether Irish or Italian. They didn't like to share, and they certainly didn't want to allow their women to stray, but if I was going to suffer the embarrassment of a cheating husband, I should at least get to have some fun of my own.

The muscles rippled along his jaw. "I suppose turnabout is fair play, but…" He angled himself forward until he was so close I could smell him—expensive cologne, wine, and masculinity so intense I could feel it between my legs. "Have you considered that you might not need one?"

I could hardly breathe with him so close. And at the same time, I wanted to bury my face in his chest and inhale until my head swam with his scent.

Damn hormones. I shook myself internally and focused on what he'd said.

What had he meant? That I could be one of his many hookups? That I could use him to scratch my itch and not feel devastated when he went off with other women? I was insulted by the insinuation. I wanted to be with a man who wanted me, not just used me for sex. But if I was married to Conner, would that even be a possibility? What honorable, loving man would be in a relationship with a married woman? And how could I, in good conscience, involve myself with a man beyond the physical when I knew I was bound to another?

The whole situation felt impossible. Frustration swelled to irritation.

I sat tall in my seat and wrote.

Doubtful.

His lids lowered to half-mast. "What is it that you doubt? That you'd want sex or that I could fulfill your needs? Because I'd be happy to prove you wrong on both counts."

I felt the touch of his gaze drift across my chest and down my body like a physical touch. It made me feel vulnerable.

Like this man could get anything he wanted from me and leave me a shell of a woman. I had to be strong. I couldn't afford to let him think I was a weak pushover. My father already controlled every aspect of my life. I didn't want to set that same precedent with my husband-to-be.

Sex with your wife? How could I refuse such a romantic offer?

His eyes sparked, then darkened. "You asked about a lover. I assumed we were talking about *fucking*, Noemi, not love."

That word on his lips followed by my name sent a skittering heat through my veins. This man was sin incarnate. Temptation and danger so intertwined that it was impossible to separate the two. What would it mean to be bound to a man like him? Heartbreak. Madness.

What if I refused the match? How would my father respond?

Fear unlike any I'd known clenched tight around my throat.

I might end up brokenhearted, but at least with Conner, I'd be alive. As far as I could tell, my best bet would be to marry him but keep my heart securely locked away. I would be free of my father and could work toward saving Sante as well.

I settled the tremor in my hand and wrote.

I'll accept the marriage, but don't ask any more of me.

Again, the tension in the room crackled to life.

"You have another man in your life?" Conner asked with a menacing calm.

I wasn't sure why he was asking. He'd made it clear we weren't to expect fidelity from one another.

I shook my head.

His chest expanded as he slowly sat back, finally giving

me space to breathe. "Then we have a deal." He stood, holding out his hand for mine.

Not wanting to be rude when I'd only just accepted his proposal, I placed my hand in his, biting back a gasp at the zing of electricity that lit my nerve endings from my hand all the way to my belly. The second I was on my feet, I pulled away from his touch. He was too much. Too consuming and disorienting.

I caught a glimpse of a smirk from the corner of my eye.

Jerk. He knew how he affected me and probably every other warm-blooded woman on the planet. Even worse, he used it to manipulate. To exercise power over his hapless victims. But not me. I refused. I wouldn't be putty in his hands to be played with, then ignored.

I surged ahead, leading the way into the living room, where my father and Sante stood talking to one another.

"I believe everything is in order," Conner announced from behind me.

"Wonderful," my father crooned. "Tomorrow, we can begin to hash out the details."

Conner extended a hand, the two shaking firmly as if closing a deal on a sale of cattle. That was all this was. My hopes and dreams meant no more than the breeding ability of livestock. It was appalling, but when Dad closed the door behind Conner, and I was once again pinned beneath my father's murderous stare, I knew marriage was my only option.

I WASN'T ONE TO SHY AWAY FROM SIN. IN FACT, I WAS RATHER fond of several of the deadliest sort, but envy had never been much of a problem. Until now. The thought of Noemi fucking another man had turned my insides as green as her jade-speckled eyes.

What if I wanted a lover?

Jesus. Just recalling her question made my skin crawl with the need to lash out. I'd told her she could do whatever she wanted, but that was bullshit. Not once she was mine. Not if I still felt this cloying sense of need that I couldn't fucking shake. It had been two damn days since dinner at her house, and I couldn't get those fuck-me lips out of my brain.

Even worse, I'd begun to wonder how her voice had sounded before, back when she could speak.

She was Italian, for Christ's sake. I shouldn't have given two shits about her, let alone daydreamed about how dirty words would sound falling from her lips. And the very last thing I should have been doing was following her around like a fucking puppy. Yet here I was, sitting at her usual coffee shop, waiting for her to arrive like a trained golden retriever.

Fuck me.

I'd gone around in my head so many times about our last exchange that I'd needed to see her again just to be sure I'd interpreted her reactions correctly. That I hadn't just convinced myself of what I'd wanted to see. That she was affected by me as much as I was by her.

When she walked into the shop, she stuttered to a stop at the sight of me. I held back a smirk and instead concentrated my stare on her pathetic babysitter. The chalk-eater glared at me, but he couldn't touch me now that the wedding contract was in place. Regardless, he was itching for a rematch after I'd taken him down without breaking a sweat. It was written all over his pathetic pouting face.

Eventually, he retreated to sit like a good dog outside the café, and Noemi joined me at the table. She was back in casual clothes but was no less seductive for it. Something about the way she carried herself made her wardrobe irrelevant. She could be sexy as hell in a fucking clown suit.

She took out her notepad from her purse, and I found myself yet again wondering what her voice had been like. Was it delicate like the distant ringing of a windchime or warm and sultry like a summer breeze?

On second thought, it was probably best I didn't know.

I dropped my eyes from her to the message she slid across the table.

Waiting for me with my usual breakfast is dangerously close to a romantic gesture.

I hated how right she was, but I'd never admit it. "I assure you, there's nothing romantic about my motivations."

She arched a brow.

Then why are you here?

I leaned forward, clasping beneath the seat of her chair and sliding her close enough to feel her shaky breath on my lips. I'd been around long enough to know fear when I saw it. It was thick and sticky and tainted the air all around with bitterness. When Noemi was close to me, fear didn't scent the air. It was something just as primal but far more intriguing. Desire. *Need.*

I ran the back of my hand slowly down her arm and reveled in the way she shivered at my touch.

"That right there is why I'm here. I felt the way you responded to me at your house, and I've wanted more since the minute I left. Call it romance if you want. I don't really care what you call it, so long as those pretty lips end up panting my name."

I leaned back in my chair, relieving the tension between us. If I hadn't, my dick would have ended up so hard that everyone in the damn café would have seen the bulge in my pants.

For the briefest second, her body followed mine, listing forward before she caught herself.

Coming here had been the right decision. I'd had no reason to doubt my instincts. The young Mancini wanted me, no matter how adamant her written refusals.

Just because my body responds to you doesn't mean I want you.

"Trust me, sweetheart. I don't want you either, but we're about to be bound together. There's no reason we shouldn't make the most of it." The truth, sort of, but as the words crossed my lips, I realized it might have been the wrong thing to say.

Noemi cocked her head to the side, and a catlike grin spread across her lips before she scooped a finger full of cream cheese off her bagel and wiped it the full length of my Brunello Cucinelli silk tie. Then she stared right at me as she sucked the remainder off her finger.

Fuck. Me.

I was so fucking turned on, I couldn't even be mad. Leaning in, I whispered close to her ear, "Keep sucking that finger. You're going to need the practice." A shit-eating grin split my face as I walked away.

"I give you a concussion, your ma's gonna give *me* a concussion." Bishop danced on his toes in the ring, his gloved fists up at his face. "Where the hell is your head at, man?"

I feigned a jab, then snuck in an uppercut that hit its mark, sending my best friend stumbling backward. "Where's your head at, besides my fist?" I grinned behind my mouth guard, entertained by the ridiculousness of my retort.

"Ohhhh, tough guy thinks he's got a sense of humor, huh?" He came at me with a wicked-fast series of swings that nearly had me on the ground.

"Fuck, man. It's sparring, not a prize fight."

Bishop chuckled, spitting out his guard. "Winning is winning."

I shook my head and tugged off my gloves. "You've been training with Torin too much. That guy's psycho."

"He's got drive. I admire that. You would too if you weren't so distracted." He squirted a stream of water into his mouth, then leaned against the ropes. "You still thinking about the girl? She's a sweet little thing. I'd probably think about her, too."

I scowled. "Watch it, fuckwad. That's my future wife you're talking about."

He raised his hands in retreat. "My bad, man."

"Besides, that's not exactly it. Something doesn't sit right with me."

"Like what?"

"It's just strange." I shook my head. "She isn't anything like I was told. And there's not a single scar on her neck from the crash—nothing to explain a permanent loss of voice. Maybe it sounds crazy, but I feel like I'm missing something."

"See what you can dig up. Better now than later, once you're stuck with her."

I grunted. I'd already decided it was time to do some research, but not because I was considering backing out. I'd made Jimmy a promise, and I always kept my word. And I wouldn't be choosing another woman because somewhere in the past few days, I'd decided that Noemi was meant for me.

Maybe it was too many years of listening to the old guys blather on about fate. I didn't buy into that bullshit, but I also didn't know how else to explain this strange compulsion growing inside me. An instinctual attraction that had my thoughts and desires locked on one woman. Nothing else distracted from my singular need for Noemi Mancini. She was mine, and I was going to prove it to her.

He wanted to have sex with me. Marriage was one thing; sex was entirely different. Intimacy came with vulnerability and trust—things that would bring emotion into the mix. The last thing I wanted was to develop feelings for Conner Reid. Being married to the man was bad enough. If I cared for him too, my heart would never survive.

Men like him—like my father—didn't love. Not the way I wanted to be loved.

I wanted a man who put his wife and children first. I wanted devotion and commitment. Conner would never give me that, and falling for him would only make the disappointment more painful.

During the next four days, I concentrated on erecting

sturdy walls around my heart and guarding myself against his alluring good looks. I knew he'd use them to chip away at my resolve, but I couldn't let him succeed.

I spent a ridiculous amount of time debating my outfit for the night and ended up selecting a dress that was sexier than I'd previously worn. I also decided not to examine my reasons for said selection too closely. Sometimes a girl needed to look especially hot. It was a confidence boost.

That was my story, and I was sticking to it.

I curled my hair into soft waves and dipped into my makeup bag a little deeper than my usual daily routine. To top things off, I dug through my mother's jewelry box and put on her favorite necklace. The small white gold bell had been her mother's before her. Wearing it made me feel close to her. It was the cherry on my confidence sundae.

When my father saw my choice of jewelry, lightning flashed behind his obsidian eyes, promising retaliation should I step out of line. The rest of my family had a far different reaction. Pippa and her mother instantly teared up and wrapped me in a hug.

Aunt Etta and my mom were fraternal twins and had been incredibly close. When the two had baby girls only weeks apart, it had been natural that Pip and I became like sisters ourselves. She had two younger sisters and a brother, but I was never quite as close with any of them. That was why our separation over the past six months had been extra difficult. I'd only been allowed a few supervised visits, which meant I never had the chance to tell her the truth. Not that I would have. It was almost a blessing that Dad had kept us apart because she was the one person who would have unearthed my secrets. She would have made me talk. Literally.

In the early days, I'd debated endlessly about fessing up to her, but it was too dangerous. She was horrible with secrets. I couldn't take that chance.

Seeing her now, an avalanche of words careened into my throat, demanding to be released. Not just that, but a swell of emotions overtook me. I'd been so damn lonely at my house. The relief of finally seeing her again after only a couple of visits in months made my chest ache.

I fought back the onslaught. I couldn't fall apart now.

"You look incredible, Em," Pip whispered before pulling back and beaming at me with glassy eyes.

"Just like Nora," Aunt Etta added in an emotion-filled rasp.

I shook my head and hugged them again before motioning to the back room we'd reserved. When we entered, my heart fluttered at the sight of my family. Pip and her dad, my uncle Gino, along with my mother's brother, Uncle Agostino, boss of the Moretti crime family, and his wife, Aunt Azzurra. This was the first time since Mom's death that I'd been allowed anywhere near my uncle for fear I'd tell him what I knew.

If I did, my father would be a dead man.

It would be an easy solution if my father hadn't been holding my brother as collateral, using him against me. Like tonight. Dad had made up an excuse to keep Sante away. I'd seen the surprise in people's eyes when Dad explained Sante couldn't join us. They wondered what could possibly have kept him away from such an important evening, but they wouldn't disrespect my father by asking.

I could have told. It would only take a second to blurt the words that would take down my father. But what about my brother? Would the Donatis be able to save him from my father's goons? Maybe. Maybe not. I couldn't take the chance.

An opportunity would come. I just had to be patient.

Everyone greeted me with warm smiles and detectable pity in their eyes. I wasn't sure what my father had told everyone to explain away my absence at family functions, but it clearly hadn't been good.

Once I'd made the rounds, I turned toward the Irish half of the room. The two groups had stayed neatly segregated—a business alliance didn't mean anyone would be vacationing together anytime soon. The second my gaze turned to their group, Conner's eyes were on me. Like he'd been waiting. And I knew why when I saw memories reflected in his eyes of my lips wrapped around my finger.

Heat blazed across my cheeks.

A small but victorious smile carved through his dark stubble as he closed the distance between us. "You look mouth-watering tonight," he murmured once he reached me, laying his hand on the small of my back.

Was that a hint of amusement in his tone?

I wasn't sure, but I also wasn't going to let him get away with unnerving me. Smiling sweetly, I discreetly slipped my hand beneath his suit jacket and pinched him. Hard.

He didn't pull away or react in any way except to chuckle lightly. A sound like warm whiskey poured over ice—both able to warm my belly in strange, alluring ways.

"Conner, it's time you introduce me to your lovely bride-to-be." An older man joined us with a smile and blue-gray eyes so sharp I felt they could stab into the darkest parts of me and unearth my every secret.

"Of course, Jimmy. This beauty is Noemi Mancini." Conner looked at me. "Noemi, this is Jimmy Byrne, my uncle and godfather."

Ah, the infamous head of the Irish mob. It was no wonder he'd elevated himself to a position of such respect. With such keen intelligence brimming in his eyes, I wondered if anything escaped him.

I smiled and bowed my head as it was my only means of communicating the proper display of respect.

He leaned in and kissed one cheek, then the other. "It's an honor, young lady." He pulled back and motioned to the silver-haired woman behind him. "And this is my lovely wife, Brenna."

I shook her hand and smiled softly at her kind but wary eyes.

"My turn!" sang another woman with giddy excitement as she wheedled her way closer. "I'm sorry, Jimmy, but I've been waiting for this day for so long."

Jimmy arched an exasperated brow at her, but she ignored him as only a wife or sibling could have done. This had to be Conner's mother, the three Byrne brother's little sister.

"Noemi, it's an absolute pleasure." The beautiful older woman clasped my hand. "I'm Mirren Reid, Conner's mother. And this is my husband, Seamus." She motioned behind her to an austere man who nodded a demure greeting.

I forced a wide grin, hoping to ingratiate myself to these people who would be my new family.

"Don't worry about saying a thing. Conner explained everything. We're just so delighted to see him settling down and to have you become a part of the family." Surprisingly enough, I got the sense she was being sincere. A glance at her husband told me he wasn't quite so enthusiastic about the situation, but he thankfully remained silent.

"All right, Ma. No need to smother her just yet," Conner said with a touch of good-humored annoyance. "Let's get seated."

"Of course. There'll be plenty of time to get to know one another soon enough," she beamed and retreated to her place at the long table.

Sixteen places—eleven occupied by my Italian contingency, leaving five for Conner and his four guests. Somewhat lopsided but only because Aunt Etta had brought Pip and her other children. I was glad she had. I needed their familiarity while sailing this uncharted course.

Conner directed me to our places at the center of the table, and we all settled into our seats. My father and Jimmy sat next to each other across from us, Umberto beside Dad and Jimmy's wife seated next to him. Pip had ensured she sat on my other side, which I appreciated, but with Conner's close presence a constant distraction, it was all I could do to focus on anything anyone said. Fortunately, I wasn't faced with many attempts to engage me outside of those seated in the immediate vicinity. And for the most part, conversation carried on without any contribution from me. No sweat off my back. I was pleased to use the opportunity to take a breather and escape to the bathroom.

The second I stood, Umberto followed suit. Our sudden movements hooked everyone's attention, and all conversations ceased.

"The restroom, sweetheart?" my father asked with a manufactured sweetness that made me want to vomit.

I nodded, taking my clutch purse from the table.

Conner rose to his feet. What had been a simple bathroom trip suddenly felt like a scene, and I wished I'd kept my ass in my seat.

"I'm happy to escort her," Conner offered, eyeing Umberto.

I wasn't his yet. It wasn't his place to intervene, which sent a flash flood of panic racing through my veins. My eyes cut back to my father, afraid of his response. But to my relief, he forced a stiff but gracious smile.

"Of course, I'm afraid I've been a touch overprotective in recent months. I'm sure you can understand, considering the circumstances. I've already lost one precious member of my family; I couldn't stand to lose another." His eyes slid briefly back to mine, ensuring I'd caught his oh-so-subtle threat.

I dropped my gaze so no one could see the hatred brimming in my eyes and stepped away from the table. I had more immediate concerns to worry about than my asshole of a father. I'd spent days mentally preparing to hold my own against Conner's charms, and he'd already made me blush with a single look. I had to be strong because each step I took carried me farther from the safety of witnesses. The restroom was on the basement level. When we reached the bottom of those stairs, we'd be totally alone.

Conner's arm shot forward in front of the bathroom door, a steel bar preventing my escape.

This was precisely what I'd feared. I knew he'd never let the opportunity pass without exerting his dominance to make me squirm.

I'd never felt the kind of heat he roused inside me. It licked beneath my skin until a river of tingles erupted in my veins. I'd had crushes before, but this was different. Visceral. Indominable. No matter how much I wanted to remain unaffected, it was impossible. My body responded to him as though it were already his to command.

Your body and mind aren't the same. You have to remember your goal, Em.

I lifted my chin defiantly, my nostrils flaring with the intoxicating scent of him.

His cool stare held me captive, eyes inches from mine. "Is your father going to be a problem?"

My lips parted in surprise.

I'd expected innuendo and manipulation. Such a direct line of questioning hit at the very heart of my worries and unsteadied me.

I shook my head and tried to dart beneath his arm. Conner wedged his body in front of the door, blocking my path completely and bringing us chest to chest. I sucked in a shock of air, then narrowed my eyes defensively.

He wasn't remotely unsettled by my display of irritation. If anything, his intensity only darkened further in the dimly lit basement hallway—a villainous storm threatening to crumble me to my foundations.

"Protective is one thing. I get the sense this is more, and I think I ought to know if it's going to be a problem." His eyes narrowed a fraction, the difference between tension and savage ferocity in one tiny twitch of a muscle. "He ever hurt you?" The words were deadly calm.

Oh *God*. Why was he doing this?

He needed to stop asking questions, and I needed to stop thinking his questions meant he cared. This was all probably about control and power, not me. I had to shut it down. *Now*. The best way to accomplish that was not to look like a scared little girl.

Taking a small step back, I opened my clutch and pulled out a pen, then took his hand in mine, palm up. It's so much wider than I expected. Rough and solid muscle. Hands that knew hard work, like squeezing the life out of an enemy.

I mentally scolded myself to focus and wrote two letters across the full surface of his palm.

NO.

Releasing him, I peered up in challenge. Conner stepped forward, placing his leg between my thighs and swiveling us until my back was against the wall next to the door. I didn't squirm or respond, knowing I couldn't show doubt or weakness if I was going to shut down his questions.

"Not so fragile as they implied, are you?" he purred above me.

I took his tie in my hand, pulling him slowly lower until our noses almost touched, and shook my head slowly side to side. His hands came to rest on either side of my head as he brought his cheek to mine, his hint of stubble creating a delicious friction against my skin.

"Good, because I'm not remotely gentle." The words were a black promise, raw and demanding and utterly intoxicating.

Steps sounded on the stairs above us, shocking me back to myself.

I stiffened, eyes widening. Conner didn't budge. I pressed my palms against his marble chest, my frantic eyes cutting toward the feet about to enter our line of sight. Looking back at him, I slammed my hands against his chest, hating the villainous grin that spread across his face.

Finally, with only seconds to spare, he pulled back and allowed me to flee into the bathroom. Heaving deep breaths, I walked to the sinks and leaned against the old vanity counter.

Holy shit, that was close.

Had my father or Umberto seen Conner so close to me, I wasn't sure what would have happened. Dad knew I was marrying the man, but he thought it was a burden. Would he reconsider if he had any idea of the chemistry that sparked between Conner and me? If Umberto had gone after Conner to defend my honor, would the Irish back out of the deal?

Without Conner, I would return to being a prisoner in my father's house. I couldn't let that happen. He would kill me if he had no use for me or decided I posed too much risk. I had to ensure nothing derailed the engagement.

A heavy sigh tugged at my shoulders just as the bathroom door flew open. I whipped around, fully expecting to find Conner filling the doorway, but it was Pippa's gleaming face that greeted me.

I rushed over and wrapped my arms around her gratefully.

"It's harder to get to you than it is the president, you know that?"

A silent chuckle bubbled up from my chest.

Pip pulled back and studied me. "What the hell is going on, Em? Why are you under lock and key, and how did you end up *engaged*? I mean, don't get me wrong, he's a serious hottie, but damn! This came out of nowhere." Her eyes bulged. "You aren't pregnant, are you?" she hissed.

I shook my head adamantly, a smile tugging at my lips. I'd given her a few tidbits over text, but without being able to explain in person, I'd kept things vague.

I pulled my notepad out of my purse.

Dad volunteered me when the alliance was suggested. I guess Conner liked the idea of a silent wife.

If Pip's eyes had narrowed any further, she wouldn't have been able to see at all. "*Excuse* me?"

Again, I had to fight back a giggle. I shouldn't have goaded her like that.

He's actually not so bad. And as you mentioned, he's easy on the eyes. That was the understatement of the century.

"Looks aren't everything." Pip glowered. "I don't know, Em. I have a bad feeling something's not right. The way those guys almost threw down over you, and your dad hiding you away. Something has felt … off." She lifted a brow and smirked. "Blink once if you need help." She leaned in and laughed.

I forced a shaky smile, fighting back the sudden sting of tears and looking back down to my notepad so she didn't notice.

Everything's fine, promise, but maybe you can look into him. Let me know what I'm getting into.

With a deep breath, I met her gaze again, finding I wasn't the only one swept up in emotion. Pip's warm honey gaze was glassy.

"I can't believe you're getting married, and Aunt Nora won't be here for it." She gently grazed my necklace, then wrapped me in a quick embrace. "Okay, we better hurry and get back out there before they send a search party."

I nodded and grinned, thanking God I still had Pip. My world was about to change, but knowing I had her would keep my head afloat.

Conner

NINE

Always trust your gut. It was the creed I lived by, and it had served me well—saved my life any number of times—so I wasn't about to abandon it now. My gut told me something was off between Noemi and her father, and I wasn't going to ignore that feeling no matter how convincingly Noemi assured me I was wrong.

Throughout dinner, I kept my senses trained on Fausto. Umberto was a pain in the ass, but he was just a lackey. If there was going to be a problem with the Italians, Fausto would be at the center of it.

I told myself that no matter what was happening, I needed to stay out of it. Inserting myself into Italian family affairs would not go over well, but the thought of anyone but me laying a finger on Noemi made me itch with the need to paint her entire family tree in shades of red. They were her family. It was their job to protect her, and if they'd failed at that task, my wrath would be merciless.

I shouldn't have cared. I'd specifically picked her as my bride in the hopes that her silence would enable me to forget she even existed. As if I could ever ignore that fiery resolve of hers. Her presence in a room was louder than most men I knew, commanding attention with every graceful swing of her hips and perceptive flick of her emerald eyes.

Each of her penned words was worth a thousand of her father's blustered conversations.

With every new glimpse of her bold personality, I wanted to know more about where her strength had come from and why I'd been led to believe she was anything short of extraordinary. Had I been told the truth, I never would have ended up in this mess. I was distracted at the best of times and growing obsessed if I was honest with myself. It was a miracle I hadn't pressed my lips against hers in that basement hallway and stolen a taste of her glossy lips. That and the approach of a witness were the reasons I'd kept my hands pinned to the wall. Had I allowed my fingers to wrap around her waist and pull her body against mine, any degree of control I'd possessed would have been shredded.

And the way she'd blushed down to her toes when she first laid eyes on me? *Jesus.*

Sweet *and* sassy. It was a fucking lethal combination, and my days were dwindling before my eyes.

Her resistance to our connection only made me more determined to have her. While her body would be easy to persuade, I had no idea what her mental hang-up was about. I believed her when she said there wasn't anyone else. In that case, I didn't see the problem. We were going to be married, and the heat between us was fucking off the charts. So why the opposition? Why not give in to the desire?

It was just my luck. Or karma. Jimmy and his belief in fate would tell me it was my own damn fault for trying to snag a wife I could ignore—that I'd doomed myself to pine after a woman who couldn't stand me.

"Something funny?" Jimmy asked, joining me on the sidewalk when we left the restaurant. Everyone else had already departed or were getting into their cars. I'd waited to watch Noemi leave with her father before getting lost in thought after they drove away.

"Just laughing at myself."

"No reason to laugh as far as I can tell. You did good tonight, Con." He clapped his hand on my shoulder. "I see great things on the horizon for all of us. My brothers and I, along with your dad, brought this organization back from extinction in New York, and now, you and the next generation will solidify our future. We'll show the world we're a force to fear and respect."

"The alliance will definitely be helpful, but we'll have to prove ourselves regardless." The Albanians and others weren't going to go quietly into the night without a display of the new power we wielded.

"Of course, but you aligning with the Italians is only the first step in redefining ourselves," Jimmy added conspiratorially, his voice dropping to a hushed whisper.

"Oh yeah? You gonna tell me the rest of this plan?"

He shrugged. "We already got the cops in our pocket—half the damn force is Irish—but if we can get a better handle further up the chain … say … in the governor's office … then, we'd really be sitting pretty."

"Evan Alexander is a respectable man. Not many politicians own that distinction, but the governor's one of them.

You'll have a hard time catching that fish." I peered at my uncle, curious at the smug quirk of his lips.

"These things have a funny way of happening sometimes." He glanced at me. "Like you and your girl in there. I saw the way you watched her."

"It's in my best interest to be observant where they're concerned."

Jimmy's smirk grew as if he already knew my excuse was bullshit.

"Look," I said quietly. "I just want to make sure you know that no matter what, I'm a Byrne. I'll always be a Byrne first and foremost." I'd worried in the back of my mind since this alliance was first brought up that Jimmy and the others might begin to see me as less trustworthy because of my ties to the Italians. I wanted to be sure he knew my Irish roots would always win out.

My godfather clasped his hands on either side of my face and stared deep into my eyes. "You're a good boy, Conner. I never would have entertained this scenario if I'd had any doubts in you. Understand?"

"Thanks, Jimmy." A strange warmth spread throughout my chest, then chilled when he continued.

"So is that the reason Mia Genovese wasn't here tonight? Seemed like she and her husband were a key part of this alliance."

I grimaced, knowing he was right. "It just felt like too much, too soon. She's not my mother, Jimmy, and I'm not ready to pretend otherwise."

He pursed his lips and nodded. "I suppose I can respect that. Alright, Brenna is probably getting pissed in the car. I better get going."

"Night, Uncle Jimmy."

"Take it easy, Con." He waved, leaving me to wander toward the street where I'd parked hours earlier.

Once I was in the driver's seat, I took my phone out of my pocket and discovered I had a missed call from Mia Genovese. I sighed heavily, then clicked on the missed message and listened to my birth mother's voice.

"Hi, Conner. It's Mia. Mia Genovese. Ummm ... I was wondering if maybe we could get coffee sometime. I'd really like a chance to talk with you, if you have the time. You know ... when it could be just us. If you're comfortable with that, of course. Anyway, I'm rambling. Just let me know. Okay. Bye."

That right there was exactly why I hadn't wanted to meet her in the first place. I had a family. One who had wanted me from the beginning. I didn't need to suffer through awkward meetups to fill some gaping hole inside me. Meeting her hadn't changed anything. And I didn't feel any sense of obligation to indulge her guilty conscience. Her emotional trauma wasn't my problem.

I closed out of the phone and tossed the irritating device into the cup holder beside me. I had more pressing matters to deal with, like how to get a certain green-eyed temptress out of my head.

I'd be smart to call up one of my regulars and remind myself that all I needed was a good fuck, but I had a feeling I had a cold shower in store for me instead. Such a fucking idiot.

And I only had myself to blame.

Eavesdropping is perfectly acceptable if your life hangs in the balance. At least, I told myself that while I stood outside my father's office door, hovering as close as I dared get without jiggling the door. I'd heard Conner arrive minutes before and hurried downstairs the second the office door had closed. The two were discussing the alliance and wedding plans—I couldn't *not* listen.

"Acceptance hasn't been an issue, but I think it would be wise to select a neutral site for the ceremony." The deep melodic current of Conner's voice flowed like silk. As always, he seemed perfectly at ease.

"Agreed," my father responded. "I suggest Saint Francis Xavier in Midtown. It's one of the few large enough to hold both contingencies and isn't affiliated with any one group. Plus, Midtown gives us the best options for the reception. I don't want to have to limit our guest list."

"I can't imagine the church would be available on such short notice."

"You let me worry about that." My father's voice was tinged with sly mirth. "We agreed on August first, and I see no reason to change it."

August first? Holy crap!

That was only two short weeks away. I knew things would move quickly now that the engagement had been officially announced, but two weeks was no time at all.

Despite my desire to escape my father's reach, the prospect of such a life-altering event happening so quickly made my head spin with tendrils of panic. I was so distracted that I was caught off guard when the door swung open, and I stood face-to-face with Umberto.

A fresh wave of heart-pounding terror overtook me.

How could I have forgotten about him? Dad always kept him close, and though the discussion had been taking place comfortably on the far side of the room, I hadn't accounted for the extra variable. I was too shocked to even improvise an excuse.

Mouth agape and eyes wide, I floundered as all three men stared at me.

"My apologies, Conner. It appears my daughter has forgotten her manners." My father slowly rose from his desk chair, eyes spitting fire my direction.

Conner's gaze slid from me to my father ever so briefly before he waved his hand dismissively. "It's natural for her to be curious," he said, voice dripping with indifference. "You know women and weddings. I'm glad she's here, actually. I needed to speak with her. Might as well do that now before I forget." He stood without waiting for a reply.

"I suppose I have a minute," Dad clipped, not attempting to mask his disapproval.

Conner continued toward me as though completely oblivious to the warning in my father's tone. I didn't buy it for a second. The Irishman knew exactly how fine a line he walked, yet he simply didn't care.

I backed away from the door, my heart an insistent drum pounding in my ears.

Once Conner pushed past a surly Umberto, he led the way to the living room and out onto our back patio. It was a warm summer morning, yet my arms pricked with a sea of goose bumps when Conner speared me with a penetrating arctic stare.

"I thought you were smarter than that, Noemi," he said quietly.

Each of my vertebrae fused stiffly together, my jaw clenching tight.

How dare he condemn me when he had no idea of the position I was in. Yes, I needed to be more careful, but it wasn't his place to reprimand me. Not yet, anyway.

I desperately wanted to lash out and spew the venomous words nipping at my tongue, but I hadn't brought a notepad with me. I was manacled by my silence.

Conner heaved a sigh and extracted his phone from his jacket pocket before opening it to the notes app and handing it to me.

He was giving me the chance to respond, though it was clear he wasn't thrilled about it. The gesture cooled my anger. Just a smidge. He was still a jackass.

You don't know anything about me.

He read my typed words, then steadied stormy blue eyes on my face. "I know you've lived under that man's roof all your life and should know better than to be so careless." His head tilted a fraction as though something had just occurred to him. "Unless … disobedience is new to you." He took a tiny step forward as though he wanted to crowd me but knew we were being watched. "Just how sheltered are you?"

How had this conversation strayed so quickly? From worry to anger to incensed embarrassment in a handful of heartbeats. Conner had a natural ability to keep me off balance.

I crossed my arms over my chest and leveled him with a stare, unwilling to answer.

His turbulent gaze flared, hungry and dark as slate. "Have you even been kissed?" His voice lowered to loose gravel on asphalt. Deep enough to make my insides quake.

The answer was yes, but I felt an intense need to stand my ground. I didn't want to set the stage for this man to see me as a naïve pushover. And besides, it wasn't any of his damn business if I'd been kissed before.

I snatched the phone out of his hand and began to type.

Did you burn a man alive?

His responding smirk chilled me to the bone.

Why? I shoved the phone back at him.

Conner typed rather than voiced his reply.

Because he deserved it.

"Now answer my question, Noemi." He lifted his thumb to drift along my bottom lip, the touch lighting a fire in a much more intimate part of my body. "Has another man had his mouth on yours?"

I refused to answer. I could hardly even breathe.

His stare lowered to my lips, and my treacherous body listed toward his like a reed helpless against the summer breeze. That was when I realized he might just kiss me there in plain sight. It was incredibly dangerous. I had no way to gauge my father's reaction, yet I was consumed with the need to know what it would be like to have someone so compelling and overwhelming lay claim to me.

Yes, I'd been kissed by two different boys in high school, but I doubted those docile encounters would compare to the way Conner would make me feel. Just the look in his eyes promised to ensnare my senses and transport me to a place without reason.

Fortunately, Conner had better control than I did. He pulled away, leaving me shamefully cold and adrift.

"We'd better get back inside," he murmured absently, the frayed edges of his voice the only sign he'd been affected at all.

As I followed him back inside, it occurred to me that his ploy to speak privately with me had been nothing more than a way of defusing my father's anger. Conner had been protecting me in his own abrasive way. I'd have to remember that the next time he irritated me, which he undoubtedly would.

I hurried upstairs without looking in my father's direction. It was a small mercy he let me go without more of a reprimand, but that was only because he had decided to wait until later when we were alone so that he could spew his venom unobserved. I'd been quietly reading in my room when I sensed his malicious presence in my doorway.

"You're just like your mother, sticking your nose into things that don't concern you." Dad stalked closer, lifted the delicate bell pendant necklace from my chest. I prayed he didn't rip it clean off me, but he only sneered instead. "You may be out of this house in two weeks, but I'll still have Sante here with me, so don't get any stupid ideas in that head of yours." He dropped the necklace and glared. "You forget your place again, and I won't care who's there to witness. I *will* teach you some respect."

God, I wanted to launch my book at the back of his head as he walked out of my room. I wished just once I could stand up to him and tell him what a pathetic coward he was. To free the acidic spitefulness that burned my tongue whenever he targeted me with his egotistical narcissism. Even better, I wished I could make him pay for what he did. Teach *him* a lesson.

Would marrying Conner lead to a lifetime of this same frustrated helplessness?

My fiancé had stepped in to de-escalate the situation with my father, but that didn't necessarily make him a good man. He was a criminal. A bully, in a way, though I didn't feel the same sense of impending doom around him as I did with my father. In a sick way, I almost enjoyed the push and pull with him. Something about him drew me in and made me feel alive. Was I naïve to think he was different?

He burned a man alive, Em. How different can he be?

Ugh. What a mess.

I picked up my phone, needing a distraction and remembering I'd asked Pip for information on Conner.

Me: You find anything?

She'd know what I meant.

Pippa: Was just about to send you an email.

Pippa: K, done!

I opened my email and clicked on the message as soon as it appeared. Dad had access to my account, but I didn't think he'd care about Pip sending me info on Conner.

Here's what I could find. Up until recently, the Byrne family was headed by Jimmy, Brody, and Tully Byrne, along with help from Conner's dad, Seamus Reid. Two weeks ago, Brody was gunned down outside one of their clubs by Albanians. Tully always had a more passive role, so now it's mostly Jimmy running things. Rumor has it, the younger generation is starting to take over—Oran, Brody's son, and Keir, who is Jimmy's eldest. Conner is right there with them staking his claim. The group operates illegal gambling clubs and runs an underground fight circuit. They've scraped and clawed their way back to power. Not gonna lie, they sound pretty ruthless.

I couldn't find much on Conner individually. He's in his late twenties. Only child. No police record, which seemed kind of surprising. He's linked to the gambling side of their operations—runs a club called Bastion. That's about it.

I hadn't known about Conner's uncle. Had they been close? No matter how irritating my fiancé could be, I felt bad for his family's loss. I knew what it felt like to lose someone close. In my gut, I didn't think he was so callous as to be unaffected by that kind of cruel turn of fate.

Me: Thanks, honey.

Pippa: Not sure how I feel about this.

Me either, Pip. But it doesn't change anything.

Me: That's the world we live in.

Pippa: I guess.

Pippa: I had just hoped after everything that's happened, you'd find your happily ever after. Not this.

My cousin was intrepid and sometimes even seemed fearless, but I knew inside she worried just like the rest of us. Instead of adding to her burden, which wouldn't help anyone, I tried to be optimistic.

Me: You never know, Pip 😊

If I'd learned anything in the past year, it was that life could change in the blink of an eye.

People died. Fortunes changed.

I preferred having some semblance of control over my life, but if I had to rely on a little luck, so be it.

Never in a million years did I think I'd find myself sitting next to my father while meeting with my wedding planner. He hadn't attended a single school performance or been present at any of the most memorable events in my life. Planning my wedding alongside him seemed ludicrous.

Then again, so would the prospect of my dad killing my mom.

But Mom was dead, Dad was to blame, and I was stuck next to him in wedding hell. The one silver lining was my soon-to-be mother-in-law. Mirren Reid was remarkably gracious and friendly. Maybe I'd swung too far toward optimism, but I had a feeling she could be a valuable ally for me. Maybe even a friend.

We spent almost two hours hashing out details. Mostly, we gave the planner as much guidance as we could, and she was going to handle the logistics of making it all happen. When we finished, Dad announced he had a meeting to get to and instructed Umberto to drive me home after we made a quick stop to drop off paperwork at Conner's office.

All traces of the exhaustion I'd felt seconds before vanished.

Would we be going to one of the Irish gambling clubs? Would I see him on our brief visit?

An undeniable sense of excitement assaulted me on the way across town. Was it purely curiosity that set my blood flowing, or something even more destructive? Was I actually looking forward to seeing him? I told myself that if the answer was yes, it was only because I was rarely allowed out of the house. Any social interaction at all was a refreshing change of pace for me. It had nothing to do with the man himself.

Yeah…

Umberto parked in front of a four-story brick building that didn't look like much from the outside. After fussing at me to stay close and behave, he led us inside. The lobby was admittedly more modern than the outside had been, but it was still nothing to write home about. The walls were painted black, and a reception desk built from the original brick sat in the center. Large artistic photos of the city at night dotted the walls, lit by dozens of small track lights hanging from the ceiling.

"Can I help you?" A beautiful woman with short dark hair greeted us. She was outfitted entirely in black satin—snug pants that sculpted perfectly to her athletic frame and a matching cropped top with one strap sweeping over her right shoulder. It was a confident, bold look that I admired.

Umberto grunted. "Hell yeah, you can." He muttered the

words under his breath but loud enough that he knew we'd both heard him.

I had the clawing urge to kick my foot into the back of his knee and send him careening to the ground. Instead, I thinned my lips and shot her an apologetic look.

The woman flashed a feline grin of amusement. "You here for Reid?"

"Yeah, he around?"

"Let's see. Follow me." She led us back through a set of double doors and down a hallway containing a series of offices.

We followed her into the last office, which contained a modern executive setup complete with monitors and a fancy fireplace but no Conner.

"Guess he's upstairs on the floor," she said breezily. "If you want, we ladies can wait here while you look for him."

Umberto peered at me as though he were conflicted, so I shot him an exasperated look that said, *what trouble could I possibly get into here?*

"Don't move," he snapped before disappearing down the hall.

The woman, whose eyes were a striking combination of turquoise and gold, laughed from deep in her belly. "What a buffoon. I'm sorry. Guess he could be a friend of yours."

I shook my head adamantly.

"Good." She held out her hand. "I'm Shae."

Once my hand was free, I pulled out my notepad and wrote my name.

She grinned. "I know who you are, Noemi. Everyone in the family knows you."

Super.

I held up the paper, relieved when she burst out laughing. "It's not so bad."

Are you related to Conner?

"Cousin, but I also work with him here at the club. My dad was Brody Byrne."

My face fell, recalling what I'd learned from Pippa.

I'm so sorry for your loss.

She shrugged and motioned to a red leather sofa in front of the fireplace. "That's just a part of the life, I guess." She sat angled toward me, one arm over the back of the sofa. "You try to guard against these things, but shit happens."

I got the distinct impression that Shae was a badass. I didn't know of many women who worked alongside the men in our family, and I figured the Irish were probably the same.

"I wasn't supposed to come in this evening," she continued. "But I'm glad I did. I've been curious to meet the silent Mancini." She tilted her head, kaleidoscopic eyes studying me. "Not exactly what I expected."

I arched a brow, encouraging her to explain.

Shae chuckled. "Guess I expected someone shy and demure, but that's not you, is it?"

I scrolled neatly on my notepad. ***No voice doesn't mean no opinions.***

Her eyes sparked with amusement. "No, it certainly doesn't. And that right there is why I think I'm going to like you, Noemi." Her fingers toyed with the long silver earring dangling from her ear. "So tell me, how do you feel about all this? Conner and the wedding?"

That's just a part of the life. I smirked when I flashed her words back at her.

"No shit." She grinned but quickly sobered. Watching how the blue and gold in her eyes fought for dominance with the change in her mood was fascinating. When she reached out to rest a hand on mine, her irises were all molten amber. "I'm sure none of this is easy. You ever need someone to talk to, I'm here. Anytime."

I was surprised by her forwardness and the sincerity of her offer. I gave her a small smile and nodded.

The door burst open at that moment. All my attention was instantly redirected to the doorway where Conner stood, murder blazing in his eyes.

I instinctively yanked my hand from beneath hers. I wasn't even sure why. We weren't doing anything wrong, but something told me it wouldn't matter to this man.

He stalked into the room, Umberto behind him. "Shae, I wasn't expecting you today."

"Looks like you have all sorts of unexpected guests," she responded boldly. "Lucky for me, I got the chance to meet your bride-to-be. She's stunning, Reid. You're a lucky man."

Conner popped his neck one direction, then the other. "You're walking a fine fucking line, Shae. I suggest you make yourself scarce."

I flinched at his harsh words, confused about why he would be so ugly to his cousin being kind to me. Maybe he was moody like that because Shae didn't seem surprised. She grinned as she stood—a victorious flash of teeth and audacity.

Yeah, I liked her.

"You too, *Berto,*" Conner barked at my guard, though his eyes were locked on me. "I'd like a moment alone with my fiancée."

"Huh?" Umberto pulled his eyes away from Shae's retreating backside.

"Out. *Now,*" Conner snapped.

Umberto scowled, his eyes sliding to me for only the briefest moment of contemplation. "Whatever, man. Just make it quick," he grumbled, then plodded from the room.

With a flick of his wrist, Conner swept the door shut. For the first time, he wasn't wearing his suit jacket, and the sleeves of his light blue dress shirt were rolled to his elbows, giving me a view of the ink covering his skin. I was surprised to see that the other forearm was bare, devoid of ink. What was beneath the rest of his shirt? I had a feeling I'd find out in two weeks' time, whether I wanted to or not.

I rose from the sofa, the mounting tension in the room urging me to my feet. I got the sense Conner was furious, but I had no idea why. I scrambled for my pad, hoping to distract him.

Met with the wedding planner this morning.

I held up the note, but his eyes never left mine as he stalked close. Never in my life had anyone looked at me with such ardent intensity. It stole my breath. In a good or a bad way, I wasn't sure.

"I don't ever want to see anyone touching you like that again."

I flinched backward in surprise. ***She was just being kind.***

"That's bullshit, but regardless, I don't care. Man or woman, I see someone touching you in a way I don't like, I'll cut their fucking fingers off."

I gaped at him, totally flabbergasted. Where had this caveman attitude come from? He was the one who'd told me we could have lovers and this whole marriage was a professional arrangement. Where had that man gone?

So many colliding thoughts bombarded me. I didn't know what to say, so I went with the first thing to rise to the surface. ***We have dancing at the reception. You going to cut all their fingers off?***

It was meant as a challenge. A means to point out how absurd he was being.

My intent escaped him.

"Then I suggest you call the wedding planner and strike dancing from the agenda." He said it with absolute seriousness.

She's your cousin, Conner. Nothing happened.

"And for that, I'll just take it up with her in the ring, but anyone else is fair game. I know her better than you, and I know for a certainty she wasn't simply being *nice*."

My brows narrowed at his insinuation. Had Shae been hitting on me?

"Now you're getting it," he murmured.

Ohhh.

I flipped the page of my notepad and scribbled again.

Even so, you said we were both allowed lovers.

I held the page out with less force, bewilderment softening my fight. I'd started to think of Conner as a somewhat better alternative than my father. Had I been wrong? Would a life with him be even more oppressive than these last months in my family home?

My de-escalation only seemed to anger him further. He got even closer, his piercing eyes inches from mine. "No, I said turnabout was fair play. That means if I stray, you can, too. But for right now, there's only one set of legs I want between, and as long as that's the case, I expect the same in return." He took my hand and tugged me out of the office, not giving me a chance for a response.

Stumbling behind him, I could hardly string together thoughts I was so beside myself in surprise. He expected exclusivity? What if I didn't want to have sex with him? My body did, but my mind wasn't so sure. He made it sound like he could lose interest one day—that was exactly the sort of thing I'd feared. If I developed feelings for him, a betrayal like that would be heartbreaking. I didn't want to hand myself over to a man who wasn't committed to me.

Conner handed me over to Umberto. I slipped into the back seat of his car but hardly registered anything around me. I thought of Conner's thumb on my lips. His hand on my thigh and his dirty words whispered close to my ear. He wanted me and had been intensely possessive in response to

Shae's hand on mine. But would that translate to long-term devotion? Or was his interest in me just a momentary craving?

His undeniable intensity made me think that maybe our relationship had potential. That it might be … more. Conner didn't strike me as the flighty type. He was more all or nothing. And if he had his sights set on me … would that mean he wanted all of me?

Maybe it was just wishful thinking. I couldn't be sure.

The strange flutter in my chest terrified me. I should have been scared of Conner himself, but it was the feelings he'd evoked that scared me more. The fact that I had any hope at all that he might care for me was a dangerous sign. He'd admitted to burning a man alive—was someone like that even capable of love? Why was I even entertaining that question?

If I didn't get control of my wayward emotions, I would land myself in a heap of trouble. The only problem was, I didn't know how. Conner was chipping away at my defenses one small crack at a time. He wasn't the sort of man to give up. If he'd set his sights on conquering me, I was doomed.

I never dwelled on what-ifs, especially when it came to my past. Unlike many adopted kids who spent a lifetime wondering what their lives would have looked like had they not been given up, I never cared because it was pointless. The past was the past. Move the fuck on.

I hadn't questioned my life before, and learning the identity of my birth mother changed nothing. If anything, it only confirmed that I was exactly the man I was meant to be. Whether Italian or Irish, I was meant to thrive on the wrong side of the law.

My moral compass was faulty from birth, and more to the point, I liked it that way.

Guilt was a pointless emotion suffered by the weak.

I knew my mind and owned my actions so that I could walk through life with confidence. When I agreed to Jimmy's request that I marry an Italian, I committed to that decision. I hadn't known at the time how deep I'd dive into that commitment, but something inside me snapped at the sight of Shae with Noemi.

I didn't just want to fuck my fiancée; I wanted all of her.

Her body and submission. Her trust and compliance. Even her fiery temper and sarcasm.

All of it was mine, and I wasn't about to share.

Shae wasn't a true threat. She never would have infringed on my territory if she'd known how I felt. She sure as shit did now, though. Not that it would stop her from pushing my buttons. She always had, like the way she called me Reid when no one else dared. I'd shut that down years ago—it highlighted that I wasn't a Byrne. No one else got away with that shit, but Shae was like a sister. A gorgeous bisexual sister who was just as good at snagging the hottest girl in the room as she was at leveling her competition in the boxing ring. Uncle Brody had taught her well.

While my brain knew she wouldn't dare steal what was mine, the archaic animal in me had been livid. I hated seeing them together and was nearly homicidal at the sight of their hands touching. It was intimate and suggested a degree of closeness between the two that enraged me.

Jealousy wasn't my thing. I'd never wanted a woman enough to be jealous.

But what had bothered me more than anything was the way Noemi's face had crumpled when I told her she was the only one I wanted. It was as if the thought of our marriage being more than a professional arrangement had crushed her.

I'd had to get her out of there fast before I said or did something I would regret. Like guilt, I wasn't a fan of regret, but I'd been dangerously close to lashing out and hating myself for it later.

There was no way this consuming need that I felt was one-sided. If I was stuck with this suffocating feeling of infatuation, she sure as hell was going to feel it, too. I would strip her bare, body and soul, to prove to her just how thoroughly she belonged to me. I'd do whatever it took.

If I had to walk this treacherous path, I wasn't doing it alone.

But Noemi was guarded. I would have to use just the right amount of force and seduction to keep from scaring her away. That had been the one surety holding my control intact. The second she was gone, I got in my car and drove straight to the gym. If I didn't work out some of the homicidal energy festering inside me, I would explode.

As usual, Bishop was already there bullshitting with some of the guys. He ended his conversation as soon as he saw me and jogged over.

"Hey, man. I was just going to call you. Got that info you wanted back from my guy."

I slung my gym tote over my shoulder and lifted my chin for him to continue.

"I ran through everything. Her school record and extracurriculars looked pretty standard. There was only one thing in the whole file that stood out to me, but it could be nothing."

"Tell me."

"Her medical records showed a broken collarbone and other contusions from the car wreck that killed her mom, but there was no real damage to her throat. A bruise from the seat belt but no physiological explanation for her loss of voice. The doc even had a note mentioning possible emotional trauma as a factor and said he recommended counseling to her father but didn't go into more detail because she was technically an adult, and that would have been breaking confidentiality laws. I read all through the accident report, and everything seemed legit. The investigator wasn't one of our guys, but nothing looked dodgy. Like I said, it may be nothing. Just thought I'd bring it up before I sent the file your way."

Trauma. The crash couldn't have been easy to process, but the woman I knew was far from traumatized. If her silence wasn't physiological, what was the reason? Why would she go six months without a word, and why would her father accept her condition without question?

Something didn't add up, and I was ready for an explanation.

"That's great work, Bishop." I clapped my hand on his shoulder. "I'll get changed and meet you in the ring."

"Let me rough you up a little, and we'll call it even." He flashed a megawatt grin.

"In your dreams, asshole." I gave him a quick jab to the gut and ducked away toward the locker room when he swung in retaliation.

My shitty day was feeling marginally better. I still needed to blow off some steam in the ring, but I wasn't quite so bloodthirsty. My focus had turned to strategy rather than annihilation. It was time to make the caged bird sing, one way or another.

SANTE STOOD IN THE KITCHEN STARING INTO AN OPEN CABINET when I came down the next morning. He was so lost in his thoughts that he didn't hear me approach until I was within reach.

I placed a hand on his shoulder, peering up at him questioningly.

He'd been staring into the cupboard that contained our coffee cup collection. Mom had been an avid coffee fanatic, addicted to an elaborate cappuccino routine she followed each morning religiously. In the summers when I wasn't in school, I spent every morning in the kitchen with her, sharing her routine. Once she was gone, I couldn't bear to have coffee at home without her. That's why I'd first started my ritual coffee outings. I needed the caffeine fix, but without the side of heartache.

"It's strange. Sometimes I almost forget she's gone. I started to get out a mug for her like I was going to start the cappuccino machine, then realized what I was doing. It was muscle memory. Like my body had somehow forgotten." He closed the door and looked down at me, his sweet brown eyes unguarded and rife with pain.

I knew how he felt. And I knew that no words would fix it, so I wrapped my arms around his middle and held him close.

God, I loved him so much. I couldn't bear to lose him, too.

"Thanks, little big," he said softly.

When I pulled away, I grabbed my notepad. ***Want to come get coffee with me?***

His lips thinned. "You know Dad doesn't like us to go out together." Every word was wrought with inner conflict. Maybe this was my chance to help him see reason.

You know that's absurd, right?

"He explained it to me, so I kind of get it. After losing Mom, he doesn't want to chance us being out together and something happening to both of us at the same time. He'd be totally alone." And that was why I adored this poor sweet boy. No matter how desperately he wanted to be a part of the Lucciano crime family and impress our father, his heart was made of pure gold. It made him seem naïve, but that innocence was derived from a purity I never wanted to see tarnished.

I nodded, wishing I could steal him away without harming that kind heart of his.

Thirty minutes later, I was seated at my coffee shop sipping a steaming cappuccino but hardly tasting it. I was still no closer to figuring out how to save my brother, and when I'd parted from Conner the day before, he'd been livid.

I didn't know what to do about any of it. A part of me insisted I needed to be patient, while another part screamed that I was running out of time.

Two weeks, and I'd be married.

I'd be out from under my father's control but have less access to Sante than I already had. And while Conner would likely give me more physical freedom, I feared he had the potential to steal my heart and leave me even more vulnerable. No matter how I looked at my situation, it felt hopeless.

I was wallowing in such a state of melancholy that I was caught off guard as I left the restroom and was yanked from behind out the back door and into the alley. A rough hand covered my mouth, my heart sinking deep into my stomach as my body broke out in a sticky coating of fear.

"Shhh, calm down. It's me."

Conner? What the hell was he doing?

I stopped fighting his hold, my ragged breaths quickly becoming the only sound in the stillness around us. When the familiar scent of his spiced aftershave filled my lungs, I relaxed further into his hold.

Once he sensed my panic subside, he lowered his hand and turned me to face him. His harshly angled brow cast his gaze in shades of midnight and ruthless determination.

My muscles returned to a heightened state of alert, coiled and ready.

"We need to talk. Alone. And since your father has that asshole breathing down your neck all the time, this was the best way."

His explanation didn't ease an ounce of my tension.

"I did some interesting reading last night. I felt like something was off, so I asked a friend to gather information on you and your family. Your school records. Family history. Medical records."

Every muscle in my body hardened to reinforced steel, keeping my lungs from inhaling even an ounce of air.

"I found it fascinating that the doctors had no explanation for your silence. Strange things happen sometimes, and I'm willing to admit that. But did you know your attending physician made a note in your chart that his impressions pointed to a psychosomatic trauma response?" Conner walked me backward until my Ralph Lauren blouse was pressed against the dirty alley wall. "Now, sweet little Noemi, I've watched you long enough to form my own opinions, and something doesn't sit right with me. You know what I think?" He paused, not continuing until I shook my head. "I think there's nothing wrong with your voice."

And there it was.

How was it this man who didn't know me at all had seen through my ruse faster than anyone? The longer my silence had extended, the more I'd feared this moment—the day my secrets unraveled like the threads of a silk scarf in a stiff wind.

I wiggled to free my hands and extract my notepad only to have Conner yank the tattered pages from my fingers and toss them inside a nearby dumpster.

I shook my head in adamant denial. A refusal to talk. To admit anything.

"No more games, Noemi. Tell me the fucking truth," he barked.

My entire body shook with panic, but adrenaline quickly triggered my fight-or-flight response.

Who does this man think he is? He has no right to do this. To demand anything of me.

My eyes narrowed as fury took hold. I shoved at his chest repeatedly, forcing him to retreat, and he let me, but only a little. I shouldn't have lashed out, but it was the only thing I could do to keep the caustic words that burned my tongue from spewing past my lips.

A few inches at a time, we move from the wall as I took out all my frustrations on his Armani-clad chest until he had enough and seized my hands.

"You can throw a fit all you want, but I'm not leaving this alley without some answers. And if you can't give me any, maybe we should ask your father."

Every molecule in my body went cold, freezing me in place.

Conner took out his phone. The sight thawed me back into action, but now my movements were frenzied with desperation. I clasped both hands on his forearm, pleading wordlessly for him to stop.

"Words, Noemi," he ground out between clenched teeth. "I need words."

I tried to slap the phone from his hands. Tears burned the backs of my eyes, and a sob clawed at my throat. I gave everything I could, but Conner evaded me easily, clasping both of my hands in one of his.

Using his thumb, he pulled up my father's contact information and displayed the screen where I could see it. "Does your father know about the doctor's suspicions?"

Dad would have had to have cared in order to ask. The reason for my silence was irrelevant in his eyes. Him finding out my muteness was selective wasn't the reason Conner's threat terrified me. I feared his questions would pique my father's suspicions about what I might or might not have said to my husband-to-be. I didn't have to tell on my father to feel his wrath. All that mattered was what he believed I might have said—that I might have told Conner what happened the day of my mother's crash.

I shuddered to think of what my father would do.

Defeat pillaged all my strength, leaving me weary and

empty. My hands fell to my sides as my tear-filled eyes locked with Conner's hardened stare. A distant siren drifted in the air along with the rancid stench of desperation.

If I did this, there would be no going back. But I saw no other choice. I had to break my silence and trust that giving him this shred of truth would be better than the alternative.

I took a shaky breath and parted my lips. "Please … don't." The words sounded as raw as they felt. Raw and vulnerable and desperate.

Conner's eyes widened with bemused fascination, as though he hadn't fully expected his threat to work. Then his hands clasped the back of my neck and pulled me close until his forehead rested against mine. His eyes bore so deep into my soul, I feared he'd cleave me in two.

"You'll give me your voice from now on?" His own voice softened, but his words were still more command than question.

When I nodded in response, his hand tightened on my neck with warning.

"Yes, I promise." Anything to keep him from asking more questions and demanding answers.

I was devastated that he could conquer me so easily but also surprisingly relieved to finally have the first of my secrets revealed, even if it was by force. For six months, I'd borne the weight of my knowledge without the slightest reprieve from the burden. My body swayed in the aftermath of such an emotional release, drawing me closer to Conner's warmth, my eyes falling to his chest.

Maybe the emotions had scrambled my brain, or maybe it was just sheer stupidity, but a part of me wanted to believe Conner was the safety I'd been searching for. My fingers curled into his designer suit jacket as I lifted my gaze back to his. The sapphire shards in his eyes were almost entirely consumed by shadow.

"You shouldn't look at me like that, Noemi. I'm not anywhere near honorable enough to resist."

I had no idea what I was doing except that it felt so good to hand over control to this man. To not be responsible for once and simply allow fate to lead the way. I'd spent every minute of every day for six months overthinking each of my actions. For better or worse, Conner was stripping away my choices and enabling me to just … be.

How could I resist that sort of temptation?

"Maybe … maybe I don't want you to."

Conner's hand fisted in my hair, gently tugging my head back.

He groaned at whatever it was he saw shining in my eyes, then nipped my bottom lip between his teeth, languid and leisurely.

I gasped, feeling the scrape of his teeth as though they'd been somewhere further south. Another part of my body aching for his kiss and swollen with need. I was desperate for more. Leaning in, I tried to press my lips to his, but he kept his mouth just out of reach.

"My name. Say it," he ordered softly.

I didn't understand what this was about, but for the briefest second, I would have given him anything if it meant keeping him close.

"Conner," I breathed.

"*Fuck.*" The violent curse tore from deep inside him before he claimed my lips with unrestrained savagery. I was rendered senseless, unable to comprehend anything beyond the taste of warm cinnamon and masculine hunger. Unable to breathe or think. Unwilling to resist.

He possessed me with unquenchable desire and lay siege to my heart in a way I never dreamed possible. Each seductive sweep of his tongue was another letter of his name etched into the surface of my soul. It would take no time at all for every thought and emotion to be centered around him.

He was too addicting. Too consuming.

A taste of his attention would never be enough. I'd crave it all, and he would become the center of my orbit. My entire purpose in life.

I pulled away from the kiss, my rational mind screaming with panic.

"I can't do this," I cried hoarsely, pulling from his grip.

"Tell me why." The undercurrent of hurt in his harsh demand gutted me.

I shook my head. "It's too much … I…"

"Then at least tell me why you were silent for so long."

My lips clamped shut, and my body stiffened with steely resolve.

Conner must have seen the iron gate come crashing down behind my eyes because his hands relaxed and allowed me to tear myself free.

I shot him one last parting glare, demanding he let the subject go.

He answered with a stare equally as adamant.

Never.

Conner

FOURTEEN

Slippery slope was the understatement of the century. Kissing Noemi was more like walking up to a black hole—I was helpless against its gravitational pull. One taste of her, and there wasn't a force on earth great enough to cleanse her from my system.

And her voice. *Jesus Christ*, her voice.

Husky but feminine, the sound of my name on her lips nearly buckled my knees. And to know I was the first to hear her speak? I didn't care that the words were coerced from her. I loved knowing I was the only one who'd reached that part of her. Who'd seen past her barriers and coaxed her out from where she'd been hiding. I could have listened to her talk all damn day, but instead, she'd run from me, which sent me spiraling in an entirely different way.

The woman made me insane. I wanted to rage against her hold on me, but a bigger part of me was too preoccupied with need for her surrender. I didn't want to bleed the truth from her like I would an enemy. I wanted her to lay it at my feet. Freely. Unconditionally.

It would happen, eventually.

For now, I'd give her the space she needed. Whatever had motivated her silence still bound her. It pissed me off that she wouldn't give me an explanation. I'd get my answers one day soon, and then I'd have her, too.

When I felt madness sinking its claws deep inside me, I tried to convince myself that pursuing her would only make my life worse. Then the darkest parts of me spoke back, arguing that the clawing insistence would subside once I'd had her. That after I'd gained her surrender, the insatiable craving would finally disappear.

Those were blatant lies, and I knew it. Something I fed myself to rationalize away my growing compulsion.

As if the darkness in me had needed a rationale.

When it came to Noemi, I was beyond reason. Infatuation had seized me like a toxin in my blood.

"If that scowl deepens any farther, it'll mar that pretty face of yours forever." Shae winked at me, seating herself on my desk.

After my exchange with Noemi, I'd busied myself with errands to keep from thinking. Once I'd run out of tasks, I came in early to the office but had found myself hopelessly distracted.

"Better than what I'll do to your face if you touch my wife again," I groused.

Shae's eyes widened. "Did you two exchange vows I'm unaware of?"

"Semantics. You knew better than to lay a finger on her." I'd already been in a dark mood, and Shae's presence wasn't helping. I'd seen her in action with women and knew she could seduce better than most men. I'd been pissed beyond measure to see them together. Hell, I hadn't even kissed Noemi at that point. I hardly even knew her, if I was honest, but none of it mattered. Nothing seemed to dilute the feral possessiveness that overcame me where she was concerned.

Shae placed her right hand over her heart and held up the other. "I swear, I won't touch Noemi from here on out." Her lips quirked with a devious smirk. "Unless she asks me to."

"Swear to God, Shae. You're walking a fine fucking line."

"Relax, Reid. I'm not moving in on your territory but think about it. She doesn't know anyone in the family. Us ladies have to stick together, and I can only imagine how isolated I'd feel if I was her, especially not being able to talk." She shoved off the desk and sauntered to the door. "I just think having a friend would be good for her." Pausing, she shot me a patronizing look that would have had me drawing my gun if it had been anyone else.

Fucking Shae.

"Just try me, woman, and I will put you on fucking bathroom duty. For life," I called after her, reclining back in my office chair with the weight of my frustrations.

"Bathroom duty? Damn! What'd she do to earn that?" Bishop filled my doorway, his too-large brown eyes shining with amusement.

"None of your business," I grumbled. "I'm surprised to see you here. I was starting to think you'd quit and moved in at the gym." Bishop could be a pain in the ass, but I'd known him all my life. He'd naturally fallen into step as my right hand and knew most everything I did about the business. I trusted him with my life. I still wasn't interested in sharing my Noemi dilemma with him.

"When the guys called and said they had a guest waiting for me downstairs, I figured I could combine work and pleasure." He raised the white towel I hadn't noticed he was carrying, blood smears staining the terry cloth.

I stilled. "You holding out on me?" A prisoner was exactly what I needed to excise some of these demons.

Bishop's answering grin was almost maniacal. "Albanian was caught sniffing around the 58th Street club this morning. Got him all squared away downstairs."

"Fuck, why didn't you tell me?" I pushed to my feet and slipped off my jacket.

"Just loosening him up for ya."

I marched from my office before I'd even finished rolling up my sleeves. It was a good thing some people never learned because I needed this today.

Our dual-purpose storage room in the basement was currently empty save for a middle-aged man tied to a chair beneath a single pendant light bulb. That, and a small metal table lined with various tools used for persuasion.

Bishop had been right. The guy was bruised and splattered with blood, but no permanent damage had been done. He'd be ready to sing soon.

All the swirling thoughts from earlier settled, and I was filled with a peaceful calm. The certainty of purpose and the joy of revenge.

"I take it our friend here hasn't been in the mood to talk yet?" I asked Bishop, moseying closer to the table.

"Nah, thinks he's a big shot."

Excellent.

I took the cordless drill into my hands, enjoying the feel of its weight. When I turned toward our prisoner, his eyes briefly flashed with terror before his pathetic mask fell back into place. That was my favorite part. Watching just how quickly they broke.

"We don't have to do this, my friend. Just tell me what your boss is planning, and this can all be over quickly." *Please, please don't.*

He glared at me through glassy black eyes, then spit at me.

I love it when they act tough.

I revved the drill and buried the tip into his knee, pushing the drill bit down into bone and cartilage.

Hysterical wails filled the room.

The drill was highly effective, so I didn't have to go too deep before they started talking. Once I heard his cries, I stood back and looked at him expectantly. The man's face was lowered, obscuring it from view.

"I don't have all day, asshole," I deadpanned.

When the man lifted his face to mine, what I'd thought were sobs was, in fact, maniacal laughter.

"I hear congratulations are in order," he said, his words lightly accented and raspy from pain. "The Mancini girl is quite the prize. Would be a shame … to lose such a … sweet little cunt." He could hardly hold up his head but still managed to smile triumphantly because he knew he'd struck a nerve by the vengeful wrath that darkened my face.

Rage like I'd never known seized me, stealing all rational thought and launching me into action.

I pulled the gun out from the waistband of my pants and shot him in the gut. I couldn't help myself. I had to punish him for spewing such filth and having the gall to speak to me about my fiancée.

"Well, shit. You really shouldn't have done that," Bishop said over the Albanian's screams.

Yes and no. I'd wanted to end his life then and there, but I wouldn't deny myself the pleasure of knowing he suffered. "You have any idea how long it takes to die of a gut shot? We still have plenty of time. And maybe, if he asks really, *really* nicely, I'll put a bullet in his brain before it's all over."

Bishop chuckled. "Guess I better settle in."

I grunted, feeling a smidge better. Not only would the Albanian die but he'd probably also tell us everything we wanted to know by the time he took his last breath, and I'd be able to send him home with a maggot-infested wound and pain etched into every crevice of his ugly face.

Life was all about finding the silver lining.

I RECEIVED AN UNEXPECTED TEXT FROM SHAE THAT AFTERNOON asking me to join her for dinner. The prospect of time out of the house with a friend was so compelling that I risked angering my father to ask for permission. I crafted a note explaining how it would be important for me to make my place among the Irish women and showed it to him along with the text. He agreed, but only after his usual barrage of thinly veiled threats and the order that Umberto was to chaperone.

I was in terrible need of a distraction after my disaster of a morning, so I didn't care what restrictions he shackled me with. I needed out of that damn house and away from my own maddening thoughts.

We met at a quaint French restaurant with low ceilings and shimmering candles at each table. Umberto was seated across the room from us. Shae eyed him curiously, and I was reminded of the way a child might study a sandcastle right before leveling it to the ground.

"You take your muscle everywhere?" She looked just as gorgeous as she had the first time we met. I wondered if she ever had a bad hair day and wore sweats or if she was naturally perfect. It seemed exhausting, but I was also a tad envious.

I took out my notepad, not ready for the rest of the world to know I could talk. Hopefully, Conner had kept that little nugget between us.

Unfortunately. I slid the pad toward her.

"It's good that your father wants to protect you," she conceded.

I wished that was all it was. Umberto had morphed from protector to jailor the day my mother died.

Thanks for the invite. It's good to get out of the house.

"Of course! We didn't get nearly enough time together at the club."

I raised my brows in question. ***Does Conner know you're here?***

He'd been pretty clear that he didn't like the idea of Shae and I befriending one another. I didn't give a crap about his ridiculous orders, but I didn't want her to get in trouble.

"No, but it's fine. He'll get over it." She grinned mischievously.

The server stopped by and took our drink orders. I went with a Pinot Grigio, relieved when the server didn't card me since I was still a year shy of the legal drinking age. Shae was a little older, probably close to Conner's age.

"You seem to be holding up well. Has a date been set?"

August 1st.

She whistled. "So soon?"

I nodded. ***No real reason to wait.***

"There's also no reason to rush, assuming neither side plans to back out."

I guess both sides were anxious to get the deal done.

"I suppose you're right," she said with a curious gleam in her eye. "I take it you didn't have a boyfriend you had to give up?"

Heat seared the tops of my cheeks as I shook my head.

"That's good." She flashed an amused grin. "Better than entering a deal like this from beneath a mountain of heartbreak.

She wasn't wrong. I sipped from my freshly poured wine admitting that things could always have been worse, then stilled when my gaze was hooked by an angry sapphire stare. Conner stood in the shadows of a hallway behind Shae, hidden from Umberto.

He motioned me over to him.

My heart scrambled to respond to a surge of adrenaline. I commanded my body to behave. Conner had bested me that morning, and I refused to give him the upper hand again.

Steadying myself, I passed a note to Shae, excusing myself to the restroom, and marched confidently into battle. Or at least, projecting the appearance of confidence. Inside, I was a quivering mess.

"What are you doing here?" I hissed the second I got close enough.

Conner took my hand and led me farther down the hall and into a small supply room, ignoring my question completely. I didn't resist, not wanting to risk making a scene. He left the door open, but the only light was what filtered in from the dimly lit hallway.

"You aren't speaking to her." His softly spoken observation was laced with curiosity and something else I couldn't name. Something intimate and seductive.

I shook my head.

"Your voice, Em," he crooned the command with honeyed authority that made my knees weak. And it was the first time I'd heard my nickname on his tongue. The rumble from his prolonged m reverberated deep into my chest like the purr of an expensive sportscar.

"I'm not ready to talk to anyone else."

His chin lifted. "Not ready, but you snuck out to dinner with Shae."

"I'd hardly say taking my bodyguard with me was sneaking. And besides, I wasn't aware I had to inform you of my plans for dinner with a friend."

Conner eased himself around me until he stood at my back. His hand swept my hair slowly over my shoulder, causing my entire body to shiver. When he spoke, his lips were inches from my ear. "The last thing on Shae's mind is friendship, I assure you. And if she has an ounce of self-preservation left in that brain of hers, she won't look twice at you again."

I turned my face, realizing too late that I'd brought our lips a breath apart. "You would … hurt her for being nice to me?" I asked breathily.

His lips quirked up in the corners as he stood tall and resumed walking back around to my front. "That woman wants what's mine. She should know better." Before I could argue, he continued in a grumble. "She can bare-knuckle box better than half of my men. You don't need to worry about her."

"I don't care how tough she is. She doesn't deserve your anger. If anyone should be angry, it's me. How did you even know we were here?"

His eyelids lowered so that only a small sliver of sapphire

was visible. "What kind of man would I be if I didn't protect what's mine?"

"I'm not yours yet." I couldn't quite hold his gaze while saying the words. The intensity of his stare was too much. Or maybe the words themselves were the challenge because I always sucked at lying and could taste the bitterness of the falsehood. It shocked me. I wasn't sure why I felt any loyalty to this man, but it was there, in the kernel of guilt sprouting in my gut.

Conner placed his hands on either side of my face and brought his lips back to my ear.

"*Liar, liar,*" he whispered, his warm breath on my skin heating my entire body. "Shall I prove it?" Then his lips were on mine, sucking, tasting, devouring.

Without the slightest objection, I became his willing victim, breathless for his touch. My entire body quivered as blood rushed to my center. When my lips parted on a moan, he sucked my bottom lip between his, grazing his teeth as he released it like he'd done the last time we kissed. But this time, he gave one last nip that ended on a stab of pain.

I jerked back and dabbed my fingers to my lips. They came away spotted with crimson.

"You *bit* me?" I shot at him, stunned.

His eyes glinted with dangerous amusement. "So nobody gets confused about who you belong to."

My hand reared back without thought, ready to strike, but he anticipated my reaction. Lightning fast, he snatched my hand midair and spun me around, hands clasped behind me. "Time to get back out there," he said wryly. "Wouldn't want that asshole out there to come looking for you."

Conner released me, then swatted my ass for good measure.

I shot him a glare that could have curdled fresh milk.

Hurrying back to the table, I licked away any traces of blood but knew my lip would be red and swollen.

Shae took one look at me and smirked. "He's here, isn't he?"

He who? I lifted my chin defiantly. ***Let's order. I'm starved.***

I was so over letting men interfere in my life. Conner. Umberto. My father. All of them. They could try to manipulate and toy with me, but at the end of the day, I was my own master. I chose to follow or fight. I decided who and what I wanted from this life, and right now, I needed to have goddamn dinner with a friend.

Lifting my wine, I clinked my glass against hers and took a healthy gulp, then scribbled a hasty toast after the fact.

Fuck the patriarchy.

Shae burst into laughter, and I was right behind her.

I DIDN'T FEEL COMPELLED TO STAY AT THE RESTAURANT AFTER MY tete-a-tete with Noemi. I wasn't actually worried about Shae, but when I heard they were out together, I found myself driving in that direction without conscious decision. I needed to know if Noemi was going to make use of her new vocal abilities, though I wasn't sure what to do with the answer.

Conflicting emotions warred at me when I saw her scribbling on her notepad. Selfish pride loved knowing her voice was all mine. I'd keep every part of her to myself if I could. The problem was, the more I learned about her, the more questions I had. I'd asked myself countless times already why she'd been silent for so long. Several obvious answers came to mind, but none explained why she would continue the ruse after being outed.

Why the fuck did she feel the need to stay silent?

Instincts told me there was a reason, and I needed to unearth it, but how? The uncertainty clawed at me, which only pissed me off. Lately, that seemed to be a constant for me, and I had far more important things to do than coax a girl into sharing her fucking baggage with me.

Agreeing to this arrangement was never supposed to unfold like it had. The whole reason I chose Noemi was to keep things simple. My wife and life completely separated. Now, I could hardly spend five minutes without thinking about her or bailing from my responsibilities to stand like a creeper in the shadows to watch her.

Shae's rolling laughter danced in the air as I exited the restaurant, giving me the perfect outlet for my frustrations. I walked to her flashy red BMW i8 and took out my switch-blade, sinking the titanium blade deep into her tread with a grin.

That's for going behind my back.

I only did the one tire. She had a spare and knew how to change it, so I wasn't worried about leaving her stranded. It was just an inconvenience. A playful lesson from her loving cousin—and no doubt she'd know exactly who to thank. It wouldn't have been any fun if she didn't.

Walking away, I spotted the black Caddy driven by the Mancini goon and considered rendering him the same service, just for shits and grins, but decided against it. I wanted Noemi to get home safely, and I wasn't looking to start a war. Though, for her, I just might.

I was so fucked.

I hadn't felt this way around a woman in … ever.

The tang of wine on her lips and the heat of her delicate curves pressed against me made my body act in ways it hadn't since I was a pubescent teen. It was maddening and ridiculous. I hated the way she challenged my control, yet I couldn't seem to get enough.

If my dick had its way, I would have fucked her against that storeroom wall. Thank God I retained some semblance of restraint. If she'd never been with a man before, I wasn't taking her virginity in a fucking supply closet. I wasn't a total monster.

What I was, though, was a hypocrite.

I'd always thought the worst of the gambling addicts that came to our clubs, night after night, pissing away every dime they had for one more turn of the roulette wheel, yet Noemi was giving me the first glimmer of understanding at the helplessness behind compulsion. There was no logic or rationale, only need and obsession.

Dice weren't my addiction, but I feared a certain green-eyed Italian just might be.

Dinner with Shae continued without interruption. Umberto never noticed my split lip, and my father didn't show up in my room to interrogate me about my night. I waited for him, certain he would appear any second. But as the minutes ticked by, and the buzz from two glasses of wine settled my nerves, I lay back in my bed and relished the brief sensation of happiness until sleep took me.

Despite everything going on around me, I'd had fun with Shae. I'd been in dire need of the escape. A chance to hang out with a friend and pretend my life wasn't in tatters.

After Mom died and I was released from the hospital, I spent days in bed hiding from the world. From my reality and a father who had gone from absent to abscess, infecting my life with his venomous cruelty. I'd always known he wasn't a good man—that his relationship with Mom was all show and no substance—but I hadn't realized just how wrong things truly were. Not until that day.

I wasn't supposed to be in the car with her, but I thanked God I was, or I never would have known the truth. I knew my father had orchestrated the whole thing and why he'd wanted my beautiful mother dead. She'd told me everything seconds before she took her last breaths.

I knew everything, and I'd been deciding what to do with that knowledge ever since.

For now, the answer was … nothing. I couldn't afford such a gamble until I could ensure Sante and I would both survive the fallout. And the more time that passed, the greater my anger and resolve. I would find a way.

In the meantime, I had a bullheaded Irishman to deal with. I couldn't believe Conner had crashed my dinner or the way he'd laid claim to me. Marked me.

Why had he felt the need to make such a bold statement? No matter how long I lay in bed the next morning and pondered his motivations, nothing made sense. I knew he wanted sex, but he'd said in the beginning that he didn't want the marriage any more than I did. So why the jealousy? Was he merely wanting to ensure others knew I was his? Men could be territorial like that. It didn't necessarily mean he truly wanted me beyond the physical. Right?

I didn't understand him, nor could I get the seductive taste of him from my tongue—cinnamon spiked with the burn of whiskey and temptation. I needed to brush my teeth and maybe Listerine my brain. I couldn't keep losing myself in thoughts of him. Scraps of memory enhanced with a healthy dose of fantasy.

Sucking in a deep lungful of air, I finally forced myself from bed and into the shower. Dwelling on the infinite mysteries of Conner Reid would get me nowhere, and I had a bridal shower to prepare for. Aunt Etta was hosting a last-minute luncheon for me. Ladies from my family as well as Conner's had been invited.

My aunt had insisted that a bride needed at least *one* shower. I knew she felt responsible for taking on the things my mother would have done, so I didn't argue with her. In her eyes, a shower was a sign of celebration. A show of support and a source of joy. Personally, I would rather have shaved my armpits with a rusty razor than sit among the awkward assortment of women, but as with most things these days, my preference wasn't important.

Umberto drove me to the tearoom Aunt Etta had booked for the gathering. There was a moment at the house before we left when I thought Sante might be allowed to accompany me. It would have provided a rare unguarded moment together away from the house, but my father ordered me to stay put until Umberto returned home to take me. My father was meticulous about keeping us apart. And if I hadn't been so certain my father used microphones and cameras in the house, I would have tried telling Sante the truth at home. Hell, even the cars were suspect. I wouldn't have put anything past my father.

Outfitted in my best designer sheath dress and a heavy swathe of confidence, I entered the restaurant with my shoulders back and a smile on my painted lips.

No soldier went to battle without armor, and this would be nothing less than an hour in the trenches. The silent freak set on a stage under blinding lights for everyone to gawk at. Hopefully, they would at least be too distracted by me and my circumstances to argue among themselves. As far as I knew, no one had ever attempted an alliance like ours.

The Italians and Irish meshed about as well as gasoline and a Zippo. They couldn't even go to the same Catholic churches. Everyone knew the old St. Patrick's Basilica was property of the Irish, while The Church of the Blessed Sacrament was Italian territory. Not even the priests deigned to cross those lines. I had wondered if anyone would even show up to such a highly precarious event as my shower, but I should have known better.

Curiosity was even more potent than fear.

The wives and daughters of New York's underworld weren't about to miss out on the tantalizing prospect of such juicy gossip. All but a handful of invitees showed up, packing the entire tearoom with women. A mountain of gifts filled two tables near the entrance, and every set of eyes in the building took turns glancing my way. Everything about it was overwhelming, but I knew better than to show any fear. Not among these people. That was exactly what they'd want to see.

Instead, I kept my head high despite my silence and pretended I was the queen who was under no obligation to talk to the peons. Ladies congratulated me and prattled on about who they were and how thrilled they were about the upcoming nuptials. I smiled and nodded, clasped my hand with theirs, then dismissed them with a glance at the next guest.

"Hey, love. How are you holding up?" Aunt Etta gave me a quick hug during a brief lull.

I nodded and grinned through the pain in my cheeks, sore from so much smiling.

"Good, good. You might not get another lull for a while, so I'd suggest you hit the restroom while you can." She didn't have to tell me twice.

I grabbed my clutch and hurried off in the direction she indicated, blowing her a kiss in thanks. Once I was in the stall relieving my suddenly full bladder, my adrenaline ebbed, making me reluctant to abandon the reprieve of my solitude.

Dropping my head into my hands, I rested my elbows on my knees and tried to motivate myself to rejoin the shower attendees. Before I could muster the energy, a couple of women entered the restroom, giggling voices hushed in confidence.

"It's such a shame—that god of a man getting shackled to a demure mute—but at least that means he'll still be available. There's no way she'll keep him satisfied. I should know." The feminine voice curled with a catty grin. I didn't know who exactly was speaking, but I knew the type well enough. Gorgeous. Ruthless. Completely self-serving.

"That's so gross, Ivy," said the other. "Isn't he your cousin?

"By marriage," the first one scoffed. "And besides, he's adopted, you prude. It's not like we're *actually* related."

Adopted? Pippa hadn't mentioned that. I wondered how that fact had slipped past her radar.

"*Still,*" said the prude. "It sounds icky." She paused. "Do you think all adopted people have to worry about whether they're dating a family member?"

The women quietly contemplated the question as they preened in front of the mirrors. I continued to gnaw on the assertion that I'd never keep Conner satisfied.

Why did that statement itch and claw its way beneath my skin?

I'd never intended to *satisfy* him. I wasn't a brokered commodity to be consumed. If my husband wasn't faithful, that was a reflection of him, not me.

Nothing these vapid women said should have mattered, but I couldn't help my need to defend myself and the relationship. Surprisingly enough, someone else beat me to it.

A third voice pipped up as the stall next to mine swung open. "What's icky is the sound of one woman tearing down another when she's obviously in a tough position already. In this day and age, we should be supporting one another, not stabbing each other in the back."

Sensing my moment had arrived, I used the pause created by her reprimand to exit the stall with my shoulders squared. Their eyes were instantly on me, but I didn't acknowledge any of them. Instead, I applied a perfect coat of crimson lipstick in the most seductive manner possible, gave my lips one good smack, then shot a wink at my audience in the mirror before walking out.

I'd never felt so triumphant and wrecked at the same time.

Everything about my display had been on point. I'd never appeared more confident. But on the inside, I was a rattled mess.

When the time came, what exactly would Conner want from me as his wife? The wedding night and weeks thereafter were intimidating enough, but what about five and ten years from then? Would we ever form any true connection? Did I care?

I imagined seeing Conner return home late at night, a touch of unfamiliar lipstick staining the skin on his neck.

Scalding anger seared upward from beneath my asymmetric neckline.

I didn't want my husband fucking other women. Why? Because of the embarrassment it would cause, of course. My stomach churned with uncertainty. Embarrassment was part of the reason but not the whole picture. I hated to admit it, but I didn't want him to stray because I wanted him to want me.

Hell, I'm in trouble.

All I should have wanted was for Conner to leave me alone. To live out our lives peaceably in parallel worlds that rarely intersected. But that wasn't the case. I wanted more from him, which meant I was opening myself up to heartbreak.

"Hey, wait a sec," called the woman who had supported me in the bathroom. She had rushed out after me and was hurrying to catch up with me. When I turned, she grinned broadly with crimson lips even brighter than mine and eyes so green, mine paled in comparison. She was absolutely stunning.

She held out her hand to shake. "Sorry about that. I got a little fired up. My name's Giada. Giada Genovese. I'm Conner's half sister. And don't mind those shrews. They're just jealous. My sisters are just over there, and they'd love to meet you if you have a minute."

If I wasn't already mute, I'd have been rendered speechless. Half sister? I wasn't sure if I was more overwhelmed by her boisterous personality or the fact of who she was. The Genoveses were Italian. How did Conner have an Italian half sister?

I nodded dazedly, stumbling alongside her when she took my arm and towed me toward a table in the back of the room.

"Cam and Val, look who I found." Giada grinned. "Noemi, this is Camilla and Valentina, my two younger sisters."

I nodded to each and smiled. More demure than the eldest, the two younger women greeted me with kind eyes and a gentle wave.

"It wasn't that long ago we discovered we had a brother, and now we get a sister-in-law, too! Crazy times, right?" Giada rambled. "We'll definitely have to get together. I don't know many people in the Moretti family, so you'll have to introduce us, though I'm not sure how much Conner wants us all around. It's all kind of new. Mom's around here somewhere. I'm sure she'd love to meet you, too."

My eyes flitted to each of them, trying to figure out what

on earth she was talking about. Before I could get out my notepad to start asking questions, the blond sister spoke up.

"There's time for that later, G. For now, I bet Noemi has guests to get back to. We don't want to monopolize her time."

"Of course, sorry. I get carried away. It's really lovely to meet you, and congratulations!" She pulled me into a quick hug, surprising me yet again.

I waved to the three of them before turning away to find my table. I was so disoriented that I hardly remembered making my way back to my family.

"Hey, Em. You hanging in there?" Pip asked cheerily.

When I turned to meet her gaze, I couldn't eradicate the dismay widening my eyes.

"Oh, sweetie. It's going to be okay—all of it. Everything." She paused, studying me. "Is it the party … or is it him that's worrying you?"

I just stared at her, unable to untangle my own chaotic thoughts.

She grimaced, seeming to understand. "It's a lot. And I never should have told you about the burning man. That's just this life, you know that, right? Just because he lights people on fire doesn't mean he's going to hurt you."

Pip didn't realize how right she was, except it was *me* he lit on fire every time he was near, and that was exactly how I'd end up hurt.

Oh, the irony.

I huffed with a silent chuckle.

Pip smiled, relieved. "Come on. Let's grab a couple of mimosas. That will make us both feel better."

I nodded, letting her lead me back to the center table before she disappeared in search of drinks. My emotions must have still been lingering on the surface because Aunt Etta also asked if I was okay the second she saw me.

I took out my notepad.

Does Conner have Italian half sisters? I peered at her questioningly.

"Did no one tell you?" she asked, brows knitted together.

I shook my head.

"He was adopted. It all came out in the open just recently. I don't know the details, really, just that Mia Genovese was his birth mother."

My head tipped back slowly with understanding before I scribbled again.

I just met his three sisters. I was confused.

She chuckled. "I suppose that's understandable." She took my hand in hers. "Hey, I realized we never talked about getting you a dress. I don't know how we overlooked it. You want to go tomorrow?"

I smiled warmly and nodded. Her answering grin was so heartwarming it could have brought back the dead. "Perfect. I'll set up an appointment as soon as we're done here today."

I nodded and gave her a hug. If I had to lose my mom, there was no better substitute than her twin sister. Being around my aunt these past few days made me realize how cruel it had been for my father to keep us apart for so long. I needed this. I needed her and all the strength her love provided.

Another hour later, I spotted a familiar set of warm brown eyes across the room when the party was finally winding down. Grinning, I hurried over to where Sante leaned against the wall and wrapped him in a crushing hug.

"Whoa, little big. Easy there." The second he had sprouted taller than me, he started to call me his little big sister. I loved it, and hearing the endearment only made me hug him tighter.

He chuckled and eased from my death grip. "I couldn't let my only sister get married without giving her a gift of my own, and I figured this was as good a time as any."

Did Dad know he was here? Had Sante come on his own?

I suddenly sobered, wondering if this could be my chance to tell him the truth about our mom. Or maybe even to run away with him.

My hands trembled as I accepted the small, wrapped package.

"It's not that exciting. No reason to get all shaky," he teased, not knowing my tremor had nothing to do with his gift.

I peeled back the wrapping to unveil a white gold bracelet. It had a delicate chain on either side of a flat plaque engraved with *Mancini*.

"So you don't forget us," he said quietly.

His gift was incredibly thoughtful. I hugged him again, this time with tears in my eyes, then signaled to the door in question.

"Yeah, we're here to get you."

We? An entire bucket of frigid water drenched me from head to toe.

He must have seen the question written across my face. "Yeah, Dad is waiting outside. You ready?"

I tried to swallow past the sudden lump in my throat. Nodding, I held up my finger for him to wait, then went to tell Pip and Aunt Etta goodbye and thank you. They assured me the gifts would be delivered to my house. I couldn't have cared less but nodded politely.

Once I got to the car, I slid into the back seat like a criminal being remanded back into custody. Hopelessness was yet another cratering dip in the roller coaster ride of emotions I'd endured that day. By the time I got home, all I wanted was to crawl into bed and sleep for a week, but I should have known better. My life wasn't my own, and my day was long from over.

"I'll be back in a minute. Berto needs my help in the garage." Sante stood from the couch. We'd been watching the most recent James Bond release together.

I pointed at the TV with raised brows.

"Don't worry about pausing it. No clue how long I'll be." He rolled his eyes, then left the room.

I decided I wasn't in a hurry, so I paused the movie anyway. I was more interested in hanging out with my brother than watching the show. The house seemed extra quiet after the explosion-filled action movie was silenced. So quiet that I almost jumped out of my skin when a knock sounded on the front door.

Defaulting to a time when I wasn't under constant

surveillance, I jumped from the couch and hurried to the front door but stilled before opening it. My father was out for the evening, but I knew he'd probably have a fit if he found out I'd opened the door with no one around. But then again, the guys were in the garage. Was I just supposed to ignore whoever had come by? I couldn't exactly yell through the door for them to wait.

I would have pulled up the security camera footage on my app, but I'd been stripped of my access months ago. I decided to take a chance and peek through the curtain covering the window beside the door. I couldn't see much off to the side, but it was enough when I spotted a familiar ring brandishing a Celtic knot on a masculine hand inked with a black rose. Conner was here.

Without overthinking it, I slipped outside and grabbed his wrist, tugging him away from the entrance and around the corner to a spot where I remembered the cameras didn't quite reach.

"What are you doing here?" I hissed at him in the dark, suddenly realizing he could have stopped by for my father and not me. After his surprise appearance at the restaurant the day before, I'd worried he had only one thing on his mind, and it wasn't business.

"I wasn't aware I had to explain myself to you." He leaned forward menacingly.

Not in the mood to be intimidated, I crossed my arms over my chest and realized I wasn't wearing a bra under my thin nightshirt. I tried not to let my fluster show. "I suppose not, so long as that little rule works both ways," I shot back haughtily.

His lips twisted in a wickedly vicious grin. He reached a hand slowly to the hem of my pajama shirt, twirling his finger until the fabric twisted around the digit, then tugged me toward him. "Nice try, but no. That's not at all how this works. In fact, you already owe me one explanation, at least. I don't care if you never speak to another living soul, but my mother tells me you were still silent at the shower today, and I want to know *why*."

Had he told his mom I could speak? Would word get around if he had? Shit. I needed more time.

"I just need to figure out how to explain things to my father. Once he knows I can talk, he'll want to know why I didn't before. I don't want him making any assumptions." More accurately, he'd want to know why I'd chosen to speak *now*. If I could manage to stay silent until the wedding, maybe I could sneak away and tell Uncle Donati everything I knew.

Yeah, and then what happens to Sante?

Ugh! I needed to come up with a plan. Dad needed to pay for what he did, but I couldn't risk losing my brother in the process. I was faced with the same damn problem every time. What if I couldn't protect Sante? What if the only way to stop my dad meant risking losing my brother forever?

I could hardly stomach the possibility.

"What is there to explain?" Conner asked, cutting into my internal argument. "You were processing your mother's death … unless it's more complicated than that?"

God, he needs to stop!

I felt frustrated and trapped. Adding to my mounting need to lash out, the words from the catty bathroom queen floated back to me. *Demure mute. Never satisfy him.*

I stepped an inch closer and lifted my chin defiantly. "Sometimes people are complicated. Like a man who chose a mute bride, presumably so he didn't have to acknowledge her existence, yet for some reason, he keeps showing up everywhere she's at." I took another small step. The heat of his chest pulled at my pebbled nipples, the fabric of my T-shirt just grazing him enough to shoot tiny bolts of lightning to my core.

The sensation of standing up to him made me breathless and dizzy in the best way. I never could have stood up to my father like this, but with Conner, I felt bold. Empowered.

If I dissected my behavior, I might have discovered the root of my confidence anchored in a sense of safety, but I didn't care to go there. Treating Conner as the enemy was the only way to guard my heart against him.

Every ounce of blue drained from his eyes as he forced my back against the wall, his hard body pressed into mine. "For someone who didn't want to speak, you sure have a lot of opinions." The rough edges of his voice scraped across my skin.

"For a man, you're awfully observant." A low blow, but I was running out of retorts.

"And for someone who wants to be left alone, you sure have on tiny shorts."

My lips opened and closed like a fish out of water as his rough fingertips grazed slowly up my left thigh beneath the fabric of my pajama shorts to the lace edge of my panties near my hip bone. I couldn't breathe more than the tiniest pants of air. My lungs, along with the rest of my body, were frozen in concentration, consumed with where his fingers might go next.

He lifted the elastic edge of my panties to slide the tip of one finger beneath, his eyes gleaming at my gasped response. With the measured calm of a practiced tactician, he slowly slid the finger down along the stretched fabric. My mind sparked and sputtered at the uncertainty of how far he might go, but as he reached the front of me, inches away from my slit, he slipped from beneath the baby blue lace and instead left a trail of embers like a comet's tail down my thigh before severing our connection.

"You shouldn't be alone in the dark with a man you hardly know." His voice had gone guttural, raw and wanting. The sound tugged at the deep ache he'd stirred between my legs.

"Will you give me that same warning on our wedding night? I doubt we'll know each other any better by then." I wanted to sound formidable, but every word was more breathless than the last.

His answering look was positively savage. "When I can smell your pussy dripping with need? I don't think so. Now get back inside before I decide to take what's already mine."

His filthy words grated against my skin and heated me from the inside out. I'd never heard someone speak to me with such crude irreverence, and I was ashamed of how desperate I was for more.

I whirled away from the wall and scurried back to the front entrance. When I opened the giant metal door, my mind a cyclone of emotions, I stuttered to a stop at the sight of Sante. He stood in the entry frozen mid step, his narrowed glare sliding from me to a spot over my shoulder. A quick glance confirmed it was Conner's retreating form in the distance that had stoked my brother's temper. I slammed the door shut and hurried over to him, tugging him into the living room where I had a pen and paper.

He just wanted to ask me a quick question, and you were busy with Umberto. I explained, my words almost illegible after rushing to get them on paper.

"You shouldn't have been outside with him alone, Noemi. Especially considering how you're dressed. Jesus, what if he'd hurt you?" His teen emotions and protective instincts quickly brewed a storm inside him.

He'll be my <u>husband</u> in just over a week. I pointed out with a surge of anger, then chided myself. I needed to defuse the situation, not pick a fight.

"Yeah, and if he took advantage of you, then backed out of the arrangement—what then?"

I wanted to rage at him that if he thought Conner was such a creep, he shouldn't sit by while Dad married me off to the man. But I knew Sante had just as little say in the matter as I did.

Nothing happened. There's no reason to get upset, okay? I'm fine. I peered at him pleadingly, then motioned to the living room. When he just stood there, brows furrowed, I took his hand and pulled him to the couch. He let me drag him but begrudgingly.

We returned to our movie, though he never fully relaxed next to me. An hour later, we were interrupted by the sounds of my father returning home. I sat up and slowly turned to peer at my brother, wary of what I might find. As I suspected, the severe cut of his jaw and harsh draw of his brows told me everything I needed to know. He planned to tell my father about Conner's visit.

I shook my head, small jerky movements, wordlessly pleading.

His lips only thinned with resigned determination as he stood. The clacking of my father's dress shoes counted down the seconds like the ticking of a bomb.

"You two and those action movies. Don't you get sick of them?" Dad grumbled, taking the lid off a crystal decanter and pouring himself two fingers of scotch.

"Just killing time," Sante said, his voice losing its familiar boyishness. "We had a visitor tonight."

Dad's eyes cut to my brother, then slid to me. I remained motionless on the couch, hoping beyond hope I'd finally learned to become invisible.

"Reid came by. I'd gone with Umberto to the garage to help him install that new temperature gauge." He paused, his gaze briefly straying to mine with a glint of apology that quickly faded into harsh resolve. "Noemi answered the door and spoke with him outside."

My father went eerily still. When his gaze cut to me, the fury in his eyes leached him of all humanity. My queasy stomach now roiled angrily, pressing dangerously high in my throat.

All thoughts of his drink forgotten, Dad prowled toward me.

"Nothing happened, but I thought you should know. That's all," Sante added as though a sudden bout of conscience had him backpedaling.

Dad ignored him completely. When he was close enough to tower over me, he struck quick as a snake, grabbing my wrist and yanking me to my feet. "Did you let him fucking touch you?" Irate spittle dotted my face, veins bulging in my father's forehead. He was as angry as I'd ever seen him, and it terrified me.

I shook my head frantically, the bones in my wrist screaming in agony as he crushed them together.

"That's all I need is for you to ruin this by letting him fuck you before the wedding, giving him reason to back out."

Again, all I could do was shake my head and pray he believed me.

"Don't you ever pull that shit again, you hear me?" He brought his cheek to mine, his next words for my ears only. "You fuck this up, and it won't be quick like your mother. I'll make you wish you'd never been born." He pulled back, and the demented rage in his black stare sealed his murderous promise.

I nodded through tear-filled eyes and tugged away from him, the need to escape clawing at my every fiber. He finally relented.

I rushed from the room, passing Sante on the way, unable to look him in the face. I knew my disappointment and resentment would shine through, but I also knew none of this was entirely his fault. He was just a boy, no matter how manly he now looked. A pawn in our father's sadistic games.

I'd thought I hated the man when I was younger for never being present, but I hadn't even known what hate was. Now, I was intimately acquainted with the emotion. Hate blistered a scorching path in my veins and flayed me open from the inside. Fausto Mancini was a poison, determined to destroy me, one way or another.

I PUT A WET RAG ON MY WRIST, UNWILLING TO GO BACK downstairs for ice. By morning, an ugly purple ring had formed beneath the surface of my skin.

I hated that this had become my life.

I'd never had to hide bruises before, but it made me wonder if my mother had. Was this the life she'd led before he'd taken her from me? Could he have been this cruel to her without me knowing?

I might never know the answer, though it would likely haunt me forever. Mom was the rainbow in a stormy sky. She was the sugar in lemonade and the pink stretchy bandage that made everything better. I had adored everything about her and hated to think she could have suffered right under my nose.

A suffocating cloud darkened my mood as I got ready for the day, but I did my best to sweep it away, knowing I would be spending the morning dress shopping with Aunt Etta and Pip. Just knowing I would see them helped lighten my heart. I briefly considered asking my aunt if she ever suspected Dad of abuse, but the question would only have stirred up an interrogation. Quelling my curiosity wasn't worth opening that can of worms. Not yet, anyway.

I selected an outfit that suited the only wide gold cuff bracelet I owned and used the accessory to hide my bruise. Hair in a ponytail and hope in my heart, I went downstairs to find Umberto. It was time to pick out a wedding dress.

The boutique dress shop didn't look like much from the outside, sandwiched between two modern buildings near Lenox Hill and Midtown East, but the interior was all modern elegance with dark wood floors and crystal chandeliers. Pippa and her mom were already inside when I arrived, along with Pip's two younger sisters. I left Umberto at the door and joined the group on a green velour sofa.

"Oh my God, I can't believe this is happening." Pip jumped up and hugged me the second she saw me.

It was so tempting to share my own disbelief by blurting all the crazy I'd experienced in recent weeks, but I forced my lips to remain sealed.

"I know," added Aunt Etta. "I swore I wouldn't say it because I don't want this to be a sad occasion, but I sure wish Nora could have been here for this." My aunt hugged me but quickly pulled away and waved her hands in the air. "Okay, enough of that. Only happy thoughts today!"

Pip and I both laughed. The other girls sat on their phones, oblivious to the world around them.

"This must be our beautiful bride!" A very tall, very thin

woman joined us in the sitting area with a smile. "I'm Stella. I'll be working with you to find the *perfect* dress."

I shook her hand, letting Aunt Etta introduce us.

"I explained when I made the appointment that we're working with somewhat unusual time constraints," Etta said.

"Noemi here isn't the first and won't be the last. It shouldn't be an issue. We may just have to be open-minded and a touch creative." Stella lifted her brows at me as if to make sure I was on the same page.

I nodded readily.

"Great! Now, tell me what you're envisioning."

🔥

Two hours later, I had a wedding dress. Even more astounding, I actually loved it. The gown was simple but elegant—no bows or bustles or flouncing skirt. The delicate lace top layer was accented with just the right amount of beadwork to sparkle but not make me feel like a disco ball. The straps of the sleeveless bodice sat at the far edges of my shoulders while the neckline plunged low between my breasts, working well with my modest chest. The back mirrored the front but dipped all the way down to the waist, and the A-line skirt flared just enough not to cling to me and trailed into a very short train.

The dress had been altered for a recent bridal expo where it was displayed, so it already fit almost perfectly. I'd walked into the shop not expecting to care about any of it and fully prepared to pick whatever looked halfway decent, considering my fast-approaching deadline. Now, I couldn't stop wondering what Conner would think of me in the dress.

That line of thinking was dangerous. It implied that I cared, and I shouldn't have.

Aunt Etta scooted closer to where I sat on the shop sofa

and leaned toward me, snagging my attention. "Em, honey. I doubt your dad has talked to you about this, and I have no idea if Nora handled it before she passed, so I thought I'd ask about birth control." She looked at me awkwardly while I gaped back at her.

She'd caught me completely off guard.

I wasn't on birth control, as it so happened, but only because I hadn't needed it. I'd never made any special pledge to save myself for marriage. Sex just hadn't come up. I didn't date much in high school, then Mom died only seven months after graduation. That was just the way my life had unfolded.

Now, I was days away from being a twenty-year-old virgin bride, and no, I hadn't considered birth control. After my first official meeting with Conner, I would have said it wasn't an issue. But things had changed. He'd made it clear he wanted me. I'd been so worried about the emotional impact that might have that I'd completely forgotten about any other complications.

I was NOT ready for children.

"...and maybe he's not even Catholic," Aunt Etta continued her rambling speech. "I mean, he's Irish, but they aren't all Catholic, and even then, he may still be okay with birth control. Sometimes we have to do what we think is right, or we'd all be swimming in a sea of children," she whispered conspiratorially.

A giggle nearly bubbled past my lips. It was getting harder and harder to keep my voice to myself now that I'd started talking to Conner.

Just a little longer. You can do it.

"But anyway, you'll have plenty of time to figure it out. I just thought I'd mention it so you could mentally prepare. And make sure you knew I'd be happy to help if you needed it." She patted my hand and nodded to herself, seemingly satisfied.

I jotted a note thanking her and ensuring I'd take care of it. I wasn't sure how, but I swore to myself that was one compromise I was unwilling to concede.

Our shopping concluded, Aunt Etta convinced Umberto to let me join them for lunch. We had such a fabulous time together that I could have mistaken it for before—before Mom died and my world came crashing down around me. Before my father threatened my life and I suddenly had a fiancé.

That slice of the past was enough to keep me distracted with happy memories for the rest of the afternoon once I'd returned home. I listened to music and watched a home renovation show. Anything to keep my thoughts in the happy beyond where there were no deadlines or fathers or fiancés.

Sometimes a girl needed to stick her head in the sand for a day.

I was remarkably successful at it, too, until the chime of the doorbell echoed into my room that evening. I moved to the top of the stairs, staying just out of sight of the entry below. We didn't get visitors often. I wondered if it was Conner but couldn't be sure. The velvet strands of a baritone voice were too soft to recognize.

I was desperately curious but afraid I'd earn my father's wrath again if I showed my face downstairs without an invitation. I had no desire to poke that dragon. Fortunately, fate intervened to assuage my curiosity.

"Noemi, come down and meet someone." My father's voice boomed in my ears, echoing inside the hollow of my chest.

I waited for just a second to ensure it didn't look like I'd been eavesdropping, then glided gracefully downstairs, nearly stumbling on the steps when my eyes landed on one of the most savagely handsome men I'd ever seen. He looked like his ancestors had only recently abandoned their Viking ship to raid boardrooms instead of villages. A heavy brow casting harsh shadows over ocean eyes gave him a foreboding look, while his thick blond hair styled back in a perfect pompadour would get him inside any upscale club. Unshaved scruff on his square jaw contrasted with his perfectly tailored suit the same way he showed just a tiny bit more incisor than appropriate when he smiled. Like the wolf greeting Little Red. Everything about this man was a contradiction. An enigma. He was utterly mesmerizing and perfectly terrifying.

I forced a smile.

"Noemi, this is Keir Byrne, Conner's cousin. You met his father briefly at the engagement dinner—Jimmy Byrne."

I tore my eyes from the man, sensing my father communicating an unspoken message. I dropped my chin a fraction to let him know I understood.

This man was important. A power player in the Irish organization.

"It's a pleasure." He extended his hand. "I apologize for missing the engagement dinner, but I was otherwise detained." Hearing his voice up close and the power it wielded sent a shiver down my spine. Every softly spoken word forced those around him to listen carefully. To dance to his tune. The subtle exercise of dominance was impressive.

"As you know," my father cut in. "Noemi here lost her voice in a tragic accident. Conversations with her aren't easy, so we can just head back to my office."

Keir didn't budge. "That's not an issue. Conner won't be here for a few minutes. I thought that might give me time to get to know the newest addition to our family. It's not every day we take in an outsider." The entire time he spoke, his eyes held mine captive. Studying. Assessing.

What was he looking for? What did he think he'd find?

I wasn't too worried because I had no malicious intent—

not toward him or his family. Any negativity I felt was reserved for my own flesh and blood.

My father agreed, albeit reluctantly. He'd clearly hoped to make the introduction and be rid of my presence as quickly as possible, but Keir had other plans.

Dad's lips thinned. "Let's have a seat in the living room. Noemi, you'll have to get your pad and paper." He peered back at Keir. "That's how she communicates," he explained as though I were a trained ape. "She should probably learn sign language at some point, but it's hardly been a priority so soon after her mother's death."

I gritted my teeth at the manufactured grief he forced into his voice. As if my father had given one minute's thought to her death except to cover up what he'd done. Suddenly realizing I was being watched, my eyes cut to Keir. He'd seen the glare I'd shot at my father's back.

I wondered if it was possible to keep anything from his keen eye. If he was curious about my reaction, I couldn't tell. He gave absolutely nothing away. The man was the Dalai Lama of calm and control. It was unnerving. Conner was contained, but his composure wasn't so absolute, at least not when I was around. Like last night. I'd had the sense he was seconds from complete chaos, and I sort of relished knowing I had that effect on him. Keir held so tightly to his reins that I didn't think anything could rattle him.

Forcing a smile, I tried to rid myself of emotion. If I didn't feel it, I couldn't show it.

"There are two more members of the family who would love to meet you," Keir informed me as he sat on one end of the sofa, an arm draped along the back cushion like a king on his throne. He motioned for me to sit with him. "Paddy and Nana Byrne, our grandparents and the founders of our family. It's hard for them to get out these days, but they've requested a visit. If it's agreeable to you, Fausto, I thought I could run Noemi over to their house tomorrow to meet them. They rarely get out anymore."

My heart hammered against my ribs, unsure of what to do.

Keir and I both looked at my father, whose black eyes cut to me.

"I'm not sure it's appropriate for her to be alone with another man before the wedding." Dad shifted uncomfortably just as Sante entered the room, inserting himself into our conversation.

"I'd be happy to go with Noemi." My brother leaned in to shake hands with Keir. "Sante Mancini, Noemi's brother. You must be Keir Byrne." He so desperately wanted to be a man and to help me. It broke my heart because he was so clueless. Dad would never agree to us going without supervision.

"That's kind of you to offer, Sante," Keir responded. "But surely your father wouldn't be giving his daughter away if he thought we didn't have the ability to keep her safe."

Displeasure deepened the creases of my father's face. Any argument on his behalf would be a blatant disrespect to Keir and the entire Byrne family. He had no choice but to agree, and Keir knew it.

"Of course, I trust you. But she is my only baby girl. I'd hate to damage her reputation so close to the wedding. If we sent one of my men along with you, that would ease my mind." Dad tried another tack.

Keir stared unflinchingly at my father. "And I would understand your concern if anyone beyond our two families had asked, but Conner is my cousin. It's hardly inappropriate for me to aid in escorting her."

I couldn't believe Keir was arguing with my father. Most men wouldn't have bothered pushing the issue, but Keir clearly wasn't most men. He wasn't about to back down, and my father must have sensed it.

"I suppose a quick visit to your grandparents won't be a problem." His eyes cut to mine, and I wondered what this would mean for me. No doubt I'd find out later once our guest had left.

My hand absently covered the cuff bracelet I'd worn over my right wrist all day to hide the mottled bruising.

"Tell me, Noemi, do you have any hobbies or interests?" Keir asked, putting an end to the debate.

Music. I used to sing all the time but only for myself. I tried to write extra neat, feeling an inexplicable need to gain the Irish mobster's respect. Something about him induced a desire to impress.

"Any particular genre?"

I appreciated that he didn't give any empty assurances that I was sure to recover my voice. Deceiving everyone was bad enough. I only felt worse when people tried to console me.

All kinds, but especially ballads with meaningful lyrics. I wasn't sure why I was sharing any more about myself than the bare minimum. Again, it was just something about him.

Before he could comment, the front door chimed. We all watched Sante stroll to the entrance, then Conner's baritone voice filtered into the room and feathered across my skin.

When he rounded the corner, he was the epitome of cool indifference. I would have believed it if his gaze hadn't burned my skin when it drifted from Keir to me.

"Did I have our timing wrong?" Conner asked casually.

"No," Keir assured him in that perfectly schooled voice of his. "I wasn't afforded the opportunity to meet your lovely bride previously, so I thought I'd come by a few minutes early."

Was that challenge in Keir's aqua gaze?

Most likely, considering the displeasure rolling off Conner

in waves. "Had I known you wanted an introduction, I would have been happy to help."

Finally, the tiniest break in Keir's icy demeanor—a smile wrought with wicked amusement. "You know better than to think I need your help with an introduction."

"Speaking of introductions," my father cut in. "Keir suggested he take Noemi to meet your grandparents tomorrow."

Keir's head slowly swiveled to stare at my father. For the first time I could ever recall witnessing, my father blanched.

"That's very thoughtful of him," Conner murmured impassively. "Gentlemen, should we get to business?"

"Of course," Keir agreed. "We can't have any hostile Albanians causing problems at such an important wedding. Noemi, it's been a pleasure. I look forward to chatting more in the morning. Say ten?"

I nodded, a wave of awkward uncertainty perching high over my head.

Keir nodded respectfully, then gestured for Dad to lead the way. The two men and my brother followed my father out of the room, Conner searing me with an angry stare on his way.

My bones dissolved like sugar cubes in hot water the second I was alone. I fell back onto the couch and stared at the ceiling, needing a minute to recover before I could throw together a sandwich and drag myself upstairs. It looked like Dad would be working through dinner, and I was more than happy to hide for the rest of the night.

Thinking my drama with overbearing Irishmen was over for the evening, I ate my turkey and cheese, then changed into my pajamas. Growing up with a little brother meant it was habit for me to change in the bathroom. Sante rarely entered my room unannounced anymore, so I was surprised when I opened the door and found my room occupied. Only, it wasn't my brother standing at my bedroom window.

"Conner, what are you doing up here?" I whispered, my eyes cutting to the open bedroom door.

He slowly turned and leveled me with his unrelenting stare.

I'd worried about dealing with my father after their meeting, but I hadn't mentally prepared for six feet two of blistering anger devouring me. "You need to stay the fuck away from Keir." The velvet darkness of his voice raised the hairs on the back of my neck.

"He's your *cousin,*" I hissed quietly, eyes again straying to the doorway. "What exactly do you think is going to happen?"

I'd known my father might force me to stay home, but I didn't have to take this from Conner, too. I refused on principle.

He stepped closer until every inch of his menacing frame towered over me. "I'm telling you to stay away, or you won't like the consequences."

"What are you going to do, cut off his fingers?" I spit back at him, recalling his earlier comment about maiming anyone who touched me.

He leaned in even closer, bringing his lips to my ear. "Try me and see." His words caressed, sensual and excruciating, before his lips tugged at my earlobe with just enough pressure to elicit an avalanche of tingles from my scalp to my fingertips and lower.

I gasped, words escaping me. Outrage mixed with crushing desire to form a dizzying cocktail that stole my breath.

Satisfied with himself, Conner smirked and waltzed away.

JUST WHEN YOU THINK YOU KNOW SOMEONE, THEY GO AND surprise you.

I would have bet money my father would have charged into my room the second Conner and Keir were gone and demanded I fake an illness to prevent me from going the following morning. I debated whether to mention how suspicious it might look if I canceled and if I should remind him how we wouldn't want to offend the Byrne family.

I waited. And waited.

My father never appeared, but my mental energies weren't wasted because I still had a fight in store.

Minutes after I turned the light off in my room, a phone began to chime. My eyes shot open, staring into the dark.

It wasn't my phone, or at least not a ring I was familiar with, but it was definitely coming from somewhere in my room. I scrambled from my bed and turned on my bedside lamp before honing in on the sound. A cheap prepaid phone I'd never seen before sat on my dresser, buzzing with an unknown number.

Where the hell had it come from? How long had it been sitting there?

I shook off my confusion and pressed the answer button. It was the quickest way to silence the damn thing without searching for the volume. Once quiet had returned, I stared at the device, unsure what to do. Without knowing who was on the other end, I couldn't speak. It was too risky. Gingerly, I lifted the phone to my ear.

"Noemi, this is your last warning." Conner's voice wrapped around me like a hot breeze before a summer storm. "Do *not* go with Keir in the morning."

I should have known. He wasn't the type of man to stay quiet, nor was he the type to allow his private conversations to be overheard. He'd correctly surmised that my phone wasn't secure and had provided an alternative. Had he simply used it to ensure my safety, the phone would have been a kind gesture. Considering the threatening tone in his voice, his interference felt more like a leash than a lifeline.

"What makes you think I'm still going?" I whispered, worried someone might hear me.

"Because I know you."

"Know me?" I scoffed. "We only met a week ago."

"Then tell me I'm wrong. Tell me you weren't planning to go." His voice caressed and coaxed as though goading me into defiance. Like he wanted me to resist him.

Uncertainty silenced me.

I was a bird in a cage, desperate to break free. Every demand was another collar around my neck. If it wasn't my father, then Conner was prodding me in one direction or another, each misstep potentially deadly.

I shook my head even though he couldn't see me, needing to escape my invisible bindings.

"No. I won't do anything inappropriate with Keir," I said in a rush. "You'll just have to learn to trust me." If I let this man control and doubt me, I'd forever be his captive rather than his wife. I couldn't let that happen. And besides, Keir's impressive resistance to my father's bullying gave me hope that maybe he might be willing to help me. As the son of Jimmy Byrne, he'd certainly be in the position to make such a decision. I had to do this for multiple reasons, regardless of my fiancé's fragile ego.

Unwilling to entertain his arguments and threats, I ended the call and flopped back on my bed. I didn't like to be difficult, but I couldn't afford to let Conner control me. If I gave him an inch, he'd take everything, my heart included.

For long minutes, I lay tense, fully expecting him to call back. But for the second time in one night, a man had surprised me with his silence. The phone never rang again. No texts lit the screen.

Assuring myself I'd made the right decision and my rising anxiety was unwarranted, I buried the phone under my mattress and turned off the light. Sleep wouldn't come easily, but I had to at least try. I had a big day ahead.

I felt like I'd only just closed my eyes when a sense of awareness tugged me awake. My clock read 2:00 a.m., and the house was silent, but the thudding of my heart echoed in my ears. Something wasn't right.

My gaze lifted to scan the room, locking on the silhouette of a man leaning against my bedroom wall. The large figure was illuminated by the moonlight filtering through the open window. I didn't have to see his face to recognize the form. Conner was here. In my bedroom.

Had he been planning this all night? He had to have unlocked the window when he'd been in my room earlier. Had he been so sure I'd refuse him? What exactly did he plan to do about it? Tie me to my bed to keep me from going?

I started to scoot up my bed and away from him, but Conner pushed off the wall. His movement stilled me. I watched raptly as he closed the distance between us. My chest rose and fell on shuddered breaths, goose bumps racing down the length of my arms.

"What are you doing here?" I finally asked, not sure I wanted his answer.

"I warned you, Noemi." His dark murmur sucked the breath straight from my lips.

I shivered. "But I haven't even gone yet."

He yanked down the covers, exposing my legs. After drinking in the sight, his dark gaze, inscrutable in the moonlight, lifted to mine.

"It's time to face the consequences."

"What—" I barely had time to panic before his arms caged me in, his lips seizing mine. He was a raging current, and no matter how hard I fought, he carried me away on his rising waters. I didn't want to want him, but he felt so damn good. The press of his body. The pull of his ravenous desire. I was helpless against him.

A masculine noise of satisfaction drifted between us when his commanding touch wrenched an unbidden moan from deep in my throat.

"You feel like a fucking dream," he rasped, lips drifting to my jaw and down to my throat.

A growing pressure began to pulse between my legs. I rolled my hips, desperately needing to ease the ache mounting inside me. The clawing need. It felt so incredibly good, and I couldn't remember the last time I'd felt pleasure

—pure joy or happiness. The dopamine drugged me, erasing all thoughts of self-preservation or strategy.

If this was my punishment, I'd happily accept.

None of it made sense, but I didn't care. I just wanted more.

When he lifted my thin pajama top and his mouth closed over my breast, I thought the world might stop turning. It would have explained the dizziness. I felt like I was free-falling with no clue which way was up or down.

How far was he planning to take this? Did I care?

No. Not really. He was my fiancé, right? And it felt so good. Wasn't I allowed to feel good for a change?

Conner rested beside me, one large hand drifting down my ribs, over my hip, then to my thigh where he coaxed my legs apart. I didn't fight him, but my heart began to jack-hammer in my chest. A part of my body that no man had ever touched was now open to him, only shielded by a thin layer of cotton fabric.

His gaze remained locked on where he touched me, his hand slowly caressing the inside of my thigh higher and higher but stopping just short of where my body screamed for his touch.

"Tell me this is mine." He slid one finger beneath the elastic edge of my panties. "Tell me no other man has touched you here." His voice was jagged as a cliff's edge, raw and unguarded. When his eyes finally drifted back to mine, I gasped at the violent need staring back at me. Like the last vestiges of his humanity clung by a thread.

Mesmerized by my effect on him, I nodded. "No other … only you," I whispered.

Fear suddenly spiked my veins with an icy-cold current.

I didn't worry that he'd hurt me—not physically, anyway. It was my heart that concerned me. How could I possibly keep my emotions out of the mix when Conner's presence was so consuming? Nothing with him was simple, least of all sex.

My lips parted on an objection, but his hand came to rest over my mouth, his head slowly turning side to side as a devious smile perched on his lips.

Then my brain short-circuited when his other hand slid fully beneath my panties and cupped my sex. I didn't remember my own name, let alone what I'd planned to say. Not when one long, scalding finger dipped inside me, then spread my arousal up to my clit and back down. I'd already been writhing with more electric need than I'd ever felt before. The addition of his touch nearly made me see stars.

One hand still pressed to my mouth, Conner fingered me with lavish, seductive strokes, building and teasing my restless flesh. My body arched and pleaded with his movements. When my chest pressed outward, lifting my back clean off the bed, he used his teeth to graze over my nipple. The sting sent an electric pulse directly to my clit like a flame devouring a fuse. When the spark reached my core, my body ignited with blinding pleasure.

Just as the liquid elation devoured me, Conner lifted his hand away from my mouth at precisely the right moment to allow a primal cry of release to burst past my lips. It was as though the energy inside me was too great to contain and had escaped in the form of sound, and Conner had set it all into motion, knowing exactly what would happen.

The cry echoed in my head, drowning out even my ragged breaths and racing heart.

Realization and panic chased away the remnants of my orgasm like angry dogs scenting a hare.

"What have you done?" I breathed, my eyes going wide.

Sante's room was right next to mine. Was there any chance he could have slept through my cry?

I held perfectly still, my lungs not even daring to draw breath.

A door squeaked in the hall. Sante.

I launched into motion, shoving Conner off me. "You have to get out. You have to *leave*!" I hissed, succumbing to the panic clawing at my insides. My eyes darted wildly to my closed bedroom door before cutting back to Conner when I realized he was refusing to budge.

"Promise me you won't go tomorrow," he demanded, no trace of remorse.

Had I not been so overwhelmed with distress about Sante hearing me, I would have been furious, but my thoughts were too scattered for the emotion to take purchase.

"You need to go, *now*!" I slammed my hands against his chest, tears burning the backs of my eyes.

"Em? Was that you?" Sante called softly through the door.

My chest hitched on a sob, frustration like a vise tight around my chest. "Okay, you win. I won't go, just leave. *Please*." This time, he allowed me to shove him toward the window, his brows knitting tight in growing confusion as though he meant to manipulate me but hadn't counted on such a visceral reaction on my part.

I didn't care what he thought. I just had to get him out of my house.

A gentle knock sounded at the door as I ushered Conner out the window. As I raised my hands to close the window, all signs of victory in Conner's stare bled to murderous rage. I lifted my gaze to see what he'd spotted and realized the moonlight had slanted over my arms to illuminate the ugly purple ring around my wrist.

Our stares collided, but I didn't have time for this. I forced the window shut, then yanked my curtains closed, all thoughts of Conner pushed aside as I readied myself to deal with the fallout of his actions.

My bedroom door swung open until Sante's wide-eyed stare met mine.

"Em?" he said with such heartbreaking tenderness and hope that my heart cracked straight down the middle.

I put a hand on my throat, knowing the ruse was over. "It was a nightmare," I rasped. My scream gave my voice the appropriate scratchiness to disguise the lie, making me sound as though I hadn't spoken in months. "It gave me my voice back." I infused my voice with as much enthusiasm as I could muster past the foreboding looming over me.

Sante rushed at me, lifting me against him in a crushing hug. A genuine smile tugged at my lips to witness his joy. He swung me around in a circle like we'd just been reunited after years apart.

"This is incredible! I can't wait to tell everyone." He set me back on my feet and kissed my forehead affectionately. "You don't know what a relief it is to hear your voice. I've missed that so damn much."

I grinned. "You sure? Now I can boss you around again."

"I'd like to see you try, little big." His smile turned the room from night to day because it was so bright.

"Oh, I will. Like now—you need to get back to bed. It's still the middle of the night."

Sante tweaked my chin between two of his knuckles. "I'll let you have that one, for old time's sake." He gave me one more quick hug, then retreated to the door. "Night, Em. Love you."

"Love you, too, Sante," I replied, emotions squeezing my throat tight.

Once the door closed, I was again alone in the darkness of my bedroom as I'd been when I'd gone to sleep hours earlier, yet nothing was the same. Come morning, Dad would know about my miraculous recovery, and I had no idea what that might mean for me.

I LAY AWAKE FOR HOURS. AT FIRST, MY BODY VIBRATED WITH anger that Conner had forced me to reveal my secret. He'd been curious about why I was still silent around everyone else, but I never dreamed he'd out me like that. Then I was hit with a wave of despair when I realized that despite my fury, I didn't hate him for what he'd done. Maybe it was the dawning realization in his eyes when he saw my wrists. He had no idea of the repercussions of his actions.

Now he knew.

He knew I wasn't just being childish. He also had confirmation that my father wasn't an honorable man. Would that cause him to reconsider the alliance?

God, I hope not.

I needed Conner and the escape he provided. He might have been brutish and been married to his career in corruption, but I knew in my gut that he wasn't the same as my dad. Not by a long shot. Conner was every shade of gray, preventing me from giving him any one sweeping label. It made it hard to know just how I should feel about him. The only thing I knew for sure was how he made my body feel. My core had remained swollen and sensitive in the most delicious way for ages after he'd left.

I'd never had an orgasm before. Maybe I was weird, but I'd never really touched myself. I hadn't felt the need when I was younger, and after Mom's death, that was the last thing on my mind. I'd made out with boyfriends and been felt up, but it had never gone any further. I'd had no idea release would cause such an explosive need to cry out. If I had … would I have stopped him?

I wasn't sure I liked the answer to that question.

My need for him at that moment had outweighed just about everything else. Perhaps somewhere down deep, I'd anticipated the relief I'd feel knowing the charade was at an end. The weightlessness of that relief helped counteract my crushing anxiety.

One more week.

Surely, I could survive a week until the wedding.

The wedding.

A shiver rocked my entire body.

On August first, I'd be forever joined to the man who broke into my room, seduced, then coerced me. Did I have any chance at holding my own against him?

I'd thought I could marry Conner and keep love and marriage separate, but now … I wasn't so sure. Nothing about the Irishman was neat and tidy enough to fit into a safe little box like I'd hoped. Like trying to contain an earthquake. Impossible. I felt like I had zero control over myself or my situation. That was why I decided to go with Keir despite Conner's objections. I needed to feel like I had a shred of control over my life.

The other reason behind my decision was more childish, but I didn't care in the slightest. Conner's actions reeked of jealousy. Why else keep me from spending time with his cousin? Conner wanted me to himself, and a messed-up part of me liked it. A shrink would probably blame years of an absentee father and substantial daddy issues. I didn't care. Knowing Conner wanted me all to himself filled my chest with a strange warmth.

And besides that, I liked knowing I could make him feel just as powerless as he made me feel. Something about misery loved company, yada yada.

I was probably poking the dragon, but I couldn't help myself. The way Conner pushed my buttons made it impossible not to push back.

Rather than dissect why that was, I finally forced myself back to sleep. I should have been hazy the next morning from sleep deprivation, but adrenaline surged through my veins the second my eyes opened.

It was judgment day.

I spent extra time on my hair and makeup. Anything to delay the inevitable. Once I'd preened and primped as long as I dared, I reluctantly made my way downstairs. Dad sat at the dining table with his newspaper and coffee like he did most mornings. Sante scrolled on his phone, a wide smile on his face when I entered the room.

"Hey, Em!" He stilled in breathless anticipation.

I gave a shy smile. "Hey, Sante."

"See, Dad! Told you. Isn't it amazing?"

We both peered at our father, me with far less enthusiasm than my brother.

Dad's stare cut me to the quick as he slowly lowered the paper to his lap. "It's astounding. After all this time."

I dropped my gaze and eased into my designated seat.

"We should have a party to celebrate," my brother suggested.

"I think we're already doing enough for the wedding," I replied, praying he'd let it rest. The last thing I wanted was to bring more attention to myself.

"Well, we could at least go to dinner," he countered.

"That's a lovely idea," Dad said, making the hair on the back of my neck stand tall. "Why don't you find Umberto and tell him to clear my calendar? Then you can see about a reservation at Carbone."

Sante winked at me, oblivious to the tension in the room. It was as though we lived in two separate parallel dimensions. In his, Dad was a tough but loving father who did his best to be strong for his family. In mine, we were both just puppets dancing to our father's maniacal melody.

Of course, as the male heir, Sante had always received more of Dad's attention. In a way, we *had* grown up in two very different realities. When I got the chance to tell him what I knew, I hoped he'd be willing to consider an alternate truth.

I reached for my water glass, hoping my tremble was too slight to notice. The table served as a barrier between my father and me. It was something, but I would have preferred several feet of reinforced concrete instead.

"Don't think I can't see beyond the coincidence in your voice returning right before you're about to leave this family." His softly spoken words snaked around my throat and squeezed.

If I played dumb or refuted him, I'd make myself a target. All I could do was play dead and hope he moved on quickly.

"Maybe you believe you hold some sort of power with them at your back."

My head shook a fraction, desperate to keep him from getting angry.

My father lifted his phone and glanced at the screen. "I suppose that would be easy enough to fix, if it were the case. I could always remind you of the precariousness of your situation." He typed out a short message, then set the phone down, his soulless stare returning to me.

I cleared the terror from my throat before speaking. "I love my family too much to ever put them at risk," I offered softly. My words seemed to freeze in the arctic air around us and clatter to the floor. It meant nothing to a man who trusted so little.

A roaring curse sliced through the tension from down the hall, snatching my heart straight from my chest. I shot to my feet, recognizing Sante's voice. The murmur of his continued curses coming closer was the only thing that kept a total meltdown of panic at bay.

"You okay?" I called out, hearing my brother enter the kitchen.

"Yeah, just my hand," he grumbled back. "Umberto accidentally caught my fingers in the door. Just an accident, but it hurt like a bitch. May have broken a finger."

The freezer door and rustling in the ice box drifted into the dining room. The entire time, Dad never moved a muscle. I glanced over at him, my eyes flicking to his phone and back at him in time to catch a glint of spite flash in his eyes.

He'd done this.

He'd hurt Sante—his son and heir—as a message to me.

I wanted to vomit all over the pristine white tablecloth. A part of me had hoped he wasn't truly as ruthless as I suspected, but he successfully shattered that delusion. Fausto Mancini was a pure-blooded monster.

My jaw clenched against my rebelling stomach, and a sudden urge to hurl a stream of insults at my wretched father.

I couldn't let him see the defiance boiling up inside me. If he ever suspected I'd act against him, I couldn't predict what he'd do.

"Perhaps it would be best if you waited in your room for your ride to show up. It would give you time to think about the precariousness of your current situation." A not-so-subtle order but I was more than happy to comply. I wanted nothing more than to escape his toxic presence forever.

An hour later, I slid into Keir Byrne's gunmetal-gray Mercedes. I'd practically dragged him from the house after Umberto let him in. Dad had disappeared, and I'd had no desire to wait around and chance an awkward encounter. Fortunately, Umberto hadn't argued when I'd fled with our guest, and Keir had wisely waited until we were in the car for questions.

"Call me crazy, but weren't you mute just yesterday?" he asked without even looking my way.

I took a deep breath, relaxing into the leather seat with each turn of the wheels taking me farther from home. "Yeah, it's kind of wild, but I had a nightmare last night that drew out a scream. It seemed to jar loose my voice." I shrugged.

"Sounds like a reason to celebrate." His eyes cut over to me, keen intelligence reflecting in those blue depths.

I got the oddest sense he wasn't remotely surprised, as though he'd already known. Had Conner told him? They seemed to be more rivals than confidants, but what did I know? These Irish men were such a flipping mystery.

"It was unexpected, for sure."

He slid on black sunglasses that wrapped around the sides, acting as a barrier between us. Not that it made much difference. His eyes were more mirrors than windows. Everything about him seemed designed to shield and confuse, like those 3D images you had to cross your eyes to see the hidden image. He was mirage and illusion, decked out in dark jeans and leather boots. His tight T-shirt exposed a plethora of colorful tattoos that were a stark contrast to his tightly controlled persona—yet another piece of the Viking's puzzle. I wondered if anyone ever saw the full picture.

"You know, not many people would push my dad like you did, arguing against his request to send one of his men with us." I was curious about him. Enough to embolden me to ask questions.

Keir smirked. "I wasn't arguing; I just didn't roll over. You'll never get anything in this world if you don't fight for it."

"That implies you didn't want Umberto with us. Why did it matter to you?"

"Isn't it obvious?" he asked. "I wanted you alone." His eyes cut to me before returning to the road.

My stomach dipped and swerved as though we'd taken a hard turn. Keir had answered my question while simultaneously remaining vague. Unease flitted at the base of my spine.

"Are you close with Conner?" I asked, hoping that if I better understood their relationship, I might understand why Conner had been so adamant against me taking this jaunt with his cousin. I prayed I hadn't overlooked a threat to my safety. I'd been convinced Conner's objection lay rooted in jealousy, but I was in trouble if there'd been more to it.

"We grew up together—all of us Byrne kids. Our family is close." Again, he glanced at me, and I got the sense he was feeling me out, but I wasn't sure in what way. "I imagine parting from your family has been an imposing prospect."

I swiped at invisible lint on my dress and shrugged. "Life is all about change. And I'm not exactly moving across the country or anything."

"Still, I can't imagine you were raised to think highly of other … families. Other organizations. This had to be a big shock."

Was he … questioning my loyalty? Did he think I was acting as some sort of mole?

"Dad wasn't around much growing up, so that type of stuff wasn't really a part of my world," I explained in a firm tone, my spine stiffening.

"Sometimes it doesn't take much. A few subtle undertones can color the way someone views the world," he pushed.

"So can cruelty. That puts things into perspective more than anything, focusing a person's priorities and redefining loyalties."

Keir stared at me long enough that I worried he'd crash the car. I hoped that if he was feeling out where I stood, my message had been received. I didn't give a fuck who worked for whom. All that mattered to me was protecting the people I loved.

When he finally looked back to the road, he grunted.

I took that as a sign that I'd passed, and we both remained quiet for the rest of the short journey.

"Nana, Paddy, this is Noemi Mancini. She's Conner's fiancée." Keir stepped aside, presenting me to his grandparents.

I extended my hand toward Padrick Byrne, who ignored my offer and pulled me into a hug.

"An unfortunate Italian birth, but with those green eyes, no doubt you were meant for the Irish." He pulled back and winked. The Irish lilt to his words added to the playfulness, but a sharpness in his eyes hinted at an underlying strength.

They had to be at least eighty, but I had a feeling Paddy had been positively ferocious in his day.

Nana shooed him away and took both my hands in hers, pulling them wide as she swept her gaze down the front of me. "Lovely from top to bottom, ya are, lass. Come here." She pulled me into a hug.

"We're delighted to meet ye," Paddy added. "But why is it not Conner that brought ye?"

My lips parted to answer, but Keir beat me to it.

"He was busy and asked me to bring her by."

"Ach, too busy for us? Maybe, but surely not for such a lovely bride. I'll have to give him a piece of my mind next time I see him." Nana looked at me as she sat back in her recliner. "That's the first thing you'll need to learn—never give 'em an inch, not these Byrne men. They'll take it and run a mile."

Paddy grunted. "You causin' problems for the boy before he's even walked down the aisle, Aine? Hold yer whist."

She shot him a look that could have withered a newly bloomed flower to ash. I had to bite down on my lips to keep from laughing.

"Now, tell me if I'm wrong," Paddy went on, "but I could have sworn I was told you were mute." He rubbed his scruffy jaw with a wrinkled hand and studied me.

"I was," I explained. "But in a strange twist of fate, my voice returned just last night after six months of absence."

Nana crossed herself. "Ain't that just the way of him? Workin' miracles we can only guess at. Why, just last week, Paddy here took out the trash without me even havin' to ask." She cut her eyes wryly to her husband.

I grinned, deciding I officially adored Nana Byrne.

We talked for several minutes before a knock sounded on the front door.

"Well, who could that be?" Paddy said to no one in particular, getting to his feet. Before he could move toward the entrance, the door opened and closed, and Conner joined our little party.

"What a lovely surprise, Paddy," Nana cried. "Do ye see who it is? Conner's come to see us."

"I'm old, not blind," Paddy grumbled. "Glad you came, son. It's only fitting."

Conner hugged his grandparents, a fondness to his soft smile. "I agree, Paddy. It's only right I'm here to introduce my bride." He shot a glare at Keir, then me.

Nana clasped my hand and grinned. "And did ye already know the incredible news? Our girl here can talk again!"

"As a matter of fact, I did know. I was lucky enough to be the first to know when she *released* her first sounds." Conner's devilish stare pinned me to my seat, where I suddenly wished I could melt into the floral fabric.

Nana and Paddy seemed oblivious to his innuendo, but Keir smirked.

Flames licked at my cheeks.

If I could have slugged him in the arm without looking insane, I would have. "I'm surprised you're here," I shot at Conner instead. "I thought you'd made other plans."

"Not at all. I try to stop in and visit Nana here whenever I can."

Nana snorted. "That's some bollocks if I've ever heard any."

I coughed out a poorly disguised laugh.

"Well," Conner continued. "If I hadn't meant to visit, would I have come prepared with these?" He lifted the paper sack I hadn't noticed he was carrying and handed it to his grandmother.

Her scowl melted to a wry grin. "Yer forgiven." She took the sack and peeked inside. "Orange slices! Ye know how I love them." She took out an orange jellied candy and bit off a corner like it was the most precious delicacy known to man. Granted, they were the nice kind of candies you had to go to a specialty candy shop to get, which meant Conner *had* planned to come. I wondered if that was out of his own free will or if he suspected I'd defy him from the beginning.

"Can't have sweets without tea," Nana said. "Have a seat, Con. Paddy," she barked. "Go an' fetch us some tea."

He scowled at her but rose to his feet and shuffled from the room.

"You have to try one of these, lass." The old woman held out the opened bag. "They're my absolute favorite."

Happy to oblige, I reached in and fished out a half-circle slice then took a bite. When I glanced at Conner, feeling his eyes bearing down on me, I was shocked at the unadulterated fury hardening his gaze. Then I realized his stare was trained on my wrist, where I still wore the gold cuff covering the remnants of my bruise. Every ounce of his control was focused on restraint. He would insist on an explanation once we were alone, but I was granted a reprieve for now.

I'd had to drag Bishop's groggy ass from bed to spar with me first thing that morning. He'd been up most of the night finishing off the Albanian, but I didn't care if he was tired. I was desperate to work through the shitstorm of emotions clouding my thoughts since sneaking out of Noemi's bedroom window.

Saying I felt like shit was an understatement. She'd told me she wasn't ready for her father to know she could speak. Instead of respecting her wishes, I'd been frustrated that she wouldn't explain herself and forced the issue. It was a dick move, and I never would have done it if I'd had any idea things were that bad.

The second I saw the dark ring marring her skin, I'd

wanted to break back inside and demand answers, but I'd already done enough. I could hardly sleep, wondering if her father had hurt her for what I'd done. I had no direct evidence he was responsible for the bruise, but it made the most sense. Her silence and the bruise were connected. I just wasn't sure how.

Why would he be upset to know she could speak? I couldn't begin to guess at the answer.

The gnawing worry and frustration were part of why I'd showed up at my grandparents' house. I knew she still planned to disobey me, and I needed to see her and make sure her father hadn't laid a hand on her. If he hurt her because of me, I'd do worse than burn him alive.

I wasn't one for regrets. I could count the number of times I'd regretted my actions on one hand, but last night added one more. I didn't regret touching her—that had been sheer perfection. Her body had come alive for me. I loved every second of her writhing beneath me, but I never should have manipulated her like I had.

The cloying guilt clung to me like salt from a sea breeze, a constant reminder of what I'd done. It was enough to keep my temper in check at seeing Noemi with Keir. He wasn't the type to steal another man's woman. Not exactly. But as one of the two men poised to assume a leadership role in our family, he outranked me. If he decided it would be better for the family for him to enter into the marital alliance, there would be little I could do.

That lingering possibility and guilt made me pull out a small blue box from my pocket. I hadn't planned to give her the ring in front of everyone. Everything about me was unpredictable where she was concerned. All I knew was that I wanted my ring on her fucking finger so that everyone knew she was mine.

Most of all, her.

"I just picked this up from the jeweler," I blurted. "Can't have a bride without a ring."

Noemi's eyes widened.

Satisfaction swelled in my chest. I liked catching her by surprise.

Taking her hand, I pulled her to her feet and opened the box. It wasn't a traditional diamond engagement ring. We weren't the standard couple. I thought the rectangular-cut sapphire had been fitting, and judging by her raised eyebrows, I was right. The platinum band was a perfect fit.

I leaned in and kissed her cheek, whispering softly, "That way, you don't forget who you belong to."

She swallowed, a flush creeping up her neck.

It was unsettling to realize how much I liked everything about this moment—seeing my ring on her finger and the way she responded to me. I couldn't even bring myself to care about the small fortune I'd spent on the damn thing.

"Well, lass. Let me see!" Nana said excitedly. "Oh, Con. It's breathtaking."

While the two women huddled together, I caught Keir's attention and motioned toward the front entry. He stood and followed me outside, a smirk teasing at the corner of his lips. We were family, but sometimes I wanted to punch that smugness off his fucking face.

"Tell me we aren't out here to fight over a woman," he said in a carefree droll.

"Not unless you think it's necessary. She's my fucking fiancée, after all."

He just stared that unnerving glacial stare of his, the tiniest lift of his chin telling me he was surprised at how quickly I'd owned that new label. I refused to give him the satisfaction of successfully goading me, so I let it slide.

"When we're done here, I'm taking her home," I informed him.

Keir arched a blond brow. "Her father wasn't quick to let her go in my custody. Not sure how he'd feel if I turned her over to you."

"I don't really give a fuck what he thinks. He's the one I want to have a word with about the bruises on her wrist."

My oldest cousin stilled into carved granite. "That so?"

"I suspect. That's why I need to stop by."

"Need assistance?" he asked calmly.

Most people thought Keir was unflappable—perfectly impassive—but I knew him better than that. I'd seen him as a kid being dragged away from fights, saliva dripping down his chin and madness in his eyes. The only reason he kept such tight control of himself now was because a storm of emotions constantly brewed beneath the surface. And in times like this, I sensed how close those emotions teased at breaking free.

"No, I've got this. I don't want to piss him off before the deal is done. Just need to lay down some rules."

Keir nodded. "You let me know if that changes."

My cousin had been happy to toy with me over my feelings for Noemi, but when it came to a woman being mistreated, neither of us had a sense of humor. I knew he'd have my back on that matter.

Now, to start getting some answers from my bride-to-be. It was going to be an interesting ride home…

NOT AQUAMARINE OR TURQUOISE—THE FLAWLESS STONE ON MY hand was a rich deep blue.

The exact shade of Conner's eyes.

That way, you don't forget who you belong to.

As I sat in his car an hour later, his words replayed in my mind, my eyes glued to the ring. It was no accident that the stone he'd chosen for me looked like it had been harvested from the same material as his striking irises.

I wasn't sure how I felt about that.

In some respects, the gesture felt personal. Intimate. Had a longtime boyfriend put such thought into a ring, I would have swooned at the romantic nature of his choice. A piece of him with me always. But that wasn't our situation. Was there any chance he could actually have feelings for me, or was I just another acquisition, and the ring his brand?

I rubbed at the strange ache that rippled through my chest.

"How often?" His quiet voice was liquid chocolate laced with arsenic.

"What?" I asked, confused.

"How often does he lay his hands on you?"

Of course. I'd known this was coming when Keir had told me Conner was taking me home, but the ring had distracted me. An eight-carat gemstone did that to a girl.

I took in a slow, cleansing breath. "He never used to bother with me," I explained, knowing I had to give him something. "After Mom's death, things changed. It's not all that bad. He just gets angry easily."

Conner kept his eyes on the road, but his fury was evident by his white-knuckled grip on the wheel. "He do that shit to your mother?"

Again, that ache burned in my chest.

"If he did, I never witnessed it. I've wondered the same thing so many times, but I don't think I'll ever know for sure."

"Your brother let him do that to you?"

My head whipped to the side, eyes wide. "No! Of course not. Sante has no idea. Don't you dare blame him."

Conner cut his eyes to me, a silent warning that he'd blame whoever he damn well wanted to. I huffed back in my seat and parted my lips in retort but never got the chance. The car suddenly lurched to the side, my upper body slamming against the door.

Conner barked out a murderous curse, clutching the wheel tightly to try to correct our trajectory.

"What was that?" I cried, trying to see what we'd hit.

"Face forward, Em. Head down," he ordered. "Someone's

got a fucking death wish." He growled the last part, eyes cutting to the rearview mirror.

Again, the car behind us swiped at our back end, sending Conner's BMW fishtailing to the side. The Byrnes lived just outside the city in one of the few areas with trees and hilly, curving roads. A couple more miles, and we would be back on the interstate, but I wasn't sure we'd make it that long.

An icy river of fear rushed beneath the surface of my skin. When a loud shot rang in my ears, my racing heart skipped a whole handful of beats.

Nothing happened for a second. It was enough time for confusion to settle in before the back of the car vibrated and bounced, warning of a flat tire.

"Mother*fucker*," Conner spat, gripping the wheel of the suddenly unwieldy car. They'd shot out one of our tires. We'd been speeding to get away from our pursuers and were now on the verge of total chaos.

Memories of flying past cars and my mother's frantic cries assaulted me. The sight of broken glass and pooling blood—metal bent and contorted as steam and smoke filled the air.

Terror wound tight with heartbreak to blur my vision and catapult my pulse to dangerous levels.

"Mama," I cried. "*No*, Mama."

An arm slammed against my chest right before my body jolted from side to side. Tires screeched in my ears, almost drowning out the stream of masculine curses.

My past and present blurred so thoroughly that I couldn't make sense of any of it. When the car lurched to a stop, I was too disoriented to think. I just knew I had to save her.

"Mama, *please* don't die." I clawed at my seat belt, tears streaming down my cheeks and my breaths puffing in shallow, frantic bursts. "Hold on, Mama. I'm coming. I'm coming." I couldn't get the fucking seat belt off. My fingers flailed and shook, unable to figure out the release, adding to my panic.

I couldn't breathe.

I couldn't see or breathe, and I didn't know what was happening.

"Emy, baby. Calm down." Two large hands clasped either side of my face and forced me to turn. "*Shh*, baby. It's okay. You're here with me. I've got you." Crystal clear blue eyes. Conner.

Not my mama.

My breathing slowed as I slipped back into reality. I was riding with Conner, and our car had been hit, but we were okay.

He wiped my cheeks with his rough thumbs, his eyes burning deep into mine. "I need you to calm down, Noemi. This isn't over yet," he said softly but urgently.

I tried to cut my eyes to the back of the car, but he kept my face directed at his.

"Eyes on me, baby. Now, I need you to get down on the floor and stay quiet. Can you do that for me?"

I nodded.

"Good girl," he whispered before sliding one hand down to release my seat belt, then clicking open the glovebox to retrieve a black handgun. He gave a look at the floor, a silent command.

I slid down into the shadows.

Conner pulled back the slide on the gun, his hand going for the door handle.

A new flavor of fear suddenly clogged my throat. He was going out there to face them. To face the men who wanted us dead. What if they killed him? Why did that thought fill me with such dread? Was I simply scared of going back to my father, or was it more?

When I pictured Conner's vibrant eyes turned dull and

lifeless the way I'd seen my mother's, my eyelids clamped shut, violently rejecting the image. I didn't want to lose him. Even the thought tormented me.

I gasped and flinched when he flung open the door. He didn't immediately go out. He waited for the round of shots being fired from behind us to cease. The second they paused, he launched upward. A series of his own blasts rang loud in the air around us.

I clamped my hands over my ears, another round of tears streaking down my cheeks. I didn't even realize I'd closed my eyes again until silence coaxed me to open my scrunched lids.

I was alone.

My eyes widened as though that might help me see what was happening beyond the confines of my mental stronghold. I strained to hear over my pounding pulse, but no sounds met my ears until a car whizzed past. The distraction triggered another string of bullets.

Was that Conner shooting or our attacker? God, I hated not knowing what was happening.

Seconds later, I heard a series of thuds along with guttural curses—a fight.

Conner must be grappling with someone.

Was there more than one man after us? What if he was outnumbered? I chewed relentlessly at my lip, overwhelmed with helplessness.

When a single shot rang out, followed by deafening silence, I had to take a peek. Slinking into the driver's seat, I did my best to stay hidden while easing myself closer to the still-open door. Once I was in a position to dart out if necessary, I peeked up and around to gauge the situation.

Conner stood with a gun in hand outstretched. His chest rose and fell in rapid succession, eyes cast to his left while his gun remained pointed at what I assumed was someone on the ground.

I gingerly placed a foot on the ground and stood to peer over the car's roof. Then a cascade of events happened in a flash.

Noting my appearance, Conner whipped his head in my direction just as a gunshot pinged off the metal roof inches from my face. I dropped to the ground but managed to catch sight of a man running away from the scene.

"Jesus *Christ*," Conner roared, shooting a series of rounds into the distance before rushing to my side. "Did he get you? Are you hurt?" His eyes scoured my body.

I shook my head. "It didn't get me. Are they still out there?"

Squatting beside me, Conner dropped his head back on a long inhale. "Not exactly. One's dead, and the other ran."

"Do you know who they were or what they wanted?"

When our gazes collided this time, wrathful vengeance was staring back at me.

"Albanians." The word was spat with noxious disdain. I wasn't sure of their past, but one thing was clear. Conner hated them. "Get back in the car. I'll put on the spare and get you home."

I did as he instructed.

While I waited for him to change the tire, the car filled with a suffocating uncertainty that bled to awkwardness. My emotions were a jumbled mess. No matter how hard I tried not to think about it, my mind kept returning to Conner's hands on my face, his eyes inches from mine, and his words a balm to my aching heart. He'd been so incredibly sweet.

Shh, baby. It's okay … I've got you.

His words played on an endless loop in my head. I'd been totally hysterical. It made perfect sense that he needed to calm me down before we ended up shot, but my heart wanted to read into his actions. I wanted him to care.

I could only imagine what he thought of me now that he'd seen me completely lose my shit. I'd been a total basket case.

Sighing, I rested my elbow on the door and placed my hand over my eyes, praying the day would soon be over.

By the time Conner slid into the driver's seat, his cobalt eyes had completely iced over. Whatever the nature of his volatile thoughts, I wasn't going to interrupt. We were both silent for the rest of the trip.

For the first time in six months, I was relieved to arrive home. Conner walked me to the door. I expected him to leave once Umberto answered, but he asked for my father and instructed me to go upstairs. I didn't have the fortitude or desire to argue. However, once I reached my room, I realized there was more than one reason Conner might have wanted an audience with my father. I'd assumed he meant to discuss our near-death experience and had forgotten about what we'd been discussing minutes before it happened.

Would Conner confront my father about hurting me?

An overwhelming surge of panic washed over me, and not for my own safety. For the second time in so many hours, I was worried about Conner.

"There a reason you're covered in blood?" Fausto Mancini asked casually when he joined me in the entry of his home.

I'd already killed one man today, and my hands were aching to squeeze the life from another. Seeing Fausto when I knew he'd been roughing up his daughter brought a murderous rage to the surface. It took everything I had to force a calm façade. "Ran into a little trouble on the way back here."

His eyes drifted toward the stairs. "I take it my daughter was returned safely?"

"She's unharmed but shaken up. I sent her to her room." I slowly stepped closer with my gaze lowered to my hands before me. "Things could have gone very differently. Noemi could have been hurt, and while we aren't technically married yet, I consider her my responsibility." I lifted my gaze to his, leveling him with a vicious stare. "If anyone ever harmed a woman under my protection, I'd tear that fucker to pieces. I put a bullet through one of those men today, and the other will wish I had when I catch him."

"And you're telling me this why?" Fausto asked, his lip starting to curl.

"Just thought it would be good for you to know, as my future father-in-law. I protect what's mine." I hadn't called him out in so many words, but I had no doubt my message had been received. "Now, if you'll excuse me, I have business to attend to." I gave a curt nod and let myself out. The last of my civility expired.

It felt good to confront him. I wanted the bastard to know that I was watching him. It was the only way I felt comfortable leaving Noemi in his care. If he knew I was onto him, he'd know he couldn't get away with any bullshit.

Just to be safe, however, I decided it would be best to reach out to the head of the family for a meeting. The Italians were all about structure and rules. As a mere capo, Fausto wouldn't be able to make any crucial decisions about the alliance. It would be prudent to ensure I kept the Moretti boss informed of my perspective in case Fausto started spreading any lies. I didn't want this skirmish to devolve into a war.

Two hours later, I'd dropped off my car at a repair shop and borrowed Bishop's obnoxious yellow Mustang to meet Renzo Donati at an office by the docks. Each of the Five Families specialized in specific fields. The Moretti family was all about the blue-collar worker—steel plants, teamsters, and dockworkers.

Renzo's father, Agostino, was the head of the organization. The Don or boss or whatever they wanted to call it. I would have liked to have spoken with him, but an audience with the boss was rare. I would have to make do with his son, the underboss.

I'd never met the man before, but my first impressions assured me he and I spoke the same language. In fact, the perceptive gleam in his eye reminded me of Keir.

Renzo was shrewd.

That was clear from the expensive cut of his designer suit to the casually assertive way he carried himself. Not pompous or flashy, just confident authority.

"This is rather unorthodox. You must know that," Renzo said by way of greeting.

"I'm aware it would normally be my uncle reaching out as the head of our organization, but this matter was somewhat delicate. I opted for discretion over formality."

The heavily tattooed mafioso raised his chin, denoting I'd piqued his curiosity.

"I have concerns," I continued, "that Fausto Mancini may attempt to withdraw his daughter from our engagement."

"Is that so?"

"It's a possibility, yes."

"And what makes you think that?" he asked.

"Therein lies the delicacy of the matter."

Renzo slowly paced in front of a large window overlooking the bay. "I understand you fell victim to a rather harrowing attack today. If Fausto fears for his daughter's safety, that would seem a reasonable concern." His insinuation that I was a danger to Noemi didn't bother me. It was his job to shake out the truth, and I knew the ground I stood upon was firm.

"If an adversary stirring up problems was enough to make us unfit to marry, not one of us would have a wife." I shot him a leveling stare. "I'll keep Noemi safe, just like I did today. I see no reason our alliance should fail because of a father's ungrounded fears. And besides," I continued a bit more warily, "I've discovered that she faces a much higher chance of coming to harm under her father's roof than in my care." I let my meaning drift in the air between us, my unyielding stare never leaving his.

Renzo remained perfectly motionless. "That's quite the accusation."

"A delicate matter, wouldn't you say?"

He raised his chin a fraction, then turned his gaze out the window. "Your concerns have been noted."

Renzo didn't give me any indication of what, if anything, he might do with the information I'd passed along. Still, my intuition told me he was an honorable man. I'd seen the tiniest of tics in his right eye when I'd called Noemi's safety into question. Maybe I was wrong, but I got the sense he wasn't any more accepting of domestic abuse than I was.

The knot coiled tight in my gut since being attacked finally eased.

"I appreciate your time, Donati. Give my best to your father."

He nodded, signaling I'd been dismissed. Fine by me. I'd said what I'd come to say. Now it was time to move on to the next course of business.

The second I was back in the Mustang, I called Bishop and gave him the license plate of the car that had come after us.

"See what you can dig up on the owner. I doubt it's directly associated with the assholes who came after us, but it might be a lead. I want that motherfucker found."

"Yes, sir. You coming by the gym today?"

I still hadn't cleaned up my knuckles after cracking them

open while fighting the Albanian. Worth every drop of blood, but I'd had enough for one day. "Maybe tomorrow."

Once I'd had a full day to think about what had happened and how terrified Noemi had been, I'd need an outlet, no matter how busted my knuckles.

"Countin' on it," Bishop said before hanging up.

God, I hoped we'd find that bastard. I couldn't lay a finger on Noemi's father or take away the trauma she carried with her, but I could make that Albanian fucker suffer, and I'd love every minute of it.

Noemi

TWENTY-FIVE

THE GUNSHOT I'D HALF EXPECTED NEVER CAME. I DIDN'T KNOW who was more apt to shoot first but considering Conner's anger and Dad's volatility, I was surprised at the remarkable quiet downstairs. Eerily quiet.

I was reminded of the silence that drew me to peek from the car. Conner's merciless intensity as he'd stood, gun still raised, had been chilling. It was no secret he was capable of murder, but seeing it play out in living color was another story, especially when he'd done it to save us. Watching him kill another man should have horrified me for several reasons. Yet all I could summon was a warm blanket of relief. I would have been dead if it weren't for his ruthless pursuit of those men.

Silenced permanently.

My father never would have paid for what he'd done, and it would have been my fault for not speaking up. I realized as I sat in the quiet of my room that I was done wasting time. I had to tell Uncle Donati the truth about my mother's death.

"What fucking *lies* have you been feeding them?" My father stormed into my room, teeth ground tight with anger. "I *knew* you were opening your goddamn mouth."

I'd never seen him so manic.

I tried to scurry back onto the bed but was too late. His hand fisted my shirt and yanked me to him, our faces inches apart. So close, I could smell the insanity wafting off him. I forced myself not to struggle, though it felt like he'd reached deep inside my chest and squeezed the air from my lungs with his fists.

"Whatever you've done, you'll fucking fix it. You hear me? If you think once you're married, you're free to do as you please, think again. We're *blood*. You're bound to me above all others, and if you forget that fact, it'll be your brother who pays. You fuck this up, and I guarantee you'll feel it."

I'd never heard the promise of violence so clearly in his words before. The man was totally unhinged.

Not waiting for a response, he shoved me away. I fell back onto my bed, my head thudding against the edge of my nightstand. I winced, scrunching my eyes shut tight, and by the time I opened them, Dad was gone.

I rubbed my head gingerly, hoping I didn't end up with a goose egg.

Why the hell was he so worried about what the Irish thought of him? Why was he so invested in this marriage and alliance?

I couldn't even begin to guess what he thought because I clearly didn't know the man at all. After twenty years under the same roof, my father was still a total stranger.

I rejected a wave of advancing remorse and clung tight to my determination. Scooting off the bed, I retrieved the disposable phone from under my mattress and shoved it in my pocket before sneaking from my room.

I needed to find a place where Dad was unlikely to be listening. Deciding the garage might be my best bet, I crept downstairs and to the back of the house, trying to look inconspicuous. I didn't want to look suspicious if anyone was watching secret cameras.

Listen to you. How did your life get so insane?

I had no freaking clue. One minute, I was a normal teen graduating from high school, then my mom was dead, my absentee father had come unglued, and I was plotting ways to run away with my brother.

Maybe I could make enough money to escape by selling my story to Lifetime TV.

I shook my head, pulling out the phone in a dark corner of the garage. I dialed Pippa's number, praying she answered despite the unknown number.

"Hello?" Her voice was tinged with uncertainty and a hint of annoyance.

"Pip! It's me." I couldn't help but grin as I envisioned the shock on her face.

"Em? Is that *you*?"

"Yes! I got my voice back last night."

"That's amazing!" Her excited exclamation trailed off. "Wait. Why are you calling me from a strange number? And are you whispering?"

Okay, here goes nothing.

"There's been a lot going on. I can't go into it all, but here are the highlights. This is the phone Conner gave me so I don't have to use my old phone."

"Whyyy can't you just use your old phone?" she asked, deeply confused.

"Dad's been … different since Mom died."

"Is that why you haven't left the house this whole time?" she blurted.

"Yeah."

"Em, that sounds a little crazy. He's so overprotective now that you can't even talk on your own phone? Is he monitoring your calls or something?"

"I know, it sounds a little wild." Not wanting to go into it further, I redirected the conversation. "And if that wasn't enough, Conner and I were attacked this morning on our way back from visiting his grandparents."

"*Attacked*? What the actual fuck? By who?"

"I'm not really sure, but they ran us off the road—shot out a damn tire—then tried to gun us down."

"Jesus *Christ*, Em. Are you okay?"

"Yeah, Conner was pretty … impressive." I bit down on my lip, but Pip must have sensed the admiration in my tone.

"Oh yeah?" she asked, full of innuendo. "Sounds like maybe things are going better?"

I paused, choosing my words carefully. "Let's just say I think things are moving in the right direction." If I didn't think about the confusing feelings I was developing for my intended, things were looking up. "I'm so glad to have my voice back. That's why I had to call. I need you to know how much you mean to me."

"That's incredibly sweet, but … you're kind of freaking me out. You sure everything is okay?" she asked.

A ball of emotion clogged my throat. "Recent events have just shifted my perspective, that's all. We never know how much time we have, and you're too important for me to risk going another minute without telling you."

Pip sniffled. "Shit, Em. Now you got me all choked up. I love you, too, sis."

"Love you more," I whispered.

"Listen," she said, sounding more like her normal self. "I don't know what all is going on over there, but you call if you need me. Okay?"

"Absolutely." I grinned. "Talk to you later, Pip."

"Count on it."

The following week passed in a blur of white lace, summer floral arrangements, and countless calls with the wedding coordinator. I only saw Conner once, and that was at our rehearsal dinner. We were surrounded by family the entire evening, preventing us from having any substantive conversations.

I wondered incessantly what he'd been thinking during the week. He hadn't texted or called. Not that he was supposed to. We weren't in love, and I would have been wise to remember that, but I'd felt like things had begun to shift between us. Then nothing. Like a summer storm evaporating into sunny skies.

The uncertainty left my stomach in knots.

I had no idea what to expect from him upon our wedding. I had hoped to get a feel for where his thoughts had taken him while we were at the rehearsal, but he was perfectly stoic the entire evening. The dinner was held two days before the ceremony rather than the night before. Our unusually short timeline meant there had to be concessions to tradition. I didn't care in the slightest. What I *did* care about was that I didn't see Sante once all week. Not until the rehearsal, and Dad made sure we hardly had five minutes together. He was sending a message. One I received loud and clear, but rather than deter me, it only made me more determined. Fausto Mancini would pay for what he'd done.

On the thirty-first of July, the day before I was set to be married, I had Umberto take me to my mother's grave. The skies were unusually dark for a summer day. One might even have said ominous if one were superstitiously inclined. I appreciated the somber atmosphere. Something about the stillness made me feel more connected to my mother than if it had been a breezy, sunny day.

I found her ornate granite headstone where I'd often visited her during those early days. The monument wasn't my favorite. Dad had ordered the design, likely thinking a lavish tribute was a good way to prove how much he missed the woman he'd killed. I knew better. And I knew Mom was too down-to-earth and unpretentious to have wanted a flashy tombstone over her grave.

"Hey, Mama." My voice was reed thin from pushing past the knot in my throat as I sat cross-legged on the grass. It was the first time I'd spoken aloud to her since she'd died, and something about voicing the words made my grief resurface. "I miss you so much, Mama."

I took several slow, even breaths to calm myself.

"I'm getting married tomorrow. I know, I should have come and told you before now. It's all been a blur, though. His name is Conner Reid, and he's Irish. Who would have thought?" I plucked free a blade of grass and slowly split it down the middle. "He's actually not so bad. I guess it's a little messed up that I can say that about a man who kills other people, but it is what it is. Maybe none of us are as civilized as we'd like to think." I paused, my voice softening when I continued. "I wish I'd known the truth about Dad earlier. I wish I knew if you'd been happy or if it was all a show for us."

My chest constricted so tight that my shoulders slouched.

"I'm so sorry, Mama. I want you to know that I'll do my best to help Sante. I know you'd want that. I won't let you down." Reaching out, I pressed my hand to the grass where I envisioned her chest would be. "Love you always."

A single tear broke free and trickled down my cheek. Something about talking to her made me feel like I was finally saying goodbye and moving on without her. Moving on to what, I didn't know, but in less than twenty-four hours, I was going to find out.

TWENTY-SIX

"THIS WAS MY MOTHER'S. YOUR MOM AND I BOTH WORE IT WHEN we got married." Aunt Etta held out a tiny, elegant cameo pin. "This can be your something borrowed. It's small enough to easily hide under your skirt, and it brought us good luck. Here, turn around."

"Thank you, Aunt Etta. That's so sweet of you." I did as she said, not arguing about the luck. She might have felt that way about her marriage, but I doubted Mom would have said the same about hers.

"With that gorgeous sapphire ring, a stunning new dress, and your mom's old necklace, you've got all your bases covered now." She finished tucking away the pin under my skirt and nudged me to turn back around. "You look breathtaking, little Emy. I know Leonora is here watching over you. She'd be so proud of the young woman you've become."

Tears burned the back of my throat because I wasn't so sure. Would she be proud? Or would she hate to see me walk the same treacherous path she walked?

I hugged Aunt Etta and thanked her through a swelling sense of panic. Impending doom clawed at me, making me feel like the walls were pressing in around me. "Do you think you could go get Conner for me?" I asked in a shrill voice.

Her brows knitted tightly together. "Are you sure, sweetie? You know the groom isn't supposed to see the bride…"

"Please, Aunt Etta. I need to talk to him before I do this."

She nodded, concern etched in the creases of her eyes as she left the room. I wanted to pace. Nervous energy coiled in my muscles, making it hard to sit still, but the train on my dress made pacing a challenge. Instead, I stood at a window and watched the leaves on a large oak beside the church sway in the breeze until an ominous awareness moved through me, lighting a fever from the nape of my neck to the base of my spine. When I turned, Conner stood in the doorway dressed in an impeccable three-piece suit, his inscrutable stare bearing down on me.

I wanted to thrash my fists against his broad chest and scream at him for being so insufferably handsome yet seemingly unreachable. I hadn't known him long, but I wasn't sure an eternity would be enough to fully understand this complicated man. But I wanted to. I wanted *him*, and I hated myself for it. For being weak enough to want what I could never have.

One measured step at a time, he closed the distance between us. "You have something to say? Because I'm pretty sure this is breaking the rules."

I swallowed, my throat suddenly parched. "I need to

know why you're doing this. Why did you agree to marry me?" The Irish would survive just fine without the alliance. It was helpful but not imperative. I didn't know what I was looking for by asking, but I needed to hear his answer.

He let the question marinate for a long minute before answering. "Duty to my family. The acquisition of power. Sultry green eyes and a fiery disposition. You pick a day; I'll give you a reason. It changes by the minute."

But at least somewhere inside him, I was a part of his decision. A piece of him wanted *me* and not just what my family represented. That was enough for now.

I nodded, the wave of panic ebbing to a general sense of anxiety. I wanted to ask where he'd been all week and why he hadn't reached out, but that felt like too much. This wasn't a real relationship; he wasn't courting me. I shouldn't have expected anything more.

Conner came even closer, wrapping his hand around the back of my neck and angling my face up toward his. "Just keep those eyes straight ahead on me. Don't think about anyone else, yeah?" He must have sensed the unease scraping my insides raw.

A fluttering warmth filled my chest as I nodded.

"Right. Now let's get this show over with." Before he moved, his eyes dropped to my lips. "You look good enough to eat, Noemi." He brought his lips to my ear. "And I'm famished." Once he'd sucked all the air from my lungs with his comment, he turned and walked away.

Seconds later, my aunt reappeared with Pippa, both brimming with excited energy.

"This entire church is filled, Em. It's insane."

"Not helping, Pip," I shot at her.

She grimaced. "It's fine, though. All you have to do is walk down the aisle and stand there. No biggie."

Then bind myself to an Irish mobster for the rest of my life and maybe have sex for the first time ever. Yeah, just any ordinary Saturday.

Deep breath in, slow exhale out.

"Your hair and makeup are perfect. The dress is exquisite. You've got this," chimed Aunt Etta. "The ceremony will be as short as a Catholic wedding can be, then you can stay at the reception as long or short as you like. At least we aren't having a full-scale dinner. Those last forever."

After much debate with the wedding coordinator, we'd decided on a cake and champagne reception at a hotel ballroom near the church. No extra catering to coordinate. No memorized vows. No special readings or performances. Just a short walk, a few repeated words, and I do. I could do this.

No, I hadn't succeeded in escaping the life I'd been born into, but that didn't mean I had to be unhappy. I could find joy in other areas of my life. Having a perfect husband wasn't everything. The only caveat was not to trick myself into hoping for more, into believing in love. That wasn't in the cards for me. If I let my heart grow attached, it would only lead to devastation.

I might end up Conner's wife, but he was married to the mob before he ever met me.

"It's time, sweet girl. You ready?" Aunt Etta looked at me questioningly with a glint of sorrow in her eyes.

I didn't want her to worry, so I forced a smile. "As ready as I'll ever be."

Pippa handed me my bouquet and brought my veil over my face before her mom led us out to the hall. The gentle strains of a string quartet playing Pachelbel's Canon grew louder as we neared the entrance to the cathedral. Almost as loud as the pounding of my heart, counting down the seconds until I was a married woman.

It was an enormous church—one of the city's largest—packed to the brim with hundreds of guests. People were standing along the walls beneath enormous panels of brightly colored stained glass. The wedding had drawn people far and wide like a traveling circus, and I was the main attraction.

The veil I wore had seemed part of an antiquated tradition at the dress shop, but I thanked God I'd let Aunt Etta talk me into it because it provided the illusion of a barrier between me and the world. A tiny amalgamation of privacy.

Hopefully, it hid the snarl that teased at my lip when I took my father's arm.

On the downside, however, the veil also kept me from seeing Conner very well. While I couldn't make out his azure eyes, I had no problem identifying his proud form at the altar. I did exactly as he'd said and tuned out everything else—my father, the audience, the expectations—and focused solely on the man in front of me.

When we finally reached Conner at the front of the church, he stepped forward and lifted my veil away from my face—a task that was usually left to the bride's father. Dad stood awkwardly as if unsure of what to do. Conner's eyes bore into mine, and I wished I knew what he was thinking. While he was a perpetual mystery, my father was undoubtedly pissed. Conner blatantly disrespected my father by usurping Dad's role in front of everyone. I could only imagine the fury brewing inside him.

It was an enormous relief to think that I never had to go home again after the wedding if I didn't want to. Of course, the hours after the reception would be rife with a different form of anxiety. It would be the first time I was alone with my new husband in my new house, and I had no idea what to expect.

Conner stared long and deep into my eyes before finally turning to my father and shaking his hand. My fiancé never even gave my dad a chance to kiss my cheek or say a single word. He kept himself angled between us, then guided me to the altar, preventing my father from getting near me.

With that small hurdle overcome, we moved on to the ceremony. I handed my bouquet to Pippa, who was my only attendant. We'd kept things as simple as possible with one attendant each. She stood at my side while Conner had chosen a friend to act as his best man rather than one of his many cousins.

The priest's words passed through me as though in another language. I couldn't hear or see or think. All I could do was focus on breathing and try not to pass out.

Word must have spread like wildfire about my renewed vocal abilities because the church wasn't engulfed in a sea of whispers when it came time for my vows.

"Noemi, do you take Conner to be your lawfully wedded husband? Do you promise to love him, comfort him, honor and keep him for better or worse, for richer or poorer, in sickness and health, and forsaking all others, be faithful only to him, for as long as you both shall live?"

I forced air into my lungs.

"I do."

Three letters. Two words. One life forever forfeited.

As a man, Conner was given freedoms in this world that a woman could only dream of. He was committing himself, but not to the same degree as me because he'd already accepted a life in the criminal underworld. By walking down that aisle, I'd sealed my fate in more ways than one. I swore to myself at that moment that I wouldn't let it be in vain. I would use whatever power I could acquire from my marriage to take down my father.

That was what I focused on when I said I do.

The silent vow may not have been spoken aloud, but it felt just as monumental as the oath to my new husband.

"You may kiss the bride." The priest's jovial proclamation

yanked my attention back to the present just as Conner's lips descended upon mine, one hand pulling me close against him, the other cupping the back of my neck firmly as though he thought I might bolt.

Running was the last thing on my mind. I was too busy trying to comprehend how a chaste kiss in front of an audience could feel so damn erotic. The firmness of his demanding lips. The gentle way he bent me beneath him, keeping me slightly off balance.

But the coup de grâce came at the end of the kiss.

Keeping our lips together, he whispered a single word.

The celebratory quartet launched into a joyful song, filling the church with music. The crowd rose to their feet and clapped while the priest announced us as man and wife. All the while, my head spun with disbelief as that one word echoed in my head.

Mine.

We exited the cathedral hand in hand. I kept a smile on my face hoping it concealed the anxiety swarming inside me like an angry hive of bees.

Conner and I were married.

I was now Mrs. Noemi Reid.

The words strung together sounded foreign in my head. Nothing about my life was recognizable.

Come on, Em. Not the time for an existential crisis.

I repeatedly blinked, shooing away the cobwebs and realizing we'd finally escaped the curious stares of the congregation.

Conner led us down a hallway toward one of the rooms

we'd used to prepare prior to the ceremony. The guests would be walking a short distance down the street to the reception while we took a few portraits. Afterward, we would take a limo to the reception for our grand entrance. Until then, we waited. Alone.

He released my hand once we entered the small Sunday school room. The window shades were drawn closed, only allowing tiny slivers of light inside. I felt like I'd wandered into the den of a hungry lion, everything inside me screaming to get out.

We should have talked in the days leading up to the wedding, but he didn't call, so neither did I. It made this moment infinitely more awkward.

"You went through with it," he said quietly, slicing through the tension in the room.

"Did you doubt?"

"I wouldn't have been shocked if I'd been stood up." He leaned against the wall, his thumb slowly gliding along his bottom lip.

"I prefer to keep breathing," I murmured.

Conner's eyes went menacingly dark. He was upset at my insinuation—though I wasn't sure if my father's abuse or my reluctance to marry him bothered him more. Either way, I didn't explain myself. I already felt vulnerable. Giving him any more of myself would flay me wide open. If I bent to the pressure and confessed that a part of me wanted him, only to discover his reaction was purely a reflection of his dislike toward my father, I would have been embarrassed beyond measure. There was only so much emotional strain I could take in one day.

Unfortunately, Conner didn't get that memo.

He stalked closer, eyes lowering at the last second to my wrist. He snaked his finger under the bracelet Sante had given me and lifted my hand until he could read the engraving.

"How could you show any loyalty to that prick?" he sneered.

"My brother gave it to me." I yanked my hand away. "It has nothing to do with our father."

My bruises had finally faded, but a phantom ache circled my wrist at the reminder.

"Your brother is proud of the name and everything it represents. How does that not involve your father and the reputation he's created?"

"Because Sante is different. He's sweet."

"Naïve."

My lips thinned, unable to contradict him. "I can't hate him for what our father has done," I explained, my defenses lowering. Dropping my gaze, I suddenly felt self-conscious and turned toward the door. "We should probably go look for the photographer."

Conner's right hand reached around to press flat against my belly and pull me back flush against him. My gown was practically backless, allowing the scalding heat from his chest to encompass my body like a plush velvet drape. Still, it was his hard cock firm against my backside that turned my veins into liquid magma. My internal temperature skyrocketed so quickly that I had to be seconds from breathing fire.

My new husband's lips came to my ear, his left hand delicately drifting down my throat. "You're so fucking sexy when you're angry." The coarse restraint in his voice scraped across my skin, teasing my nipples into tightly pebbled pearls.

I arched into him on a shaky exhale, unable to help myself. The hand at my throat traced over my collarbone to the neckline of my dress, sliding the tip of one finger underneath to drift maddeningly slowly down to the bottom of the V between my breasts.

"I'll be tasting every square inch of this after the reception. I suggest you get used to the idea before then." He punctuated his proclamation with a rumbling exhale that reverberated from his chest into mine and pooled deep in my core.

How was I ever going to resist such seductive masculinity? I couldn't.

Even worse, I didn't want to.

And where my body went, my heart would follow. I was already dangerously close to developing feelings for my new husband. A few more tender words and protective gestures, and I was a goner. I had to ask myself whether the battle was even worth fighting. If defeat was a certainty, I should at least enjoy the fall. Then when things turned ugly and something inevitably came between us, I could at least say I tried. That I'd given my husband my all.

It was a scary new perspective. One I equally feared and relished. Could I open myself up to such vulnerability? I had approximately two hours to figure it out.

We sat next to one another in total silence in the limo. Conner looked out one window while I looked out the other, both lost in our own thoughts on the short drive to the reception.

"Wait there," he clipped quietly to me before circling the car and helping me onto the sidewalk, but not before eyeing the area to check for threats. His guard was always up, and I appreciated how safe that made me feel.

Hands again clasped, we walked into the hotel lobby and around the banquet hall, smiling and nodding to a flurry of congratulations from staff and random strangers. The wedding coordinator waited for us outside the ballroom entrance. She initiated the announcement of our arrival, and when we heard our names called, we opened the doors and swept into the room. Hundreds of people cheered. More than that. There had to be almost a thousand people gathered in the ballroom. An ocean of watchful eyes studying us, ready to scrutinize our every movement.

At least at the ceremony, all they could do was observe. Now, they moved in on us like pigeons when a handful of birdseed hit the ground. I didn't even realize Conner had leaned in until his whispered words ghosted past my ear.

"Breathe, Noemi."

I forced my hand to release its death grip on his. It was no wonder he knew I was freaking out. I'd practically cut off circulation to his fingers.

I tried to let go of his hand entirely, but he clamped down, refusing to allow the separation.

For the next half hour, we received a constant flow of people offering their congratulations. Conner did most of the talking. I remained passive at his side, more than happy to let him take the lead until I caught sight of the woman at my bridal shower—the one who had called me a demure mute.

My spine shot ramrod straight.

Logic dictated that I shouldn't give a flip what anyone thought and that if my marriage was only a front, I didn't need to be jealous, but the primal side of me told logic to fuck off.

I inched closer to my new husband while we greeted an older couple and slipped my hand into the crook of his arm affectionately. As though my actions were perfectly natural, he reached his arm around my back to pull me into his side, his hand resting possessively on my hip. When the bathroom woman stepped forward next, Conner's hand squeezed me.

"Ivy, it's been a while. How have you been?"

The beautiful blonde flushed, suddenly suffering from an unexpected bout of shyness. "It's been way too long! I'm doing well, but we should grab lunch sometime and catch up," she said with a feline grin.

Conner chuckled, placing a kiss on my cheek. "Think I have my hands full at the moment. Have you spotted Shae in the mix? I'm sure she'd love to meet up." Then he turned his gaze to the next person in line, effectively dismissing her.

I couldn't have put her in her place better if I'd done it myself.

I smiled broadly. "Good to see you again, Ivy," I added, unable to help myself.

Her eyes flared before she stormed away.

Conner shot me a brief questioning glance.

"She was at my shower," I said by way of explanation, then turned to the next guest.

A few minutes later, a throat cleared over a loudspeaker. Uncle Agostino stood on a small stage on the far wall along with Conner's uncle, Jimmy Byrne. The two men toasted to our marriage and the future of our families. Both radiated a commanding presence, Jimmy a bit more entertaining than Agostino. I could easily see how the two impressive figures had gained the respect and devotion of their respective families.

Thank God my father hadn't been asked to speak. I could only imagine what he would have said.

The second the toasts were complete, the wedding coordinator swept us away to the cake table. It was more of a dessert bar than a cake table with so many guests. Our bridal and groom's cakes adorned the middle of the long series of tables, a wealth of other sweet treats filling the rest of the space in an artful display of decadence, including a bowl of candied orange slices I noted on either end. I hadn't seen them listed when we'd approved the dessert menu, which made me wonder if Conner hadn't taken it upon himself to make sure they were included for his grandmother.

The guests closest to us gathered around to watch while most of the crowd was busy talking amongst themselves. We performed the standard cake-cutting pose for the photographer, placing a slice of the lemon bridal cake on a plate.

I smiled appropriately for a new bride, playing my part, but I wasn't sure what to do once the cake was cut. We hadn't really discussed our cake plans.

Seeing my uncertainty, the photographer called out. "Noemi, give him a bite!"

The onlookers around us cheered.

Taking a deep breath, I used a fork to cut off a small piece and held it up for my new husband. Conner dutifully ate my offering, his eyes devouring me in the process.

My entire body flushed with heat.

My hand suddenly trembling, I held out the plate for him. It was his turn to feed me, but Conner had other plans. Using his fingers to break off a piece of cake, he brought the bite to my lips. Inexplicably emboldened, I peered up at him from beneath my lashes and ate the cake right from his fingers, sucking on his thumb as it slipped from my mouth.

I could almost hear the fibers of his self-control snapping with restraint as the azure highlights in his eyes glinted dangerously.

Managing a colossal degree of restraint, he wrapped his own lips around his thumb and sucked, rolling his tongue where mine had been only seconds before.

I should have known better than to play with fire. He didn't even have to touch me to incinerate me into ash, desire hitting my veins like liquid napalm.

A throat cleared behind me, jump-starting my heart back into motion. When I turned, I was delighted to see Sante grinning down at me. I set down the cake plate, then wrapped my arms tight around my little brother.

"Congrats, Em. You look totally gorgeous. Like a real princess."

"Thanks, Sante." I pulled back and tugged at his lapel. "You clean up pretty well yourself."

He grinned mischievously and wiggled his brows. "You're not the only one who's noticed. I may have to wear this getup more often."

I grinned the first genuine smile of the day, though it didn't last long. Like the moon eclipsing the sun, my father's approach loomed menacingly over Sante's shoulder.

"The newlyweds are so popular, I haven't had a chance to congratulate my own daughter on her wedding." Dad held my hands wide as if admiring his beloved girl. "You look incredible, Noemi. Congratulations."

I stiffened as he pulled me in for a hug. The second he released me, I sensed Conner's presence at my back.

"Fausto," he greeted my father dryly but extended his hand so as not to be overtly disrespectful.

"Have you two decided on a honeymoon?" Dad asked, feigning interest in our lives.

"We haven't gotten to that yet, but there's plenty of time."

"Of course, though, I know we're all excited for a little Reid prince or princess to make their debut."

Jesus. That's all I am to him. A pretty pawn used for alliances and breeding.

Did he have no paternal instincts at all?

"They just said I do, Pops. Let's give 'em a few days before we start asking about babies," Sante said, chiding my father in an uncharacteristic display of assertiveness.

My heart ached for him. For everything he had yet to learn. For the suffering he undoubtedly had in store if he continued to stay loyal to Fausto Mancini.

"Maybe one of these days," Conner said dryly. "Excuse

us." With a hand on my back, Conner led us away from them, and with each step we took, I felt the familial ties snapping.

I wasn't a Mancini anymore, but I didn't yet feel like a Reid. Thank God I still had Pippa and her mom. Without them, I would have felt utterly adrift.

I would have strangled that fucker if I could have. The way Noemi tensed up around her father made me want to shoot him on the spot. I wasn't sure how I hadn't seen it when we first met, except that I'd been distracted by the entire concept of an arranged marriage.

I would have thought Noemi would feel emboldened now that she was free of him, but I got the sense he still held some power over her. It pissed me the fuck off—so much so that it was unsettling.

How had I gone from begrudgingly agreeing to marry a woman to obsessing over her thoughts and feelings? This marriage was only ever supposed to be about duty and proving my loyalty. Somehow, my perspective had completely shifted in two short weeks.

When Noemi had asked me why I'd agreed to marry her, I couldn't tell her the truth. That she was fucking mine, and that was why. Not just in the eyes of the law or the church. I knew she was mine, deep in my bones.

How fucking nuts was that after only two damn weeks?

We hadn't even spoken to one another for one of them—partially because I'd been insanely busy, but also to keep my head on straight. I had to stay away from her to keep the growing addiction from taking over.

Fuck.

What the hell was happening to me?

I didn't even recognize myself anymore. The only thing that soothed my irritation was seeing Noemi wrestle with her own conflicted feelings. She may not have liked it, but I was winning her over one small victory at a time. Whatever the source of the magnetic pull between us, it was mutual. That helped calm my frustration.

I was even more intrigued when my new bride sidled up to me during the receiving line. When I saw Ivy step forward, I realized what was happening. Noemi was staking her claim.

Fuck me if I didn't love the way that felt.

I had no clue how she'd known I had a past with Ivy, but she couldn't have been more obvious if she'd tattooed her name on my forehead.

You wouldn't see me complaining. She could have pissed a circle around me, and I would have just laughed, pleased to know she couldn't say a damn word when I went positively primitive over my own jealousy.

It was bound to happen sooner rather than later.

She looked like a goddamn queen in her gown. Hair all piled on her head to expose every inch of her graceful spine, she was nothing short of royalty. Every man in that room had a semi for her, but I was the only one who could touch her. Taste her.

With every minute that passed, I became more rabid with desire, itching with the need to get her alone. By the time Mia Genovese approached me two hours into the reception, my well of patience had run dry. Noemi had been distracted by her cousins. Mia used the opportunity to try to get a private word with me.

"Congratulations, Conner. We're all so incredibly happy for you."

"Thank you. I'm glad you could be here." I gave a tight smile, hoping the brief encounter with my birth mother was over, but I should have known better by the desperate gleam in her eye.

"Do you think I could have a minute of your time? Maybe just a minute in the hallway?"

"I'm not sure this is really the time or place," I said stiffly. As far as I was concerned, the only right time was never.

She worried her hands and chewed on her lips. "I know. I left messages for you. It's just—"

"It's fine, Mia, really. I'm not interested in the past. I'm very happy with how my life has turned out, so no need for guilt." I clasped a hand on her arm reassuringly just as Noemi joined us.

"Mia, right?" she asked, surprising me that she knew the woman. They were both Italian but part of two separate organizations.

"Yes, it's so good to see you again. You look absolutely stunning, my dear." Mia beamed.

"Thank you so much." Noemi lifted her gaze back to me. "Mia and I had the pleasure of meeting briefly at my bridal shower."

Ah, so that explained it. I hadn't told Noemi about my newly discovered relations. Not that it was a secret. For all

I'd known, her family had already told her the sordid details.

"I brought the girls, too," Mia added. "They were so excited to meet you."

"Yes, Giada mentioned getting together sometime." Noemi looked up at me questioningly. I appreciated her consideration because I wasn't sure how I felt about the women cozying up to one another.

"I'm sure we'll have time to sort it out," I forced. "For now, we really need to greet some more guests." I nodded to Mia and ushered Noemi away, ignoring her shocked glance at my abruptness. Thankfully, she didn't push for an explanation.

Mia had reached out several times over the past weeks, but I had no desire for awkward apologies and guilt-ridden explanations that served no purpose. I truly was happy with my life. My adoption resulted in a loving family, wealth, and privilege. She couldn't care for me at the time, so she did what she thought was best. I wasn't impressed with her family for not supporting her. That fact had always colored my perception of the Italians in general. Still, I had no particularly hard feelings toward her.

The past was the past. End of story.

Exhausting the last of my reserves, I guided us toward the ballroom entrance. It was time to draw the curtain on the reception portion of our evening. I was ready to be alone with my new wife.

Noemi

TWENTY-NINE

THANK *GOD* FOR CHAMPAGNE. I WOULD HAVE BEEN A NERVOUS wreck if I hadn't had the calming effects of alcohol dulling my senses. As it was, I still swam in a pool of my own chaotic emotions, but at least I hadn't needed to throw up from the uncertainty of it all.

It took a half hour to get to Conner's apartment building, and we spent the entire ride in silence. Next to one another but alone. Husband and wife. Total strangers. But that didn't matter to Conner. He'd made his plans for me clear.

He'd claimed my life, and now my body would be his as well.

Breathe, Noemi.

Conner lived in one of the newest high-rise apartment

buildings in the middle of the city. I'd grown up in a periphery neighborhood that boasted single-family homes and a surprising allotment of trees. While I was used to seeing the close quarters of Midtown Manhattan, I'd never lived there. Even that would be an adjustment. Heaven forbid anything about this marriage feel easy and familiar.

I took in every facet of his expansive apartment as I walked inside the dimly lit space. It was modern but not overly cold. Open area living with a wall of solid windows overlooking the river. Sandy-colored cabinets with a light-gray stone countertop and rich camel wood floors. He even had several large house plants that softened the look. I wondered if he kept them alive or had a housekeeper who tended to them. My money was on a housekeeper.

I walked past the large cream leather sectional to the window displaying the city at dusk. The thirty-story view gave my alcohol-soaked stomach a lurch. Turning back around, I found Conner watching me as he rolled up the sleeves of his dress shirt. He'd removed his jacket and vest while I'd looked around and now had every ounce of his attention directed at me.

"Your place is lovely," I offered, moving to the center of the living area but leaving the sofa strategically between us.

"Your things were delivered earlier today. Some of it was put away, but you'll have to sort through the rest." He began to prowl around the sofa toward me, eyes never leaving mine.

Holding his smoldering blue gaze was terrifying yet felt essential at the same time. His unremitting stare commanded and unnerved me. Aroused and bemused me. It was more intimate than anything I'd ever experienced. It felt like giving confession, only darker, more seductive. What I imagined it might be like to confess my sins to the devil himself.

Conner closed in behind me, his confident fingers sliding

the straps of my gown over my shoulders. "There'll be plenty of time to show you around now that the place is yours."

"Is it, though?" I breathed, trying desperately to keep my wits about me. I could feel myself getting swept up in the desire he elicited.

I tried to turn, but Conner's hands kept my shoulders in place, then slowly caressed down my exposed spine. "What's mine is yours now," he replied distractedly.

My heart jackhammered against the confines of my chest. I would lose this battle if I didn't get away from him. He'd hardly touched me, and I could feel the resulting slickness of arousal coating my thong. If I gave him any more time, he'd reduce me to a puddle of wanton desire.

"I'm on my period," I blurted, my eyes widening in shock at my own words.

Adept fingers slid down the zipper of my dress, causing the heavy beaded gown to melt to the floor. I stood motionless in nothing but a thong and white satin heels. A rumble of masculine appreciation teased out an army of goose bumps down my arms and legs. When his hands came to rest at my hips, I closed my eyes, sensing I was fighting a losing battle.

Conner lowered himself to his knees, then used his hands to spin me around so that his face was inches from my belly. Before I could protest, he leaned in and ran the bridge of his nose up my slit, breathing in a long, languid breath as he did. When his eyes lifted again to mine, they shone with wicked triumph.

"I don't think so, little Emy. Not that it would have stopped me if you were."

One hand centered on my belly and pressed me backward. When I moved to catch myself, the back of my legs hit the sofa, sending me falling backward onto the cushions. Conner was between my legs instantly, his body keeping my thighs spread.

"I told you I was hungry." Then his mouth was on me, licking my core through the thin silk of my thong.

My head flung backward, every nerve in my body lighting up at his touch. "*Conner,*" I gasped, losing all ability to think.

"That's it, baby. Say my name while I devour this sweet pussy of yours."

His hands tugged the fabric at my hips, ripping away the thong before his mouth was on me again, this time with nothing between us. If I'd thought his fingers felt good, his tongue on my clit was pure ecstasy. When he pressed my thighs back to give himself better access, I clasped my hands behind my knees to help. I'd completely surrendered myself, a slave to the sensations he produced.

Conner knew how to coax my body into a heightened frenzy before pausing to graze his teeth over my inner thigh, giving my core just long enough to settle, just to work me up all over again. His hands roamed my body, plucking at my sensitive nipples and confusing my senses until my veins were flooded with pleasure.

"*Please,* Conner. I need more." The need was so overwhelming that I thought I'd go mad if I didn't find my way to that elusive pinnacle taunting just out of my reach.

He chuckled against my pussy. "That a girl," he murmured against my swollen flesh, then slid two thick fingers inside me. "So fucking *tight.*" His words were growing more ragged with waning restraint, but I was only vaguely aware because those fingers caressing my insides with his tongue on my clit sent me rocketing toward the release I'd been so desperately craving.

I didn't just cry out. I screamed.

My entire body spasmed, muscles quaking and nerves pulsing with pure electric bliss. Wave after wave, I was blanketed in a sensation so warm and overwhelming that I couldn't move or think.

Conner allowed me time to languish in the afterglow, his hands running gently up and down the outside of my thighs. As my senses returned, I wondered if he'd have sex with me. He'd want to come, too, right? I couldn't imagine he'd be satisfied walking away without his own release.

Righting myself, I bit down on my lip and peered uncertainly into his fathomless eyes. "Are we not …? Are you not going to…?" I couldn't seem to say the words, embarrassment at my naïvete crippling my self-confidence.

Conner rose to his feet and studied me from above, still fully dressed. "You're not ready yet, and I'm not fucking you before you're ready." He started to turn, but my hand clasped his, halting him.

It happened before I'd fully thought it through. Maybe it was the champagne, but I wanted to be the center of this man's attention. I wanted to be able to give him what he'd given me.

Easing off the sofa, I got on my knees and began to unclasp his belt. He speared me through with his predator's gaze. When he stepped toward the couch, I thought maybe he was rejecting my offer, but instead, he grabbed a pillow and dropped it at his feet. I moved to kneel on the pillow with a gentle smile at his unexpected kindness.

"There you go again, viewing the world through the eyes of a closet romantic," he said, his hand cupping my jaw. "Don't pretend I'm something I'm not. I just want you to be comfortable so you can suck my cock as long as I want."

Why did men always feel the need to disguise their softer side? Whatever. What he'd done was sweet, and I chose to ignore his brutish take on the matter.

Between the orgasm and alcohol, my hands barely trembled as I undid his pants. I'd never been this close to a man's penis. And judging by the impressive bulge pressing against Conner's zipper, he was enormous.

A flood of self-doubt tried to convince me I had no idea what I was doing and was about to embarrass myself beyond redemption. Still, an equally relentless surge of curiosity demanded I stay the course. I needed to feel him in my hands and see what it was like to wrap my lips around him. I wanted him to come undone and know that I was the reason.

Pants at his ankles, Conner used his thumb to stretch down his underwear, allowing his thick cock to bob forward, straining in my direction. I was instantly in awe. He was so thick that I couldn't clasp my hand all the way around him, and the smooth skin of the tip looked like it was made to be licked. Gently gripping the base, I ran my tongue over the head of his cock like a lollipop.

Conner hissed. "That feels good, baby, but I need you to give me more. Don't be afraid you'll hurt me." He placed his hand around mine and tightened my grip, moving our hands up and down the base of his shaft, then used his other hand to guide my mouth closer. Opening, I took him in and immediately gagged.

"Shh, it's okay. Relax your throat. You can do it. I know you can."

Tears burned my eyes, but not in a bad way—more like a reflex. It actually made me a little angry. I wanted to be able to do this and wasn't going to let my body throw a fit.

Rallying my determination, I opened wide and coaxed my throat to accept the intrusion. It felt awkward, but the unbidden shiver that wracked his body at my touch made it all worth it. Encouraged, I squeezed my hand and began lifting and lowering my head, sucking and licking with enthusiasm now that I felt more comfortable with my actions.

"Jesus, *fuck*, Em. I'm gonna come." His hand pressed against the back of my head, keeping me from retreating. "Your mouth feels too fucking good."

Hearing the strain in his voice, I peered up at him through

my lashes. That was all it took. The second our eyes met, he threw back his head and roared his release. His salty essence filled my mouth. It wasn't something I would have liked, except it was *him*. Masculine and untamed—a product of his desire for *me*—that part could be addicting.

I used the back of my hand to wipe the saliva from my chin as Conner righted his pants, then helped me to my feet. That was when the awkwardness returned.

It was no wonder people joked about bailing after a one-night stand. If this was what it was like, I'd want to escape, too. Except this was my house now, and I was married to the man who lived there.

Holy hell.

Conner took off his dress shirt and offered it to me. "Bedroom's this way."

I slipped on the shirt and followed him to a dark hallway. "I don't have to share a room with you if you'd rather not."

He glanced over his shoulder at me. "You saying you want your own room?"

"Um … I don't think so. I hadn't really thought it through, to be honest. I guess I'd avoided thinking about any of this."

He continued to the master suite, a surprisingly cozy affair with a fireplace and a large private balcony. The color scheme was similar but toned a bit darker. Soothing. Whoever had decorated used a grayish blue to add a pop of color. I wondered if Conner's eyes had been the inspiration.

"Your clothes are in the closet, but we can move them if that's what you want."

I turned my attention back to him when he spoke, noting tension now coiling in his shoulders. He didn't look at me when he spoke, either, just stalked to the en suite bathroom and began to undress. I followed distractedly. When he tossed his undershirt in a hamper, I took it back out and swapped it for the dress shirt I'd been wearing.

He stilled, watching my every movement.

"Is this okay? I'm not sure where any of my stuff is, and I'm too tired to go digging around tonight."

"No, I don't mind." A spark of hunger from before returned to his eyes. "I believe your intimates are in here." He pointed out a column of drawers in the closet.

Locating a pair of pink panties, I slid them on, then went to the vanity to pull the pins from my hair. It took longer than necessary because my eyes were constantly drawn to the sight of his naked chest and powerful legs. It was the first time I'd seen him in his underwear. Boxer briefs that pulled snug around his strong thighs.

Once he'd put on joggers and a T-shirt, he stood in the doorway waiting for me to finish. "You hungry?"

"Yeah. Guess I am." The ceremony had started at two, the reception at three thirty. We'd had cake and champagne but never got around to dinner.

Conner led us back through the house to the kitchen. Walking behind him, I realized that I liked the way he moved. Confident and powerful without unnecessary pretense. He reminded me of a racehorse—the underdog sort who ran swift and true despite a lack of breeding. His fortitude wasn't taught or manufactured; he was born with it, as natural as the slight cleft in his chin.

"Your place is nice," I said, feeling a need to fill the silence.

"Our place."

"Right … our place," I murmured. "That's going to take some time to get used to."

"Have a seat at the bar. You like risotto?"

My eyebrows hit my hairline. I wasn't sure if I was more surprised he was offering to cook or that he was making Italian.

He smirked over his shoulder. "Don't tell anyone, but

Ma loves Italian. She loves to cook in general, and since I was an only child, I spent a lot of time in the kitchen with her." He moved with natural ease in the modern space, pulling out high-end cooking pans and ingredients from scratch. I considered asking about his connection to the Genoveses but decided against it. We were tiptoeing into some semblance of normalcy, and I didn't want to rock the boat.

"Well, I wish I could tell you I know loads of Irish recipes, but that would be a lie. I *do* know how to cook, but mostly Italian." Rather than sit like he suggested, I took out the butter and parmesan from the fridge.

"You have a favorite?" he asked, starting to chop an onion on a cutting board.

I leaned against the counter near him, realizing I'd begun to feel almost comfortable. Probably best not to think about it too much, or I'd draw out some worry to throw me off kilter. "I guess my favorite would be this enchilada casserole Mom taught me."

"I hate to break it to you, but that's not Italian."

"I said I cook *mostly* Italian with a few other dishes thrown in to keep things fresh." I watched him cutting, feeling a tinge of sting in my eyes from the onion. "I don't even know what Irish food is."

"Potatoes," he teased dryly. "*Lots* of potatoes with the occasional sausage. Sheperd's pie or a stew. Hearty food—gotta eat something to soak up the whiskey." He tossed the onion into a warming skillet with a tablespoon of olive oil, then checked his phone.

"*Shit,*" he grumbled, frowning as he peered at the sizzling pan. "I have to go. You think you can finish this?"

"You're leaving?" The words came out sounding more accusatory than I'd meant.

"That a problem?"

I shook my head quickly. "No," I assured him. "Will there be someone here with me?"

His thick black brows drew together. "Does there need to be?"

"Not at all. I just haven't been allowed home alone in a long time. It feels strange."

A menacing shadow darkened his features. "This isn't a prison, Noemi. I'd prefer if you had me or one of my men with you when you go out, but I'd like to think you don't need someone lording over you." He studied me for a second longer. "I need to get changed."

Ten minutes later, he was gone.

Married and alone, like my mother had been. Was this how things had begun for her? Would I ever have any claim on him if Conner could be called away even on his wedding night?

As my brother's magic Eightball would probably say: outlook not so good.

I pushed aside the sinking feeling that tugged at my chest and put the finishing touches on the risotto. While it cooled, I figured out how to turn on the TV and found a music app. I considered selecting a haunting playlist that would suit my growing melancholy but refused to allow myself to wallow. My situation might not have been ideal, but it was better than before. I was alone, for the moment, which was more freedom than I'd been allowed in over six months.

I selected a summer party playlist. What better way to focus on the silver lining than pool party tunes?

Once I was done eating, I turned up the music to hear it throughout the apartment and familiarized myself with my new home. I found a stack of my boxes in a guest room that I'd need to sort through at some point and took inventory of one more spare bedroom, Conner's office, and a room dedicated to exercise equipment. Most of the house was located on one side while the master suite was on the other, allowing for privacy.

Returning to that side, I peeked through Conner's things, scoping out the closet and bathroom. Like most men I knew, he kept a loaded handgun in a nightstand drawer. I knew how to shoot, but guns weren't my favorite thing, so I left that alone. Otherwise, nothing of interest jumped out at me, mostly because he hardly had any *things*. No tchotchkes from trips or personal items. He had a couple of framed family photos and an old set of rosary beads on his dresser. That was it.

Seemed a bit lonely to me.

Not for long!

I grinned to myself, feeling devious, and headed for the guest room housing my boxes. If this was supposed to be my home, then so be it. I'd make the place feel a bit more like mine. If he didn't like that, too bad. It served him right for leaving me alone on our wedding night.

"Not such a demure bride, after all, am I, Mr. Reid?" I giggled to myself and dove into unpacking.

THE MASTER BEDROOM WAS PITCH BLACK WHEN SOMETHING roused me from sleep. My entire body stiffened when I realized a large hand was pressed flat to my belly, and that hand was attached to a very large, very warm body spooned against my back.

"It's me, Noemi. You can relax." Conner's tired voice melted around me like warm butter.

"I just picked a side," I murmured sleepily.

He grunted. "There's shit all over the dresser."

"And the bathroom, too." I grinned to myself. "My house, my shit."

Seemingly too tired to argue, he only huffed before his breathing drifted into gentle snores.

The next time I woke, light seeped into the room from the edges of the drapes. Conner was no longer curled around me, though one of his hands still lightly held my forearm from where he lay as though he'd managed to keep tabs on me even in sleep.

He didn't budge when I slipped from the bed. I wondered how late he'd come home. Not wanting to bother him and nowhere near comfortable enough for him to hear me pee, I used a guest bathroom before heading to the kitchen.

Conner had a surprising number of breakfast options, including bagels in the pantry and cream cheese in the fridge. Since he'd cooked for me the evening before, I thought I might throw some pancakes together. But first, coffee.

I opened cabinets until I found a coffee bar with an espresso machine and a Keurig. Next to it was a box of Starbuck's Pike Place Roast cups, and behind that, a box of Green Mountain Hazelnut cups. Conner didn't strike me as the type to drink novelty-flavored coffees. And because I loved to torture myself, I began to wonder if these had been purchased for someone else. Perhaps … a female someone.

My lips pursed tightly as though I'd tasted something bitter.

It had never occurred to me to ask about his prior relationships. That wasn't true. It had crossed my mind, but an appropriate time had never presented itself. Normally, in a relationship, that sort of thing naturally came up over time as a couple learned about one another. We'd gone the fast track. I was married to this man and had no idea about his dating history. Hell, he could have been seeing someone when this whole thing started.

I groaned.

"I can show you how to use the machine."

I startled at the sound of Conner's voice. "Crap, you scared me. Make some noise when you walk." The conviction in my voice trailed off the second my eyes landed on his shirtless form strolling in from the living room.

Jesus, Mary, and Joseph. Will I ever get used to that sight?

Joggers hung low on his hips. Every inch of his delectable chest and arms were on display. Ink covered his entire left arm and shoulder. The designs were done entirely in black and bled onto his chest and back. He had a smattering of dark hair on his chest and muscles for miles—the thick, mature kind that couldn't be bought in a gym.

"Um … I know how, actually," I mumbled. "My mom was a huge coffee fanatic. We had a cappuccino machine at home. This one isn't so different."

"We can switch to cappuccino if you prefer. Doesn't much matter to me." He flipped a switch on the fancy machine.

"I think espresso sounds good." New place, new routines. Having morning espresso with my husband might actually be nice.

"There are bagels and cream cheese if you want."

"I saw that. You like them, too?"

"Not much of a breakfast person myself."

"Then why …" I stopped, realizing he'd bought them for me. He'd bought all of it for me.

Well, damn.

There he went being all sweet again. It was strange. He wasn't flowery or poetic, but a softer side lurked beneath that gruff exterior.

"Um, I had thought about making pancakes for us, but if you don't want anything, a bagel works great." I pulled the bag of bakery bagels out of the pantry and hunted down a serrated knife for slicing. Once I'd cut my bagel and found the toaster, I turned and leaned my back against the counter's edge.

Conner had the coffee brewing and was retrieving something from the dining table. "Here, this is for you." He handed me a brand-new iPhone. "My number and a couple others are programmed in already. Bishop is in there. If you can't get ahold of me, call him."

"Thanks." I hadn't thought about it, but I definitely didn't want to keep using the phone my dad had given me.

"You have an idea of what you want to do?"

I stared at him blankly. "What do you mean?"

"I don't expect you to sit here all day just because we're married. What did you do before?"

"I was in school, then Mom died, and Dad didn't really let me do anything." I felt oddly self-conscious telling him that. I wasn't sure why. It wasn't my fault my father was an asshole or that I'd lost my mother, but admitting to having zero purpose in life felt embarrassing.

"What did you plan to do before all that happened?"

I shrugged. "I wasn't exactly sure. The kind of things that interested me weren't really career-type pursuits."

"Like what?"

I debated how silly I'd look telling him the truth when the toaster ejected my bagel behind me and sent me shooting away from the counter. Slamming into his hard chest, I gasped, looking up into molten sapphire eyes.

"Excuse me," I whispered.

Conner's hands moved from my arms where he'd caught me and trailed down to my lower back, pulling me snug against him. He brought his face down to my neck and inhaled. "You always this jumpy in the morning?"

Now I was jumpy *and* breathless because his cock quickly grew hard between us. We didn't have sex last night, but how long would he wait? How would I know when I was ready?

A flurry of questions rained down on me, prompting me to wiggle free.

"Gotta grab my bagel before it burns or gets cold or something," I mumbled, scurrying back to the toaster.

When I glanced over at my new husband, his mouth was quirked upward in a knowing smirk.

"This is yours also." He went to his wallet on the counter and pulled out a black card, sliding it across the island to me. A credit card. And it had my name on it.

My eyes widened.

Conner's narrowed. "Let me guess, that asshole kept your money hostage as well?"

"You say that like I had money," I answered softly.

He shook his head and returned to the coffee machine, retrieving his freshly poured cappuccino. "Well, you have money now. Think about what you want to do. I have to run some errands this morning, but I'll be back after lunch. You okay until then?"

"Yeah, of course."

He nodded and took his coffee to the bedroom, presumably to get ready. Somewhat bemused, I plopped myself on a barstool and spread cream cheese on my bagel. How very strange. I didn't know what I'd expected from Conner, but this wasn't it. Maybe I'd been hasty to assume he was incapable of caring for me. Maybe what he was offering would be enough. If I had freedom and a certain degree of respect, I could be happy. Probably. And if I had money, I could access the things I needed to get my brother away from our dad.

Then what, genius? You think Dad will just let Sante go?

The few bites I'd had churned in my stomach. Was I willing to run? Could I gather enough money to escape with Sante? Did I want to do that? And if I didn't, what did that say about me as a sister? Didn't I have to at least try to save him?

The remainder of my appetite shriveled up and disappeared.

I needed to hear Sante's voice and reassure myself he was okay. I wasn't sure why. I just needed to, but I didn't want to call when Conner was around. He already thought poorly of my brother, and I didn't want to somehow make things worse.

While I waited for Conner to leave for work, I debated which phone to use. I still had the disposable phone he'd originally given me. That would ensure no one tracked my end of the conversation, but knowing Sante's phone would be monitored made any efforts at privacy pointless. I might as well use the new phone and trust that my new husband was telling the truth about not stalking my every move.

I called my brother the minute I was alone, relieved when he answered.

"Yeah," he barked over the line, answering the unknown number with a degree of authority that made me smile.

"Hey, little brother. It's me."

"Em! How are you?" All pretense melted from his voice. "I've been so worried."

"I'm just fine. No need to worry about me." I wished I could tell him all about Conner, but I didn't want my father to hear. The less he knew about my husband, the better. "What have you been up to?"

"The usual, mostly," he said vaguely.

"Mostly?" I didn't think I was prying, but when Sante replied, his voice was strained.

"You know I can't talk about that stuff, Em." His defensive response startled me.

"Yeah, I didn't mean to be nosy. Wasn't sure if you meant you'd gone out on a hot date or whatnot." I tried to play it off, but worry knotted my stomach.

He was silent for several seconds. "There's stuff … *Ah!*" He cut himself off with an angry burst. "It's nothing. I'm just glad to hear you're okay. Look, I gotta go. This your new number?"

"Yeah. Call me anytime."

"Great. Take care, and I'll be in touch." He hung up before I could reply.

Shit. What the hell is going on with him?

I needed to have an open conversation without our father looming over us. I stared at the burner I'd dug out of my things while unpacking and wondered if I couldn't do the same thing for Sante that Conner had done for me. Could I get a disposable phone to him undetected? Surely, I could manage that. And from there, who knew what might be possible.

"THINGS TOOK LONGER THAN I EXPECTED. I HOPE YOU WERE ABLE to come up with something for lunch." Conner joined me in the living room, his hands shoved in his pockets and his eyes guarded.

"Not a problem at all. Are you done for the day?"

"No. I need to get back. I just thought I should check in." His jaw clenched, gaze cutting harshly to the side as if something had irritated him.

"Well, since you're here, I need to run an errand."

He nodded as if to himself. "You might as well come with me. We can run your errand on our way to the club."

I tensed, not expecting him to take me himself. Shit. "Okay. Let me grab my purse." I hurried to the bedroom, cursing my luck. I preferred he not know what I was up to, but now it looked like I didn't have a choice.

"I just need to run into a drug store," I explained once we were in his car. "I know parking's a pain, so you don't need to bother coming in." I tried to sound as nonchalant as possible.

My new husband didn't look at me or respond. Instead, he whipped into a driveway and stopped the car, pinning me in place with his stare. "We live in a world where everyone will be out for our blood. The only chance we have at staying whole is to trust one another. You're my wife, like it or not. Now, are you going to tell me what this is about?"

I wasn't sure why, but tears burned the back of my eyes. "I'm worried about my brother. I thought I'd get a prepaid phone to give him, like you did for me. That way, I could talk to him … without my father knowing."

Tension seemed to suck the air from the small space.

"Someone needs to kill that bastard," Conner spat. He had no idea how right he was, but he and his family couldn't possibly be the ones to do it. Such an outright act of war would end in disaster.

"I just need to be able to talk to Sante, that's all. Then I'm sure everything will be fine."

I didn't think he believed me any more than I believed myself, but he let the subject drop. After finding a parking spot, he took me to a drug store and showed me where the disposable phones were sold. He even had me pay for it with my new credit card to make sure the thing worked. A part of me kept waiting for the trap. It all seemed too easy. Too convenient and empowering. How would he control me if he gave me everything I needed, including my freedom to move about?

Well, that's some fucked-up thinking. Dad's done a real number on you.

I had to fight back a sigh as Conner drove us to his club. I didn't want to think my husband was capable of manipulating me like my father had, but it was hard to squash the suspicions. I felt compelled to be on my guard, just in case. It was mind-boggling how quickly life could be snuffed out or stolen.

The club entrance was quiet like it'd been on my first visit. I wondered what it was like at night—did people line up outside, or was it more like a speakeasy with secret knocks and lookouts? Maybe I'd just seen too many movies.

Shae was absent this time around, but the best man at our wedding was lounging on Conner's sofa when we reached his office.

"If you're that tired, man, just go home," Conner grumbled, alerting the man to our presence. I'd met him briefly before, but we hadn't had a chance to talk.

"Oh shit. Sorry. Late night." The attractive guy sat up, a sheepish smile showing off deep dimples on both cheeks. He looked right about Conner's age with warm brown eyes that reminded me of a golden retriever and curly dark hair he kept long and unruly on top. He was strong—thick cords of lean muscle layered on one another so that his traps made his shoulders slope, and the sleeves of his T-shirt strained over his curving biceps. With the boyish nature of his charm, he was even cuter in casual clothes than the suit he'd been wearing at the wedding.

"Noemi, you remember Bishop," Conner said distractedly, walking to his desk.

That's right. I extended my hand, which he gladly accepted. "Bishop ... is that your last name?"

"Nah, real name's Ewan Bohanan."

"Why Bishop?" I asked, curious.

He smirked, looking at Conner as if asking permission.

My husband rolls his eyes.

"Got the name in high school..." He blasted a radiant

grin. "Because all the girls ended up on their knees when I was around."

I had to bite my lips to keep from laughing hysterically.

Conner perched on his desk, crossing his arms over his chest. "Nearly got you killed on more than one occasion."

"How was I to know if one had a boyfriend?" He spread his arms wide, pleading his innocence. "And it never got quite that bad—not with you at my back."

"Yeah, you dragged me into more shit. It was a good thing I lived in the ring."

"The ring?" I asked, cutting in.

"Boxing ring," Conner clarified.

"Did you box professionally?"

"Did he box?" Bishop gaped. "My man could have been a champ—just look at him!"

I smirked, trying not to be too obvious in my perusal. Conner *did* have an impressive build. "Guess that explains why your knuckles are all scarred."

Conner smirked. "That's one of the reasons."

I shook my head, not wanting to know what else would lead to that kind of damage. It was enlightening seeing the two men interact. Bishop brought out a different side of Conner that I hadn't seen before. I imagined they'd been hell on wheels growing up.

"Alright, that's enough bullshitting." Conner stood, shoving some papers in a drawer, then looked at me. "There's always a few tables open around the clock upstairs. You want to go up and check it out?"

"Really?" I'd figured he needed to work, and I'd be stuck entertaining myself. A tour was an unexpected treat.

"Come on. Bishop, go make yourself useful somewhere." Conner led me to the elevator and up to the second floor, which housed what looked like a small hotel ballroom decked out for a Vegas-themed event. The walls were dotted with crystal sconces, and matching chandeliers hung from the ceilings. Textured satin fabric decorated the walls in a rich burgundy, the same color used throughout the space combined with gold and mahogany wood grains. A dozen card tables sat in the middle of the open room. Only two seemed to be open at the moment, and I wondered what the atmosphere would be like at night during peak hours.

"You'll have to come sometime at night to see the full effect," Conner mused, looking over his kingdom as if viewing it from my perspective.

"I was just thinking the same. It's beautiful, but I bet it comes alive at night."

He rumbled a sound of agreement.

"How exactly is it that you can run a place like this? Isn't it illegal?" I recalled Shae telling me everything on his floor was above board, which had me curious.

Conner's head inclined almost proudly. "The Bastion club is a private charitable organization. Essentially, it entails some very creative accounting."

"I see."

"You know how to play blackjack?" he glanced over at me.

"Oh yeah. I've played a bunch with my brother—not for money, although sometimes we'd play for leftover Halloween candy."

Stifling a smile, he shook his head. "Let's see what you've got then."

He motioned to one of the tables. I took the only open chair, smiling at the attractive redhead in the dealer's seat, though she hardly gave me a glance because she was too preoccupied with making eyes at my husband.

"Mr. Reid," she said in a sultry tone. "This is a pleasant surprise."

The nerve! It's like I'm not even sitting here.

Conner placed a hand on my shoulder. "Wanted to show my new wife around. Noemi, this is Lena. Lena, Noemi."

The woman smiled and dealt my cards, a dagger sheathed in her eyes. "Best of luck."

Was this the attention he got at work every day? If so, it was no wonder he was dedicated to the job. I knew that women often threw themselves at powerful men, but it was another thing to see it in action. With my husband.

I swallowed back the acrid taste of jealousy and looked at my hand. Two eights. A decent enough hand to split. I managed to get face cards dealt onto each eight, giving me two winning hands when the dealer held at seventeen. I grinned, beaming up at Conner, who was able to join me at the table when the man sitting next to me grumbled and withdrew from the game.

Lena dealt again, including Conner this time. We played several hands, and I'd begun to genuinely enjoy myself despite the overt attention Lena showered on my husband. My tolerance hit its limit when her hand trailed seductively over his for the second time as she collected his cards.

"You know what? I think I'd like to eat," I blurted, turning to Conner. "Can we grab dinner?"

His narrowed blue gaze cut to me. "Yeah, of course." He dropped his cards on the table. I walked to the elevator, not taking time for goodbyes.

"Is there something you need to say?" Conner asked once we were in the car. He'd detected the downturn in my mood, but I wasn't ready to admit the source of my irritation.

"No, just hungry." I kept my eyes cast out the side window.

A short time later, we pulled up to a restaurant by the name of Neary's. It looked small on the outside but opened up deep into the back of the building on the inside. If I'd had to guess, I'd have said the place had been open as long as the building had been in existence—possibly the thirties or forties—but in a good way. The Irish-style pub had loads of charm. Red vinyl booths lined the walls, along with Irish memorabilia and ancient-looking sconces that cast a warm glow throughout the cozy space.

"It's family-owned," Conner said, leading me to a vacant table in the middle of the long room. "This okay, Tally?" He lifted his chin to a cute curly-haired server nearby.

"Of course, Mr. Reid." She walked over and pulled out a chair for him, flashing a seductive smile. "Can I grab you your usual?"

Un-fucking-believable.

Was this what it would be like? Always feeling like a third wheel in my own damn marriage?

"That would be great, thanks. Noemi, what would you like to drink?"

I huffed and plopped into my seat, refusing to look in Conner's direction. "The house red works."

Once *Tally* left us, Conner scooted his chair closer to me, one corner of the small table between us. "You jealous?" he asked curiously, a hand rubbing at his stubbled chin.

"I just think it's disrespectful. All these women fucking you with their eyes like I'm not even here."

Something dark and primal crossed behind his eyes. "You're jealous." He said the words this time with predatory amusement, like a cat watching a mouse squirm in a trap.

"That what you'd call it if Bishop and every other man we encountered was blatantly picturing me naked?" I had his attention now, so I continued in earnest. "If this relationship was real, then a few ogling eyes wouldn't bother me. But it's not real, and that just makes everything so much more confusing."

Conner's face turned volatile—his features more stark, his anger more acute. "What do you mean *if this was real*?" Every clipped word dripped with venom.

"Well, we're married, but it's mostly a show, right? An

arrangement for our families." I was digging myself deeper with every word but wasn't sure how.

My husband leaned forward in his seat, his body seething with temper. "A *show*? Do I strike you as some kind of actor? Because I'm pretty sure you coming on my tongue and fingers was as real as it fucking gets. I told you this was more than some goddamn arrangement."

Heat seared my cheeks as I peered around the restaurant, praying no one heard him. "Yeah, but what does that mean?"

"It means you're *mine,* and I'm yours."

"You say that," I offered quietly, gaze lowered to my hands. "But I don't know anything about you." When I peered back at him, I allowed him to see through to my uncertainty and fear. It had the desired effect.

Conner's shoulders visibly relaxed as he leaned back in his chair. "What do you want to know?"

"Can you tell me about the Genoveses? I didn't realize you were adopted."

He nodded, giving the server a moment to deliver our drinks. "Several months ago, my birth mother reached out and initiated contact. I wasn't interested, but when my uncles discovered I was the son of Mia Genovese, they pushed me to meet with her."

"I can't even imagine what that must have felt like."

"It's not so bad. I've had a good life, and I don't begrudge her choices. Mia was only sixteen when she got pregnant with me. Once I was born, she dropped me off along with a set of rosary beads at the Catholic church my adoptive parents attended. Mom knew at a young age she wouldn't be able to have kids, so when the opportunity struck, she jumped at the chance to adopt me. It worked out for the best."

"I guess all of this is making a bit more sense now—the Irish and Italians coming together."

"Did your father not tell you any of this?" He shook his

head with a roll of his eyes. "Never mind. Of course, he didn't."

I shrugged. "It was unusual for the two groups to unite, but I was taught that it wasn't my place to ask questions."

"Well, you can scrub that bullshit from your mind," he grumbled. "You're my wife, not an employee. I expect you to ask me if you have a question."

I paused, deciding if I wanted to test his assertion. "What does it mean for you to be part of both the Irish and Italian families?"

He sighed heavily. "I'm not exactly sure. It doesn't change much as far as the organizations go. Even our marriage doesn't give me any special privileges with the Five Families. I'm fine with that. It's the personal stuff that's more of a complication. Mia keeps wanting to get together, and I'm not interested. I don't know what the hell to do about her."

My heart both constricted and soared at his explanation. I hated that he was in such a tricky situation, but I was also thrilled he'd confided in me about something so personal. He was showing me a degree of trust I'd never expected.

"I don't think there's any reason you can't take things slowly. It sounds like you've been very accommodating so far," I offered gently.

He studied me, blue eyes boring into mine until the server joined us and broke the spell holding us captive. We took a minute to look at the menu, then ordered. I chose a traditional Irish dish he recommended, interested in knowing more about the culture he grew up in.

"I'd like to hear more about your mom," Conner said once we were alone again. "But not if it upsets you."

"I'm happy to tell you about her. She was an amazing mother—always showering us with love and attention. We made gingerbread houses at Christmas and dyed our own eggs at Easter. She was the type who encouraged us to read and loved to try new craft ideas she picked up on the internet. She took us to farmers' markets and movies and Broadway plays, and was happy to do it. I never felt like a burden to her. With a Mom as involved and loving as she was, I hardly noticed my father's absence; although I think as a boy, Sante felt it more."

The sapphire light in Conner's eyes warmed as I spoke. "I think our mothers would have gotten along well. And while my father isn't the asshole yours is, he was definitely the authority figure in the house."

"He struck me as a little scary, I'll admit."

He smiled softly. "Nah, not scary. He was the only brother-in-law in a very tight-knit family. I think he's always felt he had to prove himself." Conner's eyes dropped to the table where his fingers slowly spun his whiskey-filled low ball glass on the white tablecloth. He seemed to withdraw into his own thoughts. While I wondered what those were, I didn't want to push and derail the easy flow of our conversation.

"And what about Bishop. Tell me more about your history with him."

A devilish glint lit his eyes before Conner launched into a number of tales that made me feel for his poor mother. I loved hearing about his life and appreciated the thoughtful questions he asked about mine. The hour we spent passed so quickly I was reluctant to leave, but Conner seemed to have somewhere to be. He initiated our departure as soon as we were done eating and ushered me to the car.

"Did you have to go back to work tonight?" I asked once he pulled away from the curb.

A simple no was all he gave me. When he parked again but not at the apartment building, I caved and pushed for more information.

"Where are we going?"

He motioned with his head across the street. I confusedly looked at the row of ramshackle businesses but followed him from the car. When he led me to the door of a small tattoo parlor, I froze.

"What are we doing here?"

"What do you think?" He took my hand and pulled me inside as I stumbled to mentally catch up.

"If it isn't Mr. Reid," called out a bald man covered in tattoos at a computer behind the counter. "What's up, man?"

The two did a manly handshake hug combination.

"Wanted to stop in and introduce my new wife. See if you had a minute for a couple of small ones."

Wait, a couple? A couple of tattoos?

I was suddenly on high alert.

"Shit, man. Congratulations." The guy looked at me and grinned. "Name's Paco."

I smiled warily in return. "Noemi."

"It's a pleasure, Noemi." He turned back to Conner. "I've definitely got time. You going first?"

"Wait. What's happening here?" I blurted, no longer able to contain my panic.

"Yeah," Conner answered him, glossing over my obvious distress. "That'll give her a minute to decide where she wants hers."

If my eyes went any wider, I risked one popping right out of the socket.

"Excuse me? I can't just roll up and get a tattoo."

"Why not?" Conner asked, both men staring at me like I'd grown a third arm.

"Because … Because …"

Well, shit.

Why couldn't I get a tattoo? Did I *want* a tattoo? That depended on what it was.

"What are you getting?" I asked, growing more dismayed

by the second.

"I'm putting your name on the inside of my wrist." He leaned in, his eyes anchoring me to the spot. "And we aren't leaving here until my name is somewhere on you. That way, you know this is real. Nothing more real than blood and ink."

I was speechless. About the tattoo. About everything.

Conner was trying to tell me he was committed to this marriage.

I watched in awe as he sat down and placed his right wrist on the table, surprising me yet again. That was the arm without a drop of ink. My name would be the one and only adornment.

I pulled up a chair next to him and watched as Paco cleaned the area, then used transfer paper to adhere a painted template to his skin. It was fascinating to watch. I'd never seen a tattoo being created, let alone my name etched into someone's body. I knew in theory it could be removed, but it was still incredibly moving. This was a statement—one I wanted to reciprocate despite an army of nerves battling in my belly.

Once the tattoo was complete, gel was slathered over the elegant script, and his wrist was bandaged.

Then it was my turn.

"I'll do my wrist as well." My voice was breathy, my lungs working overtime to keep pace with my racing heart.

"Right wrist?" the man asked.

"No, my left." I placed my arm on the table.

Conner looked at the wrist, then back at me, understanding in his eyes. It was the wrist my father had mottled with bruises. Now, it would forever bear Conner's name instead.

My heart thundered in my ears. "How bad will it hurt?"

Paco grimaced. "Not gonna lie, there's definitely discomfort, but the wrist isn't nearly as bad as other places."

It was a good thing I had no plans to ever get another tattoo because *shit,* that hurt. If it was worse in other areas? Hell, no.

When Conner's name was complete, he took my arm in his hands and examined the artistry, stroking the angry red skin with a gentle caress. "Now it doesn't matter what name's on your bracelet; it's my name you'll always carry with you."

I had to blink back the moisture that pooled in my eyes. How strange to think this man, who was so stoic and even abrasive at times, could also be so gentle and sweet.

We left the shop with our new ink and the formation of a fragile bond between us.

I was willing to entertain his notion of a real marriage, though I wasn't sure what exactly that meant to him. Was he talking about our commitment to one another or something more? Could he possibly mean love? And even if he did develop a love for me, could our relationship ever come first when pitted against his duty and ambitions?

There was only one way to find out.

I had to take the leap and try to trust in him and open up my heart.

On the entire way home, I debated whether I could take that risk. When we reached the building lobby, I was still lost in my thoughts when the sight of Mia Genovese brought Conner to a stop.

"Em, I need you to head upstairs," he said in a low, wary tone.

"Is everything okay?" I asked, worry gnawing at my gut. I wasn't sure why she'd show up at his home, but something felt off.

"I'm sure she just wants to talk. I'll be up in a few." He pulled his frustrated gaze from her and gave me a pointed stare, urging me to comply.

Nodding, I left them alone, not remotely reassured.

Conner

THIRTY-THREE

I DIDN'T LIKE SENDING NOEMI UPSTAIRS BY HERSELF, BUT EVERY ounce of intuition I possessed was prickling at the sight of Mia Genovese. She was practically vibrating with nervous energy. Something was up, and it wasn't simply a case of a guilty conscience.

I steeled myself for whatever she had to say and walked to her. "Mia, this is a surprise."

Her smile was kind, but the apology creasing the corners of her eyes had my attention. "Conner, I'm so sorry to show up like this, but I need to talk to you about something. Something important that you need to know." She clutched her phone in her hand as though it had the power to transport her away from the remorse eating at her.

"Let's have a seat." I reluctantly led us to an unoccupied sitting area. Residents passed through the lobby periodically, but our conversation wouldn't be overheard. I kept my posture as relaxed as I could and allowed her to say what she'd come to say.

She sat perched on the edge of her seat, eyes dancing between me and her phone. "I know it seems strange for me to come here. There's never exactly a good time for a conversation like this, but it's been eating me up inside."

"Okay, you have my attention."

She sucked in a gulp of air as if to fortify herself. "I don't imagine you know much about the circumstances of your adoption."

"Just that you were sixteen and unable to care for me," I offered without judgment.

"My family was very devout, you see. I volunteered at our church when I wasn't at school. One summer, our youth director asked if some of us older kids would be willing to help out a sister church with their vacation bible school. They'd had an unexpectedly large enrollment of little ones and needed a few extra hands for a two-week day camp. Of course, I was happy to volunteer." She paused, the fondness of a treasured memory relaxing her features. "The church was St. Patrick's, and it's where I met your father."

If I stilled any further, I might have been mistaken for dead.

St. Patrick's was the church where I'd been taken as a newborn. The church where my adoptive parents were members. Mia Genovese was going to tell me who my father was, and something about that terrified her.

"We didn't know each other long. He was so charming, though, that I fell hard and fast. I was so naïve at that age that I didn't think I could possibly get pregnant before I was married. My parents were so conservative and proper that they never talked to me about sex. I was a full six months along with you before my mother figured out my condition. I'd been clueless. I was terrified, so I did exactly as they told me.

"I didn't leave our house for the next three months. Not until the day after you were born when I snuck out and took you to the church along with my grandmother's rosary. My parents had made arrangements with a non-secular adoption agency, not wanting to work with any Catholic services that might leak information into our community about how I'd shamed them. I felt so powerless, but the one thing I could do for you was get you to that church where I knew you at least had some family."

I could have stopped her right then and there—could have told her I didn't want to know and to leave it in the past—but the words wouldn't come. I sat in rapt silence, watching the train wreck before me unfold.

A tear trickled down her cheek.

"When I found out who you'd become, you couldn't imagine how happy I was for you. To know you hadn't been alone." She wiped at the tear, her words growing shaky. "I thought we'd meet, you and I, and then I could tell your father about you. He had a family, you see, so I wanted to go about it carefully, but then ..." Her words caught on a sob, but she continued as though the avalanche of truth was now too powerful to hold back. "How could I have ever known that the same night ... the same night we had our dinner ..." She squeezed her eyes shut, grief overtaking her.

The same night we had our dinner. That was all she had to say, and I knew.

"Uncle Brody," I breathed.

Mia lifted her glassy eyes to mine and gave a single sorrowful nod.

My uncle Brody had been my biological father this whole

time, and we'd never known. He never knew, and now he never would.

The harshness of reality slammed into me, stealing the air from my lungs.

I thought I'd been okay with how my life had unfolded. With the adoption and my family. I'd thought nothing Mia could say would have changed the past, but I'd been wrong. The truth changed everything.

"I'm so sorry, Conner," Mia whispered. "I had no way to find you before. I would have told you if I'd known how close you already were. I would have wanted you to know. These last two weeks have been agonizing to know how everything unfolded. It was so unfair. I didn't want to keep the truth from you for a minute longer."

"It's not your fault," I murmured distractedly, surprised to realize I believed what I said. I didn't blame her for any of it. Her parents, perhaps, but more than anyone, my ire was zeroed in on the group of people who had taken my father from me.

The fucking Albanians.

They'd stolen my chance to ever connect with Brody Byrne as father and son. And for what? A pathetic attempt at intimidation? I'd show them intimidation. I'd burn their entire organization to the ground.

Fury took up arms with a vengeance and rattled the bars of my control.

A volcano of hate erupted inside me, spewing rivers of molten rage through my veins.

I had to get out of there. I had to find an outlet for the vicious monster seething inside me before he aimed his bloodlust at an innocent.

"Thank you for sharing this, Mia." I stood, my movements stiff and uncoordinated. "I know it wasn't easy to come here, and you don't have to feel guilty about anything.

The adoption. Brody. None of it was your fault." I managed to force my gaze to hers in an attempt to project my sincerity, then gave her a hug. The first hug we'd ever shared. She'd been through just as much turmoil as I had, if not more. I had no desire to magnify her pain. She wasn't the one who deserved to suffer.

"Thank you for listening," she said in a quivering voice as she pulled away, a small smile on her thin lips. "I won't bother you anymore."

"It's not a bother, Mia. Truly. All of this has been a lot to process, but you're never a bother."

More tears pooled in her eyes before she smiled and retreated to the doors.

Opening my phone, I dialed Bishop.

"Hey, man. I—"

I cut him off before he could say another word. "You got anything on that license plate yet?" Each clipped word was seething with aggression.

"Uh, yeah. I have an address, but—"

"Give it to me."

Bishop's voice sobered. "You need backup? I don't have any other intel on these guys yet. I'm not sure it's a good idea to—"

"*Address,*" I ground out with enough savagery to silence him, then hung up the second I had what I needed.

Noemi was waiting for me in the living room when I got upstairs. I walked right past her toward the bedroom.

"I have to go out," I told her when she jumped up to follow. "You need to stay here."

My lethal intensity magnified her worry.

"What did Mia say?" she asked, her voice small as though she was scared to ask.

"Nothing I want to talk about right now. I have something I have to do." In the master closet, I took out my unregistered handguns from their hidden compartments and slipped on my chest holster.

"Is this about my dad? You aren't going to confront him, are you?"

I wasn't sure what had given her that idea, but I didn't have the capacity to discuss it further. "I already did that before the wedding," I said distractedly as I checked the chamber of each weapon and put extra clips in my pockets.

"What? You confronted him about hurting me?"

I grabbed a jacket bulky enough to cover my weapons, ignoring her questions.

"Conner," Noemi called more forcefully. "Don't leave here without telling me what's going on."

I whipped around to face her, unable to leash the feral nature of my anger. "You going to tell me why things changed with your father? Why you need a burner phone to talk to your brother, or why the *fuck* you didn't speak for six goddamn months?" I knew there was more she wasn't telling me. I would have been fine to let it sit on the back burner had she not pressed me, but I didn't have the time or patience for bullshit.

Noemi's lips clamped shut, a door slamming behind her wide green eyes.

Seeing her shut me out like that pissed me off even more, despite the fact that it was my own damn fault, yet I still couldn't stop myself. My emotions had taken over.

"Didn't think so," I bit out, walking past her and storming from the apartment.

THIRTY-FOUR

SOMETHING WAS HORRIBLY WRONG.

What could Mia have told him that would have upset him so much? Something about his Italian family? Could it involve my family? Why else would he not have told me? Conner was the one insisting this relationship was real and suggesting matching tattoos. He wanted me to open up and share, so what could have upset him so much that he couldn't do the same? That he could hardly even look at me?

Had he learned something that made him regret marrying me?

The uncertainty was maddening. But most of all, I was desperately worried for my brother. If Conner's anger had anything to do with my family, I had to ensure Sante was safe. I had to talk to him.

Hurrying to my new phone, I dialed Pippa.

"Hello?" she answered harshly, not recognizing yet another new number for me.

"Pip, it's me."

"Hey!" My cousin's voice calmed me instantly. "How are you? How's married life? This a real phone or another burner?"

"This is my new number for good. And all things considered, I'd say it's going okay. Conner had some work stuff come up, and I wondered if you could pop by. You could see our place and visit for a bit." Explaining what I needed from her would be much easier in person.

"I'd love that! I won't be able to stay long—you know how my dad gets about me being out late—but I can definitely swing by."

I gave her my new address, then went to my closet and found the gold cuff bracelet I'd used to hide my bruise, this time using it to cover my new tattoo. I had to remove the bandaging, but I preferred for the sensitive skin to be exposed rather than for Pip to see what I'd done. If she happened to tell her mother and word got around to my father, I couldn't be sure how he'd react.

For the next thirty minutes, I paced the wall of windows in the living room until the front desk rang to announce her arrival. I informed them she was expected, and the doorman helped her with the elevators, which required either a security code or a key card. Once she arrived upstairs, I showed her around my new home. She oohed and aahed over the place as I knew she would.

"It's gorgeous, Em. I've been so worried about you, so it's such a relief to see that you aren't miserable here on your own."

"Not at all. We're still just getting to know one another, but it could definitely be worse." I gnawed on my cheek for a second before continuing. "I have a favor to ask while you're here."

She turned away from the gorgeous view of the river, her attention now squarely on me. "Oh yeah?"

"Do you think you can pop by my house and give this to Sante?" I held up the prepaid phone. "You'd have to make sure my dad didn't know the reason you were there."

Her sharp eyes pinned me to the spot. "And why exactly would we be doing this?" Her eyes shot wide before she leaned in and whispered, "Is this about Conner? Is he hurting you?"

"No, not at all!" I assured her. "It's actually my dad who's the problem, but it's nothing."

She seemed to settle but still studied me intently. "Nothing? You ask me to slip your brother a burner phone, and you think it's nothing? I know you said your dad had gotten overprotective, but this feels off."

I sighed, deflating. "It's a long story, and something I can't really talk about yet. I'll tell you when I can, but until then, I could really use your help."

Pip's shoulders sagged. "Of course, I'll help, Em." She pulled me close, hugging me tight. "But you have me pretty worried."

"I know, and I'm really sorry about that. I'm sorry to drag you into any of this."

She took the phone from my hand and dropped it in her purse. "Please. I was made for this shit. Remember when I snuck into the boys' locker room one night to put itching powder into Brandon Swanson's jock strap?"

I smirked. "That was pretty epic." Seeing a bully finally get what he dished out had been awesome.

"He deserved every miserable minute of it."

"Hell, yeah, he did." I sobered, squeezing her arm with my hand. "Thanks, sis."

"Always." She winked, then turned for the door. "Love you, babe."

"Love you more," I called back at her.

🔥

A half hour later, I hadn't heard from Conner and was a tangled ball of nerves when my phone pinged with a reply message from the burner. I'd already sent an initial text before I'd even given the phone to Pippa, just to make sure it worked.

Sante: Em? You ok?

Me: Hey! Yes, but I wanted to talk to you.

Sante: Call?

Me: No, in person. Think you can get away from the house without Dad knowing?

Sante: ?? Why can't he know?

Me: Please, it's important.

I waited anxiously as the conversation dots appeared and disappeared three times before his reply appeared.

Sante: Where? Now?

Me: Yes, now. I was thinking of that diner Mom used to take us to. Romeo's.

Sante: See you in fifteen.

Me: 🩶

Conner had told me not to go out, but this was too important. I finally had a chance to talk to my brother and couldn't waste the opportunity. Plus, I was worried whatever Conner was doing involved my father. I had to find out what was going on.

The diner was halfway between the new apartment and my old house. While waiting for Pip to arrive, I'd decided it would be a perfect place to meet up, should I get the chance. Mom used to take Sante and me there to get milkshakes when we were little. We'd all three share, alternating turns to pick a flavor. I was hoping the good memories might make the difficult conversation easier.

When Sante spotted me in one of the glittery green vinyl booths, his answering smile didn't reach his eyes. "What's this all about, Em?" he asked as he slid in across from me.

"I needed to talk to you without Dad listening in. You know how paranoid he's gotten since Mom died. He's actually the reason I wanted to talk."

"Yeah, but for good reason. He worries about us." He glanced around the half-empty diner. "This feels deceptive, and I'm not crazy about going behind his back."

"We're adults, Sante. We should be able to have a private conversation." Frustration washed over me. How could I ever convince him of the truth if I couldn't even get him to talk to me freely?

He caught my eyes, the corner of his mouth snagging upward. "So now you're willing to admit that I'm an adult?"

I coughed out a laugh, relieved to ease the tension between us. It was the tiniest of first steps—not anywhere near enough to unload the bomb I was carrying. He would freak out and cling to denial, then I'd never reach him.

"Yeah, I'd say we've both grown up a lot in the past year." I smiled, and when the server came to take our order, I told her a milkshake and let him choose the flavor. "For old times' sake."

"So what's worrying you about Dad?" Sante asked without his earlier defensive tone.

"Some stuff has gone on recently that you don't know about, and it's made things tense between Dad and Conner." I decided to tiptoe into safer territory rather than cannonball straight into Mom's death.

My brother peeled the wrapper off from around his silverware, his eyes suddenly engrossed in his task. "I wondered what exactly he had against the guy. I guess that's why I was worried Conner had hurt you."

"Not at all." I placed my hand over his, stilling his movements. "Sante, has Dad talked about Conner?"

His eyes flitted to mine before dropping again. "Some, but it's just talk. You know he has a temper."

"But you'd tell me if he was planning something, right? Please tell me you'd warn us."

Sante pulled back, slipping his hands from mine. "I don't know, all right? I don't know what it is he's got going on."

"But … there is something?" I pushed, needing to get answers and sensing my brother was holding out.

"He's working on something big, but … that could have nothing to do with you guys. I just know he's been really stressed, okay?"

I leaned back and forced a soft smile. "I believe you. He's not really the type to tell anyone his plans, anyway. I just hope that if you find out something you think I should know that you'll tell me." It wasn't exactly what I'd come to say, but I'd pushed my brother as far as he would go. I'd opened the line of communication and at least had a lifeline to him. That was enough for now.

Arriving at the perfect time, the server set down our vanilla shake and helped guide us back to shallower waters. We reminisced about past days at the diner and other fond memories from our childhood until I realized it was nearly eleven thirty at night.

"I better get going. Thanks for coming tonight." I slid from the booth and gave my brother a big hug.

"Anytime, little big. You need a ride home?"

"I hate to keep you out any later than necessary. I don't want you getting in trouble."

Sante grinned. "Nah, no one knows I'm gone. It'll be fine. Come on."

I followed him to his car, preferring not to mess with getting a cab at that hour. He dropped me at my new building, promising to come by soon for a guided tour of my new place. The lobby was empty except for the security guard stationed at the front desk. I used the key card Conner had given me to get to the thirtieth floor and punched in the access code to the apartment.

Once inside, my veins filled with ice at the sight of Conner sitting in the living room waiting for me, a murderous glint in his eyes and blood splattered across his chest.

Noemi

THIRTY-FIVE

"I TOLD YOU TO STAY HERE. I TOLD YOU *NOT* TO LEAVE WITHOUT one of my men or me. You didn't call. You didn't text. You just … disappeared." Conner downed the last of the golden liquid from the crystal glass in his hand.

Each softly spoken accusation both cut me to the quick and terrified me.

"I'm sorry. I was worried about my brother and ended up getting ahold of him. He offered to meet up to talk, so I went. I should have texted." I could have lied and said I'd forgotten, but the truth was, I hadn't forgotten. I just hadn't wanted to chance Conner refusing to let me leave. It was better to ask forgiveness than permission. And when I hadn't been certain he'd let me go, I didn't take that chance.

I set down my purse and crossed the room, sitting on the edge of the sofa across from him. "What happened tonight?" His sudden departure. The blood. The menacing calm he exuded. All of it made the cold from my milkshake seep from my stomach throughout my body until I couldn't hold back a shiver.

"That's not your concern." His words were a door shut in my face.

I was about to argue with him when I noticed his eyes narrow and realized he was staring at my hands in my lap—more precisely, at the gold cuff bracelet still hiding my tattoo. My other hand reflexively closed over the offending jewelry as if hiding it now would make a difference.

"I didn't want Sante to see it and tell my dad," I hurried to explain.

"Why the *fuck* should it matter if he sees it?" The tenuous grip he held over his anger flexed and bowed with strain. His loss of control spurred my own, dialing up my frustration that I was being blamed for more than my crimes deserved.

I stood, hands on my hips. "That's not your concern," I shot back at him, feeding him his own line. I was getting sick of tiptoeing around the men in my life.

Conner rose from his chair and, in one swift motion, threw his glass into the fireplace across the room. The sound of shattering crystal pierced the air, heightening the tension between us.

"The fuck it's not. Your father is a threat to you, and your safety is *always* my concern."

I took a lunging step forward, undeterred by his outburst, and shoved a finger into his chest. "Ditto, Conner. You've got blood all over you, and as your wife, I deserve to fucking know if you …" My breath hitched, the emotion of the night suddenly getting to me. "If you … were hurt." I wiped furiously at my treacherous eyes, frustrated tears leaking free without my permission.

"Fuck!" The guttural curse rebounded off the walls before Conner's mouth slammed into mine. Hands on either side of my face, he plundered my mouth like I was the very air he needed to breathe. Tongues tangling and teeth nipping, we both punished and savored one another.

"You drive me fucking crazy, baby." He brought our foreheads together, our heavy breathing all that lay between us. "Blood's not mine. It's that Albanian fucker who got away after attacking us."

"You found him?"

"Yeah. He won't be a problem anymore."

I nodded, my fingers moving to unfasten the buttons on his shirt. "I'm glad you're okay," I breathed, spreading his shirt wide. He slid it the rest of the way from his body, then took off his undershirt. I trailed my hands over his taut skin, and he patiently allowed me to walk a slow circle around him so I could verify he was unharmed.

Once I was facing him again, I lifted my gaze to his as I removed the cuff from my wrist and dropped it onto the ground. An apology and a promise. I hadn't wanted to hurt him, and I'd try my hardest not to do it again.

His eyes blazed liquid sapphire. Grabbing the hem of my dress, he lifted it over my head, discarding the offending fabric to the ground.

The air around us thickened, pregnant with meaning. With intent and desire.

We were on the precipice of a shift in our budding relationship. A fork in the road that could change everything. The implications were so far-reaching that we stood motionless across from one another, unsure whether to leap the divide or slowly back away.

"My dad killed my mom," I whispered, freeing the words for the first time in almost seven months.

I'd chosen to leap without ever really choosing. The need to open up to him was simply too great to resist any longer.

Conner stood stock-still as I bared the ugly truth about my family.

"Dad orchestrated the accident, and he knows that I know. He's been threatening harm to Sante to keep me quiet. He's a bad man, Conner. I was worried about Sante. About you." The words faded to a near whisper by the time I was done.

My new husband took a shuddering breath, then growled as he lifted me in his arms. I circled my legs around his waist and pressed my lips to his, greedy for his touch.

I wasn't sure how it had happened, but the barriers between us crumbled. I'd gone from despising him to seeing his worth to craving his approval—all in a handful of weeks. It was the very best and worst of outcomes because no matter how much we wanted one another, there would always be secrets between us.

He had an entire life beyond my reach.

Nothing exemplified that more than the fact that he still hadn't told me what had upset him about Mia's visit. Something had triggered him to go after the Albanian though he hadn't admitted as much. And I couldn't fault him because I wasn't being entirely forthright either. I had omitted the reason my father had killed my mother, allowing him to assume her death was a product of his abusive nature, but there was so much more to it than that. If Conner knew the truth, it would give him even more reason to move against my father. The situation could devolve into an all-out war.

Secrets were the essence of Mafia life and the reason I'd wanted out.

How could a man ever claim to value his wife and children above all else when he kept a world of secrets from them? It wasn't possible. Secrets paved the road to treachery and distrust. A road I wanted to avoid but was instead running toward full steam ahead.

I couldn't help myself because, despite it all, I wanted Conner Reid.

And even more importantly, I wanted him to want me. To choose me above all others.

That was why my body came alive when I was the focus of his brutal intensity. I craved every ravenous stare. Each mercurial thought that passed behind his eyes and the protective weight of his devotion. When I felt the full force of his desire, my body wept with happiness, the evidence soaking my silk panties as he walked us back to the bedroom.

He unclasped my bra before we reached the secluded master suite so that when he did finally set my feet down, the lacy fabric slipped from my shoulders, leaving only my most private parts covered.

"You're fucking gorgeous," Conner murmured, eyes roving hungrily over my body. "Take off your panties and lie back on the bed. I want to see all of you."

I did as he commanded, all the while spellbound at the sight of him shedding the last of his clothing. Everything about him radiated raw power. He was so much larger and stronger than me that I wondered at my own sanity. It seemed crazy not to be a little terrified of this man—not to fear the vulnerable nature of what I was offering him—but I wasn't scared. Call it female intuition, but I knew he wouldn't hurt me. Not physically, anyway.

Once he was bare, he took his engorged cock in his hand and began to stroke himself. "Spread your legs for me, baby. Show me what's mine."

Knees bent, I dropped them to the sides.

Conner's abs seized as his grip tightened around himself, practically throttling his cock as if to keep himself in check.

"Tell me you're on birth control, Em." His words were as coarse as gravel tumbling across the asphalt. I felt each word scrape against my skin, heating me from the inside.

"I got a shot before the wedding."

"Thank *fuck*." He released himself and prowled onto the bed, his lips latching briefly to my nipple before raising to capture my lips. "I don't want … anything … between us," he said between kisses. "I want to see you stain my cock red." He rocked himself, rubbing his shaft against my folds.

His heavy warmth felt incredible. I was already so damn wet at the sight of him that he glided smoothly over my swollen clit, aching for more.

"Conner, what about … other stuff?" I didn't want to derail our moment, but I had to ask. "Are you clean?"

"Baby, it's my job to protect you in every way. I'd never put you at risk like this if I wasn't." He pressed my hands together above my head and wound a seductive path with his lips down my body. The scruff on his jaw tickled and teased while his lips caressed and teeth devoured. I felt like a goddess beneath him, worshipped and adored.

When his mouth closed over my core, hunger like I'd never known clamped down on my lungs. I gulped in air, eyes wide yet unseeing. He licked and sucked, teasing up the intensity of my pleasure to a heightened frenzy. While he owned my body with his tongue, his fingers worked at my entrance. First one, then two. He hooked them inside me, stretching and soothing at the same time.

The pressure felt so damn good. So full. Before long, I came with a burst of thunder, pleasure pouring down on me, drenching me to the bone. He coaxed the last drops from me before moving up my body. I felt too sensitive for more, yet the gentle nudge of his cock at my entrance stirred a renewed craving to life. Like my body knew it had yet to receive the heart of what it wanted.

His hands again found mine, keeping them raised above my head, my chest thrust upward toward him. His lips remained parted as though each breath of restraint plunged him further into madness. His luminous blue eyes sparked with the conflict between mindless lust and a protective devotion.

"Fuck me, Conner. I'm ready. I need it."

And with my simple plea, all pretense of restraint dissolved. Conner eased inside me until he bumped against my resistance. He wasn't even all the way inside, yet I felt bursting with fullness. I gasped for air, struggling to adjust to the foreign sensation. He used the opportunity to seize my mouth, his tongue delving deep against mine as a distraction just before he thrust his cock deep inside me. He stole the cry from my lips, soothing the stab of pain with his shower of affection.

"That's my girl. The worst is over, baby."

I nodded, chest panting with exertion. The burn quickly ebbed, however, and I explored the situation with a squeeze of my inner muscles.

Conner hissed, his back arching involuntarily. "Do that again, and this will be over way too soon."

I smiled, a small chuckle bubbling up from my throat, only intensifying when it caused me to squeeze again and coax yet another moan from him. Though my laughing died a quick death when he turned the tables, his own chuckle causing him to swell inside me.

Good God, he felt incredible.

I moaned unabashedly.

How was it I could somehow feel him in every part of me? As though from the inside, he'd gained access to the highways and byways of my body and could command me like a master puppeteer.

Conner began to ease in and out of me. Each back and

forth motion was punctuated with a zing of pleasure when he rubbed over that extra sensitive bundle of nerves deep inside me. I began to move along with him, lost to an ancient dance my body seemed to know without instruction or direction.

He placed a hand under one of my knees and pressed my leg back, curving me in on myself in a way that intensified the effect of his movements.

"I'm ending this quick so I don't make you too sore, but next time..." He nipped at my bottom lip, then began to thrust inside me with the ferocity of the devil pounding on the gates of hell.

A velvet promise of something more coiled deep in my belly. It seemed to hover just out of my reach like the moon on a cloudless night. Already sated from my orgasm before, I wasn't bothered by my inability to grasp that amorphous spark. If anything, I was intrigued and fully awash in a shower of pleasure.

When a guttural rumble tore from deep inside Conner, I was amazed that I could feel his shaft swell and pulse inside me. His entire body shuddered as his movements slowly ebbed.

Without allowing himself much time to recover, he lifted back to his knees and watched as he pulled from inside me. His eyes gleamed with satisfaction.

On the other hand, I began to panic as I felt the evidence of what we'd done seep from my core. I started to close my legs together, but Conner's hands quickly anchored me in place.

"I'm going to make a mess of the sheets," I reminded him, embarrassment creeping up.

His eyes never left my pussy. "Don't give a fuck. There's nothing sexier than watching my cum drip from your wet pussy." He ran a finger gently along my opening, swiping up and breathing in the essence of our combined juices. The lights in the room were low, but it was still enough that I could make out the red tinge to the glistening moisture.

"I'd never expected to marry a virgin or felt a particular need to fuck one, but hell if I don't love knowing my cock is the only you'll ever know." His eyes finally lifted to mine.

My lips quirked up in the corners. "I never intended to save myself for marriage, but hell if I'm not glad I did."

A strange intimacy passed between us while our eyes remained locked on one another. It heated the room with a frightening electric current.

Jaw clenching, Conner slipped from the bed. "Stay there," he murmured before heading to the bathroom. When he returned, he had a wet washcloth in one hand and a dry one in the other. I was pleasantly surprised to discover when he gently wiped at my slit with the wet cloth that he'd warmed it to a soothing temperature. Once he was satisfied with his work, he patted me dry, then held out a hand to help me up. "You need to pee, then take some painkillers."

"Yes, sir," I said playfully, which promptly earned me a smack in the ass.

He got me a glass of water while I went to the restroom. Then we brushed our teeth and returned to the bedroom to curl up beneath the blanketed weight of the secrets still looming over us.

Conner

THIRTY-SIX

"YOUR MOTHER WAS AGOSTINO'S SISTER, WASN'T SHE?" I'D meant to let the subject rest until morning but couldn't settle my racing thoughts. Noemi had yet to fall asleep herself, so I decided maybe a brief talk would be necessary before we could find rest.

"Yes. She and Aunt Etta were twins, and Uncle Agostino is their older brother."

That was what I'd been afraid of. "He and Renzo would want to know the truth, but I'm not sure it's our place to say something." I'd been debating the issue in my head for the last ten minutes. As far as I could tell, one crucial bit of information was missing. "Why did Fausto kill his wife, Noemi?"

I'd been holding her cocooned against me, so it was easy

to feel her body stiffen in response to my question. I wasn't surprised. When she first unveiled the truth about her mother's death, I'd sensed she was holding something back.

"Does it matter why?" she asked quietly, her voice worn from months of anguish. It had to have been hell living with the man who'd inflicted so much pain in her life.

"I'm afraid it does. I need to know what happened." Yet again, I sensed the tension in her body intensify, so I continued. "Normally, we don't involve ourselves in the domestic disputes of people outside of our organization. But if there's more to her death than a violent husband, your uncle may need to know."

"You would get involved if there was more to it? My father would likely know that you were the source of that information."

"Yes, but we owe a certain loyalty to the Donatis. I don't like inserting ourselves into a Mafia matter, but if we're the only ones who have that information, it may be necessary."

She was silent long enough for unease to prick at the back of my neck.

"I agree that it's a delicate matter," she finally said. "That's why I think you should leave it to me. Let me keep this in the family."

My reaction was visceral. No way in hell was I sending my wife into the middle of a potentially dangerous situation. "It's not happening, Em, so don't even try."

Noemi wrestled out of my hold to turn and face me in the dark. "*Please*, Conner. I'm the one who should talk to my uncle. I wanted to from the beginning but was so worried about protecting Sante that I held off. I should be the one to do it, and then you and your family won't be thrown into the middle of it."

I didn't like it one bit, but she wasn't entirely wrong. Had I been in her shoes, I would have argued the same.

"You know your brother is no safer now than he was before."

She sighed, relaxing back into my arms. "I know, but it needs to be done. And I'd rather this way than … well, let's just say that bringing you and your family into it would only make things worse."

I grunted, irritated that she made sense. "I'm not making any promises, but I'll think about it."

Setting up a meeting for her to talk to her uncle wouldn't be so bad, but I couldn't imagine not attending. And if I was present, I might as well handle it myself. The whole thing was a shit situation. I didn't like any of the options but knew we had to commit to something, even if that was to ignore the whole thing.

I lay there and continued to think as my young wife relaxed into sleep. She might have felt better after our talk, but I was all too aware that she'd avoided answering my question about why her mother was killed. Fausto hadn't lashed out and accidentally struck his wife with too much force. She'd died in a car wreck, which meant her death was premeditated. That wasn't domestic; that was murder.

But how could I fault Noemi for holding back when I'd done the same?

I still hadn't told her about my father. I should have, but the words were bottled up inside. The truth still felt too raw. Too unbelievable to be real.

And if I wasn't already overwhelmed sorting my feelings about Mia's revelation, the jumbled storm of emotions my wife evoked would have certainly pushed me over the edge. I'd been so fucking angry when I got home and found the place empty. Angry and worried and frustrated as hell. Yet the second I saw the genuine fear she'd felt for me, for my safety, all of it had melted away and left nothing but scorching desire.

It was a good thing she offered herself to me because I'd been so damn ravenous for her, I wasn't sure I could have resisted what I'd wanted. What I'd *needed*.

I trailed my fingers down the delicate indentation of her spine. Pliable yet strong, just like her.

I'd never met a woman who was so deceptively resilient. I had thought I'd wanted her gentility, but it was her fierce tenacity that hooked its claws into me. I couldn't help but respect her strength.

In my world, respect was everything.

It prompted the question whether I'd earned her respect. Apparently not, considering she was still keeping secrets. Respect went hand in hand with trust. What did I have to do to prove I was worthy?

A dull ache radiated in my chest at yet again finding myself faced with that question.

As a boy, I'd spent years asking myself why my birth mother had given me away. Once I'd matured and learned she'd been a teen mother, I'd accepted that her actions weren't a reflection of how she felt about me; however, the echo of those feelings still stirred down deep in my memories.

I wanted to be certain of Noemi's feelings for me. I wanted to know she was just as irrevocably drawn to me as I was her, and there was only one way to accomplish that—I would have to become the air she breathed. Make myself so indispensable that she couldn't imagine a life without me. And the first step in that process was eliminating Fausto Mancini from her life, no matter the cost.

I had to face the fact that I could lose him. No matter how strategically or artfully I laid the groundwork to reclaim my brother to my side, there was a definite possibility he'd reject all my efforts. I'd felt the probability of that outcome increasing ever since I'd gone to the diner with Sante. He was so damn idealistic. His desperation for our father's approval was almost palpable. It made him blind to Dad's faults, even the most egregious.

Sante wasn't ready to hear the truth, but I'd run out of time. The reprieve Mom's death had provided was at an end. Judging by Sante's cryptic hint that Dad was moving forward with his plans, I had to make a decision. I could allow Conner to involve himself in my family drama and put him at risk, or

I could step up and make the first move, which would almost certainly push Sante out of my reach, possibly forever.

I couldn't guarantee how either scenario would play out, but it felt like having to choose between my husband and my brother—a choice I never dreamed I'd have to make. And I certainly never imagined, if faced with such a dilemma, that my brother would be the one I'd allow to slip away.

I'd laid in Conner's arms as certainty warred with heartbreak, carving out a hollow chasm deep in my chest. I knew in my gut what needed to be done.

I had to choose Conner.

How could I ever hope to have a husband who would put me first if I wasn't willing to do the same for him? That was why, when Conner asked about the reason for my mother's death, I couldn't tell him. Not if it meant he'd get involved. If he and the other Irishmen drew my father's wrath, they'd all be in danger. It wasn't worth it if I could handle the matter myself without putting them at risk.

With Conner sniffing around, interjecting himself, I needed to make my move.

Whether procrastination of the inevitable or exertion from the night before, I was slow to rise the following morning. Conner was long gone by the time I plodded into the shower. My limbs were filled with lead and the weight of responsibility. But offsetting the troublesome burden was an erotic soreness between my legs that reminded me of hope and better things to come. It reminded me that the reason for my decision was worth the potential consequences.

An hour later, I was ready to face my day, no matter what that might entail. I'd gotten such a later start that it was already approaching noon by the time I entered the kitchen. Stomach still churning to keep pace with my tumultuous thoughts, I only managed to force down a banana before I decided to get the ball rolling and call Pippa.

"Hey, sis. What's up?" she answered warmly.

"I just need Uncle Agostino's phone number."

Silence.

"Whyyy?" she asked warily.

I had worried this would happen. "It's not really something I can talk about."

"Nope," she shot back. "Not acceptable. Not again. You're telling me what the hell is going on. I'll be there in ten."

I stared at my phone, the line dead. I never even had a chance to argue.

Well, shit.

Pip would see right through any lies, and I doubted she'd let it drop until she'd wrung something from me. I considered what I might tell versus hold back, but suddenly, it all seemed pointless. I was going to talk to Uncle Agostino as soon as I was done with Pip, so I might as well give her the truth.

True to her word, Pippa was at my door just over ten minutes later. As soon as she was seated with me at the kitchen table, I started from the beginning. The trickle of information became a burst dam, every incident, and emotion from the prior seven months spewing out from its prison deep inside me.

"That son of a bitch." Tears pooled in Pippa's eyes, but it was fury that sparked in her golden irises. "I'm glad you're going to make him pay because someone needs to."

"I know."

"This is just too much. I need a fucking drink before I drive there myself and gut that pig."

I huffed out a small laugh. "I could probably use a drink myself." I was so damn worried about Sante and how this would unfold. If my father got word that I'd gone to the Donatis and my uncle didn't act quickly, there was no telling what my father might do before he was stopped.

"What do you want?" I asked, scouring the liquor cabinet. "There's loads of whiskey."

My cousin grimaced, doing a full-body shiver.

"Yeah, same. Vodka or tequila?"

"He have any Patrón?"

"Ah ... yeah, there is some in the back." I got on my tiptoes to retrieve the wide glass bottle then brought it to the table where Pip sat with two plain shot glasses. "Salt and lime?"

"Nah." She waved off the suggestion. "Feels too much like a celebration. Think I need the burn."

I couldn't argue with that. After filling our glasses, I raised mine in the air and threw back the clear liquid. Pip followed suit, both of us coughing as the fire scorched our throats.

Once we recovered, a heavy silence joined our little party.

"This whole time, huh?" Pip finally said, her voice hollow.

"Yeah."

"I feel awful that I didn't know."

"You couldn't have," I tried to assure her.

She shook her head. "But I did, in a way. I felt like something was off about you not leaving the house. I just didn't listen to my gut. Pisses me off."

"Listen, I've known what he did for over six months and still haven't done anything about it," I said more forcefully, pouring us two more shots.

"How could you?" she gawked. "He kept you *prisoner* most of that time."

"I could have found a way," I muttered.

"We can't play that game. Hindsight being twenty-twenty and all that crap." She threw back her shot, and I did the same before turning on the stereo and syncing my phone to play music off one of my playlists. I had them organized by mood, and today called for the darkest, most depressing of songs.

"How are things with Conner?" she asked when the music started.

"Surprisingly well, actually." Heat bloomed across my cheeks. I prayed she would chalk it up to the booze, but no such luck.

"Oh my God. You're blushing. You guys had sex, didn't you?"

I met her gaze, mine glinting with erotic memories of the night before.

"Hell yeah! That calls for another shot." She grabbed the bottle and began to pour.

"Holy crap, Pip. You trying to get us blackout drunk?" I gaped at her but couldn't fully quash the smile teasing the corners of my lips.

"Hey, if we're lucky, we'll forget how fucked up our family is."

What could I say except, "I'll drink to that."

After that, I refused any more shots, but my near-empty stomach absorbed what alcohol I had consumed straight into my bloodstream until my head was spinning, and my brain-to-mouth filter had broken down. Pip and I talked about all the little things we'd missed chatting about during my absence. We'd covered the big stuff when we talked, but this was different. This was the way things used to be—talking about the dress she'd considered buying for a cousin's baby shower and discussing why the new season of our favorite show wasn't quite living up to our standards. Our conversation was easy and light and flowed like a summer breeze. That was until my phone began to ring.

"Oh God. It's Conner." My eyes bulged wide.

"Just don't answer if you don't want to."

"Right, and get my ass spanked?" I bit down on my lips when I realized what I'd said, and we both burst out laughing. "*Shh* … stop it," I hissed through my laughter. Picking up my phone, I took a deep breath and accepted the call. "Hello?"

"Hey. You have a good morning?"

"Uh, yeah. Pip came over, and we've been visiting." I tried my very best to sound perfectly sober, almost cracking when my cousin doubled over in a fit of giggles.

"What was that?"

"Oh, just Pip being silly. What's up with you?" I now had tears in my eyes from the strain of holding in my laughter.

"I talked things over with Keir this morning about your father, and we decided too many factors are in play to let you handle it. I said I'd consider what you said, but it's not possible. We have a plan, though, and it won't be much longer until he's a distant memory."

"Wait ... what?" My sluggish brain struggled to process what he'd said. "A plan? You can't plan when you don't even know ... No, Conner. This is ... not at all ... you can't." Emotion and alcohol jumbled my words until I couldn't get out a complete thought.

A silence darker than shadow drifted over the line.

"You been drinking?" Conner finally asked, low and menacing.

I lifted my chin defiantly, though he couldn't see it. "I'm a married woman. I think I can have a drink if I want to."

"Care to tell me why you'd want to get shit-faced before lunch?"

"Nope." I popped the P proudly. "If you get to do whatever the hell you want, then so do I. I mean, where do you get off? I chose *you*, Conner. Not Sante. *You*. And you're just gonna go fuck it all up ... I mean. *Ugh*!" My mini rant bubbled up from deep inside, a geyser I couldn't hold back.

"I'll be home in ten."

The line clicked dead.

My eyes cut to Pippa, who had her hand over her mouth and brows touching her hairline.

"Oh shit," she breathed.

Oh shit was right.

My cousin stood. "Well, it's been fun, but I should probably go."

"Sit your skinny ass back down." I shot to my feet and pointed at her chair. "You are not abandoning me now. You brought out the liquor that made me flap my lips. You can stick around and act as my buffer."

"Em, that's going to be crazy awkward."

I shook my head, one-hundred-percent adamant. "Nope. Don't care. You. Are. Staying."

Noemi

THIRTY-EIGHT

PIPPA AND I WERE SITTING ON THE COUCH TOGETHER WHEN THE front door clicked open. We both sat as still as statues. Conner slowly stalked inside, his gaze trained on me the second he came into view. He left the door open, which seemed strange until he spoke.

"Time to go, Pippa. Bishop is in the lobby to take you home." He spoke to my cousin but never took his eyes off me.

"What if she doesn't want to leave?" I asked stubbornly.

"I'll have Bishop remove her."

Pip's hand squeezed mine. "I told you this wasn't a good idea. I'm sorry, babe, but I'm gonna bail. You and your man need to talk this over."

Logic told me that she was right and I'd asked too much,

but I still felt a smidge betrayed as I watched her scurry away. The door clicked shut behind her, leaving me alone with all six-foot-something of pissed-off mobster.

I wasn't even sure why he was so upset. I hadn't done anything wrong. I hadn't broken any of his rules, and I certainly hadn't burned anyone alive or fed information to the police. That made me damn near a model mafia wife, in my humble opinion. So why did my skin feel hot and itchy under his scrutinizing stare?

"You want to tell me what made you decide to start drinking before the sun was all the way up?" he asked as he prowled closer.

"You make it sound worse than it is." As if he'd never started the day on a rough patch.

"Far as I can tell, it's a pretty huge deviation from the normal. I assume it has something to do with your father, considering your reaction to learning we had a plan that didn't involve you. I'd say it sounded like you were upset that we'd infringed upon your plans. You have something planned I should know about?"

I couldn't take his penetrating stare any longer, so I shot from the couch and began to pace. "I *did* have a plan. Like I told you, I was going to handle things with my father. Then you had to jump in like a damn knight in shining armor coming to my rescue." My arms waved about as I worked myself into more of a frenzy with every word. "And if you go getting yourself killed, my choice will have all been for nothing. I'll lose both of you, don't you see?" I slowed and looked at him pleadingly, hoping he'd come to his senses.

"Not even a little bit." Exasperated, he crossed his arms over his chest and breathed deeply. "Explain it to me, Noemi. What choice will have been for nothing?"

"Choosing you," I whispered. "I'm the only one Sante has left. I should have picked him, but I couldn't because I was most worried about *you*. If you get involved, he'll *kill* you."

"Your father?"

"Yes. He'll kill you and anyone who tries to stop him. That's why I couldn't tell you the truth, don't you see? Because if you knew what my father had planned, you'd have to tell the Donatis, and then you'd be in danger. I couldn't have that. I couldn't sit by and watch you get hurt. And it pisses me off that I had to decide between protecting you or my brother because it wasn't supposed to be this way. I wasn't supposed to fall for you. I told myself I'd never end up like my mother. I told myself not to marry a man like my father. I know I'll only get my heart broken because this was never supposed to be real, and even though you say it *is* real, the oath you made to your organization will always come first. I know how these things work. I knew better than to care for you…" My breathing hitched, the angst and worry of so many months catching up with me and the realization that what I'd said was true—I was falling for Conner Reid.

Tears blurred my vision as I finally lifted my gaze to my husband. He hadn't moved an inch while I'd unloaded my fears and uncertainty, vomiting up every unfiltered thought at his feet. I wasn't even sure what all I'd said, but I knew it hadn't gone over well when his seething glare pierced through me. His body vibrated with every silent curse and violent thought he bit back.

"If you think I am *anything* like your father, then you haven't learned a damn thing about me." His words rattled and shook with forced calm, each barbed with pain. They carved their way through my heart as I watched him walk away, leaving me hopelessly shredded and alone.

THIRTY-NINE

My knees gave out first. Then the sobs took over before I melted to the ground.

What had I done? I'd been trying to tell him that I cared for him—that I'd chosen him over my family—but it had all come out wrong. I *did* know him. And what I said was true, wasn't it? His oath to the Byrne brothers would trump all others because that was how it worked with men in that line of work.

Right?

A terrifying uncertainty filled my insides like an icy fog until my bones rattled and shook.

Had I unjustifiably condemned Conner? He'd agreed to a marriage for the benefit of his organization. That seemed to be a telling indicator of what he valued most—that he'd be willing to set aside his chance at love for an alliance. But did his willingness to agree to the arrangement necessarily preclude the possibility that he would value love over duty?

I thought back to the ways he'd subtly or overtly confronted my father. Each of those actions undermined the purpose of the alliance and put the Irish-Italian relationship at risk. But he'd done those things anyway. For me.

He'd been showing me the whole time that he valued me beyond a simple contract, but I'd been too scared to see it. Too terrified of being hurt to admit that Conner could never be like my father. I'd seen what I wanted to see in order to protect myself, and in doing so, I'd hurt the man who'd stood loyally at my side. The man who kept his birth mother's rosary beads on his dresser and knew his grandmother's favorite candy treat. If I'd looked closely, I would have seen that the duty he felt was purely by virtue of the family he worked with. The people, not the organization, were important to him.

What have I done?

I had to fix it, but how? I wiped away the salty remnants of my tears and looked around the empty apartment. I needed to talk to Conner and apologize. He wouldn't want me to leave, so I'd have to call him and hope he answered.

Grabbing the phone he'd given me, I dialed my husband's number. The alcohol had long since leached from my system, and in its place was a blossoming sense of determination.

"Yes." His voice was as hard as polished steel, yet my eyes drifted shut at the relief that he'd taken my call.

"I wasn't supposed to be with her that day," I began, deciding to give him everything I had and hope it was enough. "I had vocal coaching on Tuesdays and Thursdays, but she'd asked me to go with her to visit Uncle Agostino. I could tell she seemed anxious, so I agreed. As soon as we were in the car, she began to tell me how she'd overheard my dad plotting to kill my uncle. How Dad had been furious for years that Agostino outmaneuvered Dad for the role of boss. Dad was outraged when Renzo was promoted to underboss last year at only twenty-seven years old. He felt it was his due, and from that day on, he began to plot his takeover. I could tell Mom was terrified. She told me that she had to warn her brother, but every muscle in her body was tense from the fear of the repercussions. I remember it like it was yesterday," I whispered, my mind replaying the scene in vivid detail as tears trailed down my cheeks.

"I don't know how he knew she'd be in the car that day or how he made it happen, but once we were on the freeway, her foot started pounding on the brake pedal. Nothing happened. We kept going faster and faster. She had to weave around cars, the whole time chanting, 'Oh God. He knows.' The crash happened in slow motion. Someone didn't see us speeding up and moved into our lane. Mom swerved, lost control, and we spun. And spun. Until the car wrapped around a light pole on the driver's side." I had to pause for air. I couldn't seem to get enough air. "There was so much blood. She'd never had a chance." My eyes closed to shut out the gruesome sight, and when they opened again, Conner was there, standing in the entry.

"You came back," I breathed, the phone slowly falling away from my ear.

"I never made it past the lobby. I didn't want to leave you alone." He was here, but his face was still set in harsh angles, his body rigid with restraint.

"You were right. My dad has hurt me and used threats of hurting Sante to control me. Every day since my mom died has been a nightmare. I'm so sorry I didn't tell you before. I was scared that if you knew, you'd put yourself in danger, and I'd already lost ..." My breath hitched. I swallowed back the emotion and pushed myself to continue. "I'd already lost one person I cared deeply about. I couldn't lose another." I stood but didn't approach him. "I'd never been close to my father, but what he did was such a betrayal. I never imagined he was capable of hurting us like that. It made me scared—of him and of being hurt like that again. But you were right; you're not like him. I never would have given myself to you if, deep down, I'd ever believed you were. You would never hurt me," I whispered. "And I'm so sorry I hurt you." I held out my arms at my sides, my face stained with tears. "So here I am, giving you everything. This is me. All of me. No more secrets."

Time stood still.

Conner's eyes burned with intensity.

"Take off your clothes." His voice was devoid of emotion, but I wasn't scared. I would do anything he asked to repair what I'd broken.

I lifted my shirt over my head and dropped it to the floor. Then my bra, jeans, and panties. Until I stood naked before him. No doubts. No reservations.

"On your knees." His black command licked down my spine.

I obeyed without hesitation.

"Now close your eyes." This time softer. Almost hypnotic.

My lids dropped shut as my ears pricked at the sound of him finally coming closer until he was there, sinister and seething like an angry viper.

"Why did your father volunteer you for the alliance?"

The question surprised me, but I didn't show it. I simply gave what he asked. "I think because he wants the connection to help him solidify his role as a boss once he kills my uncle and cousin. He doesn't want to risk the capos supporting anyone else."

"Is he still plotting to kill the Donatis?" The question was cold and detached.

"I think so. I talked to Sante, and he seemed worried. He wouldn't say why, but I think my dad has started making plans again. He had to put everything on hold after Mom died so he didn't raise suspicions."

Silence nipped at me from all directions. A primal instinct within writhed at the vulnerability and pleaded for me to take a small peek at my surroundings, but I paid it no heed.

"Stand up," Conner finally instructed from nearby, slowly circling around me.

I rose to my feet, swaying the tiniest bit from the headiness of the situation.

"Had you been kissed before me?"

"Yes," I whispered, not holding back like I'd done the first time he'd asked.

"How many?"

"Two."

"Did they touch you here?"

I gasped when his warm palm cupped my sex. I turned my head side to side. His hand drifted up my body, his other joining at my breasts, where they cupped my heavy flesh and pinched my nipples.

"And these?" His voice was frayed at the edges.

I desperately wanted to open my eyes and see him—to verify my sense that his anger was fading—but it was more important that I bridged the chasm that had opened up between us. "Yes."

"How many?" he bit out.

"Just one."

A grunt sounded in response. "Turn around." He was close enough to touch if I could just reach out, but I did as he instructed and turned my back to him. He moved closer until the heat from his body became an intoxicating lure, begging me to step back and seize what was just out of my reach. "I need your trust, Noemi. Show me that I can trust you." The gravelly murmur caressed my skin, drawing out a legion of goose bumps down my arms and legs.

I nodded again, ready to give him anything.

His body slowly pressed against mine, his front to my back. "Keep your eyes closed." His hands reached around to take mine, his body coaxing mine forward one small step at a time toward what my mind's eye knew was the wall of windows.

My breathing grew jagged and shallow with uncertainty. It was broad daylight out, and though the windows were tinted, we could be seen if someone was looking.

And in the city, there was always someone looking. Waiting. Watching.

Conner pressed my palms flat against the warm glass and used his foot to command my legs apart.

I felt so open and exposed. My nipples pebbled excruciatingly tight under the imagined spotlight of an audience. My body responded to the erotic nature of my situation, whether I wanted to put on a show or not, and I preferred not to. I wasn't an exhibitionist by nature, but I wanted to prove myself to Conner. He'd asked for my trust, and I was desperate to give him what he wanted.

The clink of his belt buckle sounded behind me, along with the rustle of fabric. When his hands finally came back to me, they were commanding yet gentle. He placed a hand at my belly, tugging my ass backward while his other hand cupped the back of my neck, keeping my face close to the glass. My inner muscles clenched and ached when the soft skin of his cock drifted against my folds.

"You sure you trust me, even if I fuck you up against the glass where the world can see?" His harsh words held the last vestiges of his anger, worn ragged and roughed by desperation.

"Yes, Conner. I trust you."

"Then open your eyes." He released the words on a breath a second before pressing himself deep into my entrance.

My eyes burst open, bemused wonder and heady relief stealing my breath as I took in the sight of the now frosted glass before me. I wasn't sure how he'd done it, but the entire wall of windows had turned opaque.

He'd never risked exposing me. It had all been a ploy.

I turned my face to see him just as he thrust again, drawing a moan past my lips. Conner cupped my throat and brought our mouths together in a kiss so moving it could have ended wars and toppled kingdoms.

"I will never endanger you, body or soul. You understand?" he asked, an urgency to his voice.

"Yes," I breathed, aching for more of him.

"Then hold on, baby, 'cause I need to fuck you fast and hard." He returned his hands to my hips and began plowing into me. Hungry for his touch, I pushed back into his thrusts, reveling in the feel of our bodies connecting.

I felt as though we were weaving a spell—something profound and monumental that would bind us far more than any oaths or vows.

Conner suddenly stopped, spinning me around to face him, then lifted me in his arms. "I need to see you."

I wrapped my legs around his waist as his lips molded against mine, and his cock found its way back into the welcoming embrace of my weeping core.

While my back was pressed to the glass, Conner fucked me with abandon. The whole time, his eyes never left mine. Our bodies were positioned just right for my nipples and clit to rub against him with every bounce of my body onto his throbbing cock. When his fingers beneath me edged closer to tease at the forbidden pucker of my backside, the erotic rush of it all was too much.

"*Conner,*" I whimpered, my body erupting in a cascading avalanche of pleasure.

"That's it, Emy," he growled. "Fucking come for me." He briefly doubled his efforts before roaring with his release, gripping me tightly against him as his body pulsed with pleasure.

My head spun in the wake of the thundering orgasm. When Conner moved to walk us away from the window, I shuddered from the stimulation of my over-sensitized flesh.

"I can walk," I murmured, knowing his legs had to be tired.

Conner only grunted.

"Stubborn." I grinned against his skin. "Where are you taking me?"

"The shower. First, I'm going to watch my cum drip down your thigh, then I'm going to wash it away and replace it with more until you start to understand that you're mine."

I slowly eased back to see his face, and he could see the sincerity on mine as I whispered, "I'm getting there."

THE HEARTBREAK IN HER VOICE HAD BEEN TOO GUT-WRENCHING. Despite my lingering anger, I'd had to go back to the apartment when she called. I'd had to be near her, even if I couldn't bring myself to touch her until I was sure she understood the gravity of her mistake.

Her father and I were nothing alike. Absolutely *nothing*.

I would rather die than let my family come to harm, let alone harm them myself. Fausto Mancini was fucking scum. I was glad Noemi had told me the full truth because it justified the events I'd set in motion to take down the bastard. His reign of terror was over. He just didn't know it yet.

"Keir and I have a meeting set up with the Donatis." I set

Noemi down on the bathroom vanity, keeping my body between her legs. "You trust me to handle this?"

"I do." She nodded. "I'm just worried about Sante."

"I know, and I'll do my best to keep him out of it." I couldn't get enough of the unguarded innocence she offered in her mossy green gaze. Leaning back, I looked down at her inner thighs and trailed my fingers through the sticky wetness coating her. The sight brought new life to my softening dick. "This terrifies me, too, you know." I peered up at her through my lashes.

"It does?"

"Of course, it does. I feel like I could walk away from everything—spend every day fucking you senseless—and die a happy man. That wasn't how this was supposed to go. I wasn't supposed to want you either," I confessed.

"The mute Italian?" she teased with a smirk.

"That's the one." I touched my lips to hers with the hint of a kiss, bringing my body back to hers. "Italians gave me away. Why would I want anything to do with them?"

"You still feel that way?" she asked, a tinge of worry in her eyes.

"Nah, not really. And it doesn't matter because you're not Italian. You're *mine*."

Her lips hooked upward. "And you're mine?"

I hated that she had any doubt. "Hell yeah, I am. And that means I owe you an explanation as well. It was shitty of me not to tell you, and I'm sorry. When Mia Genovese came over, she told me that my uncle Brody had actually been my biological father." Saying the words brought back a renewed wave of frustration and loss. "All that time, and we'd never known. And now, it's too late. He's gone."

"Oh, Conner. That's heartbreaking. I'm so sorry." Her body softened with the weight of realization. "That's why you went after the Albanian last night."

"I'd needed to make someone pay for what I'd lost. What had been stolen from me."

"And when you got back, I was gone." Her small hand came to rest over my heart.

My jaw clenched at the reminder. "I should have told you what I'd learned, but I couldn't. I couldn't even comprehend it myself, let alone tell anyone."

"I shouldn't have left without telling you. I won't do it again."

"I don't want you to feel like you're in prison, but I need to keep you safe, and I can't do that if I don't know where you are. Tell me you understand."

Noemi nodded, a golden hunger warming her green gaze while a shiver shook her. I wasn't sure if it was desire or cold or a little of both.

The primitive inside me let loose a feral rumble. "Let's get you in the shower before I fuck you again."

My wife was equal parts innocent and seductive siren—the combination was beyond intoxicating. Bishop had called me obsessed, but that wasn't it. My desire for her went beyond that. It was a chemical in my blood, overriding all logic and reason.

I was addicted to the mere thought of her.

She was all that mattered, and anything that threatened her would face my wrath. Fausto Mancini thought he was tough, but he had no fucking clue about the beast he'd unleashed.

Ready or not, fucker. Here. I. Come.

Noemi

FORTY-ONE

WE SPENT HOURS TOGETHER THAT AFTERNOON NAKED IN THE bedroom. After we showered, he brought us a tray of food, telling me he didn't want me to leave his bed because he wasn't done with me. True to his word, he proceeded to eat me once I'd eaten my fill.

We had sex and talked and even laughed. Neither of us checked our phones, giving one another our full attention. While we talked, he let me trace the intricate lines of his tattoos and told me their meanings. Aside from my name on his wrist, my favorite was a candle on his back. It was inked in relief on solid black, the light from the small flame seeming to shine through his skin. The artistry was incredible, and he told me it symbolized his Byrne family and how they were always his light in the dark.

My throat had clogged with emotion.

Conner truly did value his family in ways my father could never comprehend. Unlike the large mafia families who weren't truly related, the Irish organization's origins sprouted from a set of brothers and was now primarily composed of blood relations. Conner and the others weren't as apt to face issues of conflicted loyalties because family and work were one and the same.

My Mafia ties introduced a complicating factor into his life. Mafia ties that I'd never wanted to be a part of. Did I feel the same about the Irish organization? Could we ever come to a crossroads where Conner would have to choose between me and his Irish family? If so, how would I fare in the aftermath?

I wouldn't end up dead like my mother, but I wasn't sure beyond that where his allegiance would fall. Hopefully, we wouldn't ever have to find out.

When my stomach eventually began to growl again, Conner ordered me to get dressed and took us to dinner. I was reluctant to break the spell of our fairy-tale afternoon but also liked the idea of a date. Our first dinner out had been good, but this felt different. More intimate. Meaningful.

Aside from the incident when he'd first come home, the day was one of the best I could remember. My chest had a strange warmth to it as though that candle of his had somehow lit a twin flame inside me.

Buoyant from our time together and two glasses of wine, I sat back in my chair after eating and decided to ask Conner a question I'd been itching to ask.

"Why me? I assume you were presented with a number of eligible Italian ladies to choose from. Why did you pick me?"

His sapphire eyes sparked as he sipped from his wineglass. "A lot of reasons. At first, I paused on your picture because of your eyes. I grew more interested when I was immediately warned away from you because of your silence. I was ... intrigued."

"Is that when you spoke to me at the coffee shop that first time?"

He dipped his chin in confirmation. "I was told you were traumatized and wanted to see what that meant for myself."

"And what did you find?" I asked, endlessly curious of his early thoughts about me.

"That if they thought you were traumatized, they didn't know the meaning of the word."

"Not mute either. You sure didn't get what you bargained for." I dropped my gaze, a tinge of uncertainty making me shy.

"Better to get what I needed than what I thought I wanted." His unwavering stare stripped away my insecurities and painted me in shades of perfection.

"You don't give yourself enough credit, Mr. Reid," I said softly. "There's a budding romantic in you somewhere."

He swirled the last bit of wine in his glass. "Debatable, but I suppose the right woman might see my mangled efforts as sufficient, Mrs. Reid."

Our server interrupted just in time. Had our combustible stare extended any longer, my panties might have gone up in flames smack in the middle of the restaurant.

"Is there anything else I can get you two?" The young woman flashed a wide grin, laying her hand on Conner's shoulder. She'd been friendly throughout our meal, and while I could overlook her frequent glances in his direction because the man was freaking gorgeous, there was only so much I could allow.

"You could take your hand off my husband," I said firmly but cordially. "Then the check, thank you."

Her hand snapped back so quickly I'd have thought his shoulder had burned her. "Yes. Yes, ma'am. I'll get that right away." She scurried away, head down.

"I must say," Conner mused. "I'd always thought a jealous woman was stifling, but you wear it well. In fact, I'm not sure I've ever seen anything hotter."

A flush warmed my cheeks.

"I don't like the way they all flirt with you."

"They?" he asked, his good humor fading.

"Waitresses, the women at the club, and probably any heterosexual woman who encounters you. It's like they can't help themselves. I imagine that would make it easy to … well, for things to happen." My cheeks had to be positively flaming. I couldn't even force myself to keep eye contact.

"Look at me, Noemi," Conner coaxed, his voice a sensual caress. He only continued once his eyes were again on mine. "I can't speak for the men you've known in your life, but that shit doesn't fly in my world. If you're mine, I expect to be the only man in your bed; the same goes for me. If their flirting bothers you, I'll put a stop to it. I don't want any question in your mind as to my faithfulness."

I swallowed back the emotion swelling in my chest like a saturated sponge. "Okay," I breathed shakily.

"Good," he said, comfortable that his point had been made. "Now, I need to run by the club. It won't take long."

"Not a problem at all."

A half hour later, we were walking into Bastion. It was my first visit after dark. The outside didn't look much different, but the edgy music playing in the lobby introduced a new vibe. It was still early, as far as city nights went, but things were definitely picking up.

Shae was stationed at the front entrance, a grin splitting her face when we arrived. "This is a pleasant surprise." She walked over and hugged me. I half expected Conner to go all caveman and jump between us, but thankfully, that didn't happen. Shae seemed to note the change in his demeanor as well, shooting him an arched brow. "You two joining the festivities this evening?"

"No," Conner said quickly, resting his hand at the base of my spine. "Just stopping in to grab some papers."

"Sometime soon, though," I assured her.

Shae's eyes danced from me to Conner, her grin returning. "I don't know what's happening here, but I approve."

"What's happening here is you're minding your own business." Conner's hand coaxed me forward.

I bit back a smile and gave her a finger wave. "Lunch sometime?"

"Absolutely."

I led the way through the double doors and back to Conner's office, the clacking of my heels echoing down the hallway. As I walked, it occurred to me that Shae's father was Brody Byrne, which made her Conner's half sister. The two had already thought of themselves as cousins, but it seemed strange to think of her not knowing she had another brother.

"I know it's all new to you, but do you think you'll tell them?" I asked once we were alone in the office. I knew he knew what I'd meant when he didn't answer immediately.

Eyes locked on the papers in his hand, his features hardened. "I haven't decided."

I joined him at his desk, placing my hand on his arm. "I can only imagine how frightening that would be," I offered softly. "Someone in your shoes might worry they'd deny the claim or see you differently. I haven't been around them a ton, but I don't see that happening. I think they'd be thrilled to know you've been a part of the family you were born into from the beginning."

His gaze lifted to mine, and he offered me an unguarded view into the volatile depths of his feelings on the subject—a desperate yearning for acceptance, a life-long fear of abandonment, and an unconditional devotion to his family. It left me awestruck.

Without thought, I lifted to my toes and pressed my lips against his. He abandoned his papers and met my advance with equal enthusiasm.

I'd had no idea how much more there could be to a kiss when emotion was involved, but I did now. Conner infused every sensual glide of his lips with passion and promise. He imparted a potency of adoration that stunned my senses.

When he pulled away, I was well and truly breathless.

"Time to go home," he rumbled. He got no complaints from me.

Conner

FORTY-TWO

My mother, Mirren Reid, the woman who raised me, would have had half a dozen children had she been able. Despite being the youngest in her family, she was a born caretaker. From what I'd gathered, she'd kept her three brothers in line almost better than their parents had. That probably had something to do with their adoration of her. Still, it was owed in no small part to her natural ability to be the glue that bound us together. When people met Mirren Reid, they subconsciously wanted to make her happy.

That devotion she instilled made me most apprehensive about telling my family. Noemi was right. I was worried about how the news would affect the others, but more than anything, I was afraid of hurting my parents.

Dad busted his ass to fit in with Mom's brothers. As the only girl and brother-in-law of the family, they constantly had to prove themselves. With this information, I would take the one thing that was theirs alone and give partial ownership to the brothers who already had everything.

Or at least, that was how it felt to me.

I wasn't sure my parents or anyone else would see it the same, but that was my fear. The last thing I wanted to do was hurt the two people who had loved me unconditionally.

I considered keeping my identity a secret and moving on, but that option didn't sit right either. When I saw Shae at the club and thought about how she was my sister, I didn't want to hide that. I'd always wanted siblings like my cousins had. We weren't children anymore, but that desire hadn't faded. I wanted them to know the truth.

In my gut, I knew I would tell them, but I needed assurance that what I was doing was the right thing. That was how I found myself sitting in Paddy and Nana's living room two days later.

"You keep showing up with orange slices, and I'll be big as a house in no time," Nana teased.

"I could come less frequently if that'd help."

"Don't be daft. Just leave the candy with that pretty wife o' yours. She's young enough to eat her weight in the sweet stuff and not gain an ounce. How is she, anyway?" Despite her fussing, Nana took out a candy wedge and ate the whole thing in one bite.

I stifled a grin. "She's better than I had expected, actually."

"Oh! Hey, now. So things are going well, are they?" Her eyes gleamed. "Paddy, did you hear that? Conner and that new wife o' his are gettin' along well."

Paddy grunted. "Of course, they are. Never met a Byrne

man who couldn't charm the pants off a woman if they wanted to."

I gave a dry chuckle. "Funny you should say that. It's actually the reason I'm here."

Nana's wrinkles congregated on her scrunched face. "You need charm lessons?"

"No. I wanted to talk to you about the Byrne men—specifically, about Brody." All humor faded from my face as worry set in. "I haven't told anyone yet, but my birth mother came to me a few days ago and told me who my father was." The words caught in my throat, making it hard to continue.

"Well, now," Nana breathed. "It suddenly makes sense. You were the spitting image of him as a baby. Never could explain it."

My lips parted in shock. "Uncle Brody?"

"Aye. His eyes darkened through childhood to a gray-blue, but when he was born, his eyes looked just like yours." The fondness in her smile wavered with grief. "Such a shame he never knew. Did you hear that, Paddy?" She called over to her husband in a raised voice.

"Never could keep a leash on that one," he grumbled, making me grin. "Not that it matters. You were one of us regardless."

Fuck me.

I hadn't cried since I was six years old and broke my wrist jumping off a skateboard, but a few words from my grandfather, and my sinuses were burning like a motherfucker. He had no idea how much his comment meant to me. Or maybe he did. It was hard to say with him.

I took in a slow, even breath. "I appreciate that, Paddy, and I'm hoping everyone feels that way, but it still worries me to share the truth with everyone. I guess that's why I'm here. The last thing I want to do is hurt the family, and especially my parents."

Nana's eyes softened, the creases in the corners deepening. "Yer a good lad, Conner. Everyone thinks my boys are tough as nails, but my wee little Mirren had them all beat. She's a tough one, she is. Don't underestimate her. She and yer da will be thrilled to know they were lucky enough to raise their nephew and call him their own."

I nodded, hoping she was right. "I suppose the cat's out of the bag, now. I'll have to tell everyone before you get to them first."

The old woman's flinty eyes narrowed. "You sayin' I have loose lips, Conner Reid?"

"Wouldn't dream of it." I grinned, snagging an orange slice from her brown paper bag. I tossed the candy in my mouth and stood when I heard Paddy mutter, "I would," and Nana sucked in a lungful of air.

"Well, that would be my cue to head out."

"Probably best," Nana grumbled. "I'd hate for ye to see a grown man cry."

I chuckled, giving her and my grandfather hugs before letting myself out. I didn't make it to the car when my phone vibrated in my pocket.

"Yeah," I said after seeing Keir was calling.

"Everything's been set up. It's time."

The blood in my veins chilled so fast that a gallon of antifreeze wouldn't have kept them from icing over.

"On my way." I despised what I was about to do, but we'd discussed the options and decided it was the best way to cut the head off this particular snake. I just hoped we didn't get bit in the process.

Noemi

FORTY-THREE

THAT WAS THE LAST OF IT. I'D UNBOXED MY THINGS AND FOUND new homes for everything. I still felt a little strange filling someone else's house with my things, but the apartment felt more like mine each day. Conner had even offered to bring in a decorator if I wanted to make any changes to the place. I didn't think that was necessary, but I appreciated the offer. I was still considering converting one of the guest bedrooms into my own personal space. A place to read or do yoga that was all my own.

I was standing in the doorway, trying to envision the options when my phone began to ring. Like an idiot, my face split in a goofy grin when I saw Conner's name on the screen.

"Hey," I answered warmly.

"Hey, I wanted to let you know it's happening." His unexpectedly severe tone had me instantly on alert.

"What does that mean?" I knew he was talking about my father, but I needed more information.

"It means the Donatis looked deeper into your mom's death and agreed that your father was behind it. We'll meet with them and ensure your father can never hurt you or anyone else again."

A tidal wave of relief rippled from my head to my toes.

They knew. My family finally knew the truth, and the burden was no longer on my shoulders. My uncle would make sure Dad was punished for his crimes.

"Thank you," I whispered, tears pooling in my eyes.

"It's not over yet," Conner cautioned me. "What I need from you is to stay put while I handle this. All of us are coming together to pull this off, so I won't have any men available to protect you."

"I'm not going anywhere, but please call to update me when you can."

"It may be a few hours, but I'll be in touch."

"Be careful, Conner."

"Fuck, you're sexy when you're sweet." His voice dropped an octave.

I grinned. "Focus."

He grunted, then the line went dead. I chuckled, but the laughter quickly dissipated as the reality of the danger set in. Conner was going to plot with the Donatis to take down my father. Dad wasn't as powerful as them, but he was experienced and had connections. He wouldn't go down without a fight.

I wasn't overly religious, but I closed my eyes and said a silent prayer that Conner and Sante would be okay.

Going back to the living room, I wondered what the hell I could do to distract myself. I'd planned to scavenge the fridge for lunch, but that wasn't an option now. My stomach was entirely too disgruntled with nerves to eat. Deciding TV was my best bet, I curled up on the couch and began to scroll for a movie that might hold my attention.

Ten minutes into a murder mystery on Masterpiece Theater, my phone rang again. It was Sante calling from the burner I'd given him. All my senses pricked with alarm.

"Sante?" I answered, muting the TV at the same time.

"Em, I need to talk to you. Can you meet up with me?"

"I'm sorry, but I can't. It needs to be in person?" I asked, hating the strain I heard in his voice.

"Fuck, I don't know. I just really need to see you. You told me to talk to you if something was up."

"What if you came here?" I asked reluctantly. I knew Conner wouldn't be crazy about me inviting Sante to our home, but I knew my brother, and he was more distressed than I'd ever heard him sound.

"Yeah, I guess that works."

I gave him the address before we ended the call, hoping it wasn't a mistake. I didn't think my brother would set me up, but I'd been wrong about my father in the past. People were unpredictable.

On the other hand, I liked knowing that if something went down today, my brother would be far from the action. Just to be safe, though, I retrieved the handgun Conner kept in his nightstand and put it in my purse. I'd make sure to keep it near me when my brother arrived, and I wouldn't let him in if anyone came with him.

Confident with my precautions, I sat on the sofa in silence, chewing my nails to the quick until the front desk buzzed to notify me of my brother's arrival. They confirmed he was alone, and I gave permission for them to send him up.

He looked terrible when he arrived. Shadows darkened his eyes, hinting at sleepless nights. Even his ordinarily curly hair was matted and dull. What made me most uneasy was how he avoided me when he entered. No hug. No eye contact. Sante was completely overcome by whatever he had to tell me.

"Thanks for seeing me," he finally said, peering at me hesitantly.

"Of course. You're always welcome here." I placed a comforting hand on his arm. "Can you tell me what's wrong?"

He took a deep breath, seeming to gather his courage. "I think something's going down today."

"Does it involve Conner?" I asked, assuming this had something to do with him meeting the Donatis. I kept pushing when he didn't answer right away. "*Please*, Sante. If Conner is in danger, you need to tell me."

"Dad knows he's meeting with the Donatis. He thinks they're conspiring against him. I don't understand why, but it's serious. I've never seen him like this."

I felt the blood drain from my face.

"I think he's planning something, but…" Sante continued.

"But what?"

"I just can't see him doing it. Why would he risk the alliance like that?" My brother looked at me for understanding.

A calm sense of certainty settled in my bones, telling me it was time.

I lifted my chin and looked deep into my brother's eyes. "I didn't know how to tell you before. I wanted to, but the time never seemed right, and I was struggling with my own emotions. I quit talking because I knew that Dad was behind Mom's death. He orchestrated the car crash to keep her quiet."

Sante's face contorted with shock and horror as I continued.

"Before the crash, Mom told me in the car that she found out Dad was putting a hit out on Uncle Agostino and was going to take over the family. That's why we were on our way to see him that day—to warn him. Dad must have found out and sabotaged the breaks. I wasn't supposed to be with her that day, but Dad assumed Mom told me everything when I survived the crash. That's why he kept us apart all those months and didn't let me out of his sight. He didn't want me to try to escape with you or get word to the Donatis about what had happened."

"Escape?" He shook his head. "What the hell are you talking about? None of this makes sense."

I tried to reach for him, but he shrugged off my touch. "I know you have a different relationship with him than me, but if you try to set that aside and look at it objectively, you'd see the truth—the way he treated me after her death. The odd behavior. The secrets."

I could see the uncertainty setting in. I was making progress. "If Dad knows about the meeting, is he planning to do something about it?"

Sante's brows drew together worriedly when he finally looked at me again. "He didn't tell me, exactly, but I overheard him talking once."

"Sante, tell me, *please*."

"I couldn't figure out why he'd be talking to the Albanians, but now, I'm wondering if he hired them for this. Like mercenaries."

My heart dropped all the way to my feet.

The Albanians had it out for the Irish. They'd jump at the chance to kill Conner. Sante had no idea of the catastrophic news he'd just unleashed.

"Oh God. Sante. We have to warn them." I yanked my phone from my back pocket and dialed Conner's number. The line rang, each unanswered tone sounding longer than the last. Once I was sent to voicemail, I tried Bishop with the same results.

Fuck! Fuckfuckfuck.

What was I supposed to do? What if the meeting was already in progress, and they had no idea that my father was coming for them?

Panic sandblasted my insides until I felt helplessly exposed.

"*Shit*! What do we do?" I cried.

As though my meltdown had the opposite effect on Sante, his self-assurance and conviction seemed to grow by the second. Spine stiffening, he squared his shoulders. "I know where they're at. The meeting shouldn't have started yet."

"I'm going with you," I asserted, grabbing my purse.

"It's too dangerous, Em."

I glared at him. "There is no way I can sit here now. You have to take me with you."

His lips thinned harshly. "If I do, you have to stay in the car. Period."

"Fine." I wasn't crazy about it, but at least I wouldn't be left behind. I'd told Conner I wouldn't leave, but this was too important. He needed to know he was being set up. I just prayed that we weren't too late.

FORTY-FOUR

Sante called Umberto once we were in the car. The man who had acted as my jailer wasn't thrilled about Sante joining them but eventually conceded and gave instructions on where exactly to go. The meeting was happening at an old warehouse by the mafia-owned docks, but we'd needed to know where our father was hiding out in wait.

I could see why they chose the location. Aside from the abandoned nature of the warehouse, the entire area was piled with crates and equipment, not to mention cars parked everywhere. It appeared the dock workers used the lot for parking though it was far enough removed from the river to keep it isolated. So long as we didn't encounter a shift change, the place was vacant.

We parked a ways out, not wanting to be seen.

Sante instructed me to duck down into the floorboards. "Stay here, understood?"

A part of me was proud of how mature he sounded, while another part wanted to insist I'd do what I damn well wanted. I wasn't happy about being stuck yet again hiding in a car while a man I cared about went out into danger to protect me, but I wouldn't help matters by arguing.

I didn't follow him, but I did peak out the window enough to watch my brother slip away from the car. He walked to an old shed at the entrance to the lot—probably some sort of security checkpoint when the factory had been operational. Once Sante was close enough, Umberto exited the shed between them and the warehouse, keeping them hidden from the men inside.

The two talked, and even from a distance, their discussion looked heated. I suddenly regretted not discussing what Sante had planned. Was he confronting them about the truth?

Crap, I hate this so much!

My hands trembled, and a sticky nausea filled my belly. The feeling of impending chaos clawed at my skin with little barbed hooks.

My brother puffed out his chest as he flung an angry comment at Umberto, who responded by lifting a gun to Sante's head.

This was it. This was what I'd been terrified about for months.

I couldn't sit by and watch him get killed. I had to help him.

Grabbing the gun from my purse, I clicked off the safety and chambered a bullet before sneaking from the car. I left the door open so I didn't make any extra noise and snuck up behind Umberto.

"Don't move," I ground out angrily, my gun pointed at him from a safe distance away. "Drop the gun."

"What is it, princess? You want me to hold still or drop the gun? I can't do both," Umberto shot back at me with the unbothered swagger of a man who had completely dismissed me as a threat.

"Now, Umberto." My father's eerily calm voice touched my ears before he appeared on the other side of Sante. "Do you think sarcasm is really appropriate at this little family reunion of mine?" He was the epitome of cavalier nonchalance as he lifted a gun to Sante. "What will you do now, Noemi? You can only point a gun at one of us."

I was in over my head. I knew it. He knew it. I had no freaking clue what I should do. Luckily, my father continued with his narcissistic banter, giving me precious seconds to think.

"I expected this from her, Sante. She's headstrong like her mother. But you? I'd thought better of you." He shrugged a shoulder as though discussing a restaurant's wine selection. "I really don't need either of you, so I suppose it's no great loss."

Before Dad could do or say any more, Sante lashed out at Umberto. He was a good size for his age but no match for a mature man. The gun went off in the struggle, taking me by surprise. It was so damn loud, my hands reflexively went to my ears, gun still clamped tight in my right fist.

The distraction gave Dad a chance to grab me and put his gun to my temple. "Stop right *fucking* now," Dad hissed at Sante, then clamped his hand tight around my throat. "And you, drop the fucking gun." His voice dripped with malice.

In a handful of heartbeats, we'd gone from a standoff to utter failure.

Umberto again had his gun pointed at Sante's head, but

Fausto Mancini was no longer amused this time. His darting eyes flashed with raving madness.

I did as he ordered, flinching at the sound of my gun clattering to the concrete.

"You're going to fuck up everything. Just like your goddamn mother. I was days from owning the entire Moretti family when she had to try to be a hero." He shook my neck, pressing the gun harder against my head. "This time, though, I won't fail. I've made sure of it."

"Put the gun down and let her go." A new voice entered the fray, and I recognized that sound of cool indifference.

Keir and several others stepped out from nowhere, guns drawn. My heart pounded so ferociously that the beats echoed to my fingers and toes. With every passing second, our situation worsened. I was terrified we were headed for an all-out bloodbath.

My father laughed maniacally. "You think you can get one over on me? I've been at this longer than you've been alive."

The Albanians. He drew his confidence from the knowledge that he'd hedged his bets by bringing in hired guns, and our guys had no idea.

I stared pleadingly at Keir, desperately wishing I could somehow warn him.

The words pressed against my lips, demanding to be released, but the gun at my temple effectively silenced me.

As if the fates knew there was only one way to make this situation worse, Renzo Donati and Conner appeared in our circle of destruction.

Conner's eyes were a merciless black, every ounce of blue eclipsed by his wrath. "Let her go, Fausto, or this won't end well for you."

My father tugged us away from them. "You're pathetic, all of you. You think I came here alone?" he whistled loudly through his teeth, summoning yet another cluster of armed bodies that emerged from behind cars and seemingly out of nowhere.

The Albanians were here, and they had us completely surrounded.

How had this happened? How could the Byrnes and Donatis both fall victim to this man?

Despair clamped tight around my rib cage, my eyes darting from one murderous face to another until a humorless chuckle drew my focus back to Conner.

"You know, I have to give you props. Hiring Albanians when you knew we were already at odds with them was a clever move. You could put a hit out on your daughter without anyone being the wiser. You worried when she started talking that she'd leak your secrets, and you were right to be concerned. If you'd been successful, you would have lost the power the alliance would have brought, but your secrets would have been safe."

Shock rang in my ears. The men who'd come after us in the car—they'd been sent to kill *me*? I'd assumed they were after Conner, but that had been the whole point. My death was supposed to look like collateral damage in the war between the Irish and Albanians, a convenient way to tie up loose ends.

While I reeled over his unveiling, Conner continued. "The thing is, you didn't count on me capturing one of the men you hired." Conner slowly stepped forward, arms crossed over his chest. "I found the man who ran from the scene and learned about your involvement."

Conner's eyes cut to the side. I followed his stare over to Sante, whose face twisted in disgust.

"It's time to open your eyes," Conner urged my brother. "Your father isn't the man he wants you to believe."

"Don't listen to the lying bastard," Dad spat. "They'll tell you anything to turn you against me. Look what they already did to your sister." Fear setting in, my father was trying to rally Sante back to his side.

My brother only looked more pissed with each word our father spoke. "You tried to kill Emy? Mom wasn't bad enough, you fucking psycho?" His face grew red and blotchy with fury, and I prayed he didn't do anything brash.

Our father snarled. "You're barely old enough to get your dick wet. What do you fucking know about anything?"

"Sante," I hissed, demanding he look at me. "It's okay. I'm here. He didn't hurt me."

"Not yet," Dad spat. "But I'm the one in control here. You don't shut your fucking mouth, I'll put a bullet through it."

"Now, Fausto," Conner continued, drawing our attention back to him. "There's something you need to consider. Mercenaries are a dangerous business. You go outside your loyal organization, and it becomes hard to trust the people you work with. Take these men, for example." He motioned to the small army around us. "They have no real loyalty to you. Should someone have learned of your arrangement with them and negotiated a better deal, your entire plan could be in jeopardy, not to mention, your life."

My father stiffened behind me.

One by one, the outer ring of soldiers lowered their weapons.

I was stunned. Conner had known what my father was up to and managed to get one step ahead of him.

"This is *bullshit,*" Dad hissed, desperation now oozing from his pores. "I paid you! You can't do this."

While he spewed his outrage, my eyes stayed locked on my husband. His cobalt stare bore into me, urging me to be ready. Receiving his message, I sucked in a lungful of air and clenched my eyes tightly shut.

In the same instant, a gunshot rang out so loud that I couldn't hear beyond the ringing in my ears.

I shrieked, returning my hands to my ears and noting warm sticky droplets in my hair.

I knew what had happened. I never heard his body hit the ground or saw the bullet that hit him, but I knew my father was dead.

Slowly, I peered over my shoulder at Fausto Mancini's motionless body, a crimson-lined hole in his forehead. The sight should have made me nauseous or relieved or something, but an eerie cold settled over me instead. A shiver wracked my body as I turned back around to see where the shot had come from.

Conner stood with his arm outstretched, a black pistol clenched tightly in his fist.

What he'd done had been risky, but every ounce of him radiated undiluted confidence. I'd sensed what he was about to do and was shocked at my complete confidence in him. A few inches off, and it would have been my body limp on the ground.

Another shot pierced the air around us, all eyes turning to my brother. Sante held Umberto's gun outstretched as the hulk of a man collapsed to the ground. My brother had stripped Umberto of his gun and shot him in cold blood. No tremor to his hand. No remorse in his eyes. His face was so harsh with violence that I almost didn't recognize him.

Lowering the gun, he aimed it at our father's body, unloaded one more shot into the dead man's chest, then spit on him.

Sante was no longer the boy I'd known.

I walked over slowly so as not to startle him and gently wove my arms around his middle. Sante held me close, a hand pressing my head into his chest.

"I'm so sorry, little big," he said on a ragged breath.

"Me, too."

When he let me go, he walked directly to Renzo and handed over the gun. "I hope you'll believe I had no idea about this. If I'd known what he did…" Sante's jaw clenched against his anger.

Renzo dropped his chin. "Don't worry about that now. You're still family in our eyes, and there's time to work through the rest."

"This is all very touching, but I'd say our job here is done." A man with a heavy foreign accent stepped forward, along with several others who held the rest of my father's men at gunpoint.

The Albanians.

Conner moved, placing his body between the foreigners and me. "Our organization appreciates what you've done for us."

"As does ours," added Renzo.

The man smiled, holding his hands wide. "Well, hopefully,

this can be the start of something new for all of us, eh? We work together, is much better for all." He barked a string of commands to his men, who turned over their captives to the Italian soldiers nearby. "Until we meet again." He bowed his head before leading his men away from the scene.

I watched Conner, blistering hatred in his eyes. Those very same men had tried to kill us and had succeeded in killing his biological father. He had no intention of ever again working with those men. They'd made a life-long enemy in my husband, but he'd done it this once. For me.

I couldn't even grasp the magnitude of what that had cost him.

I flung myself into his arms. "I'm sorry I left the house," I said hoarsely. "Sante told me Dad was setting you up, and I had to warn you. I tried to call. I was so terrified."

Conner pulled me back and peered into my eyes before lowering his lips to mine. Neither of us cared about the men milling about or the two dead bodies at our feet. All that mattered was the press of our lips and a promise of another tomorrow.

"Don't look in the mirror." I did my best to keep Noemi facing away from the bathroom vanity. The last thing she needed to see was her father's blood splattered across her face. She knew it was there. That was bad enough. She didn't need to see it. "Arms up," I instructed softly.

She did as she was told, having slipped into a state of shock as I whisked her away from the warehouse scene. The others could handle the fallout—cleanup and the authorities. I'd had to get my wife out of there. Her poor little body was shaking like a leaf.

Once I stripped us both down, we stepped into the steaming shower. Her eyes drifted shut under the hot spray of water. Even blood splattered and wrecked, she was incredible. Smooth, creamy skin over soft curves. It was mesmerizing to watch the water run in rivulets down her body.

I let her absorb the water's warmth for several long minutes before I lathered her in soap. For once in our short relationship, she handed me complete control. We both needed it. After discovering she had wound up at the warehouse and feeling like all of our plans had erupted into total chaos, I needed to feel a sense of control. I needed to feel her unharmed body warm and alive beneath my fingers.

Noemi angled her head back so I could wash her hair. It wasn't something I'd ever done before, so when I finished, and she opened tear-filled eyes, I had a moment of panic that I'd gotten the damn shampoo in her eyes.

"What is it?" I asked, my entire body tensing.

"Conner, I'm so sorry. I left your gun at the warehouse. It was the one from your nightstand," she said, her words growing frantic.

I huffed out a breath, smiling softly. "Don't worry about that, baby." I cupped her face in my hands. "The guys will take care of everything. I'm just glad that if you were going to go, you went prepared." I pressed my lips to her forehead, temple, and the bridge of her nose. "You scared the shit out of me, Em." The words were as raw and broken as my insides felt. I hadn't wanted to fuss at her, so I'd kept my mouth shut, but I needed her to know how terrified I'd been.

"I know, and I'm so sorry. I would never have gone if I hadn't been so worried about you."

I pulled her against me, wishing my damn dick understood the difference between comforting my traumatized wife and shower sex. "I'm just glad it's over."

"Me, too." She pulled back, brows drawing together. "You said over the phone that my uncle had verified Dad sabotaged Mom's car—how?"

"They got ahold of the detective working for Fausto. He

doctored the investigation. He admitted to removing the incendiary device that took out her brakes and had modified the accident report. We're connected to half the NYPD. I'd say your father was lucky one of ours wasn't the first to respond to the scene, but I imagine he planned that as well and had his guy on call."

"It all blows my mind." She shook her head just slightly. "And those men who came after us in the car. They were sent to kill me. What kind of father does that?"

"The kind who doesn't deserve a second thought." I brought her eyes to mine, holding them until she nodded. "I'm just glad he was dumb enough to take our bait."

"Bait?"

"We intentionally leaked information about our meeting today. Keir and his men were stationed around the perimeter to let Fausto think he'd successfully surrounded us, but we knew we had the Albanians in our pocket. Of course, there was always a chance they wouldn't uphold their end of the bargain, but it was a risk we decided to take. Their leader knew they'd fucked up making an enemy of us, and working against the Italians would only have made things worse for them. Agreeing to be bought was the same as saving their own asses. It won't buy them indefinite immunity, but there's peace for now."

"You paid them?"

I nodded, hating how worry etched into her face.

"How much?"

"Totally inconsequential when compared to your safety." I smiled, hoping to reassure her. "And besides, everything we did has strengthened our ties to the Italians more than any abstract alliance could have."

Finally, a smile formed on her lips. Small, but it was a start.

"I'm glad. We're really not a bad lot." As soon as the smile formed, it faded. "I feel so bad for Sante, though."

"It wasn't an easy lesson," I admitted. "But Renzo took your brother home with him. I think the two will talk. He'll be a much better role model for Sante in the long run."

"Yeah." She peered innocently up at me, forest green lined with inky black lashes. "Do you think you can take me to see him tomorrow?"

Fuck, look at me like that, and I'll take you to the goddamn moon.

"Yeah, we can do that." I brought my lips to hers, slow but ardent. "Now, let's get you dried off and dressed before you prune into nothing."

"But you didn't even wash up."

"This wasn't about me." I gently smacked her ass and smirked. "Now, move."

Two Weeks Later

"I NEED A DRINK, AND YOU'RE GOING WITH ME," PIP SAID IN LIEU of a greeting when I answered her call.

"Excuse me?" I replied, still processing her words.

"We haven't had a girls' night in almost a *year*, sis. It's time. And after everything that's happened recently, we could both use some fun."

"I suppose you're in luck. I just talked to Sante, and I could use a drink myself."

"Oh yeah? What's my sweet cousin up to?"

I groaned. "He's retracted his promise to stay in school. I

think he's doing pretty well, but I'm disappointed he won't get his diploma."

"He still staying with Renzo?"

"Yeah, but he's signed a lease for an apartment, and our old house goes on the market next week." It shouldn't have bothered me because there was nothing at the house I wanted to keep. I'd gone over and taken everything of Mom's that I wanted, but something about letting go of the past was still hard.

"He'll be fine, Em. It's not like he has to go out and find a job. As long as things are good between you two, that's all that matters."

I smiled, glancing down at the new bracelet he'd given me a couple of days ago. It was the exact same as the one he'd given me before, but this one read *Little Big*. He'd been equally ready to cut ties with our father as I'd been once he'd heard what Dad had done. Sante struggled with his anger, but overall, our relationship was stronger than ever. "Yeah, we're good. So about drinks. When and where were you thinking?"

"Tonight, and I don't give a crap where so long as the vibe is right."

"The vibe?" I ask, smiling.

"Yeah. I'm not talking chardonnay at a tapas bar. We're going *out*. To a club. Somewhere with music we can dance to and hot guys who will buy us drinks."

"Uh, married over here, remember?" I held up my ring-clad hand even though she couldn't see it through the phone.

"Whatever. You don't have to sleep with them."

I rolled my eyes. "Okay, let me check with Conner and get back to you."

"And that *right there* is why I'm not interested in bossy men," she groused out of nowhere. "Think they own everything they touch."

Okaaay. Someone's a little sensitive.

"Text you in a bit," I said, keeping my thoughts to myself.

"Sounds good, but we're going, whether he likes it or not." Then she hung up. I had to laugh. My cousin was a little crazy, but she was also the best.

I walked back to Conner's office, where he spent most afternoons until it was time to head into Bastion. It was a Friday afternoon, so he likely had plans to work. That was the only drawback about his business—weekends were peak hours of operation.

"Hey, you," I greeted softly. "Mind if I interrupt for a minute?"

"You don't even need to ask." He leaned away from the desk and let his hungry gaze sweep over me. "What's up?"

"Pip called. She wants me to go out with her tonight, like … a girls' night." I told myself to be assertive, but the words still sounded like a question. I was a little worried about how he'd react.

Conner steepled his fingers together. "I don't see a problem with that, so long as you take Shae with you."

"Really?" He hadn't seemed as bothered by my friendship with Shae anymore, but I was still surprised he'd send us to a club together.

"Really. Unless there's a reason I should be concerned?" He raised a masculine brow.

I suppressed a grin. "Not at all. Though, I'm not sure if she'll be free tonight."

"She was slotted to work. I'll let her know the plans have changed. And don't forget we have Nana's birthday gathering tomorrow."

"It won't be a problem. Guess I should start getting ready. Pip may want to grab dinner before we go out."

"I'll take you on my way to work. Just let me know the plan, and I'll pass it along to Shae."

I walked around the desk to him, bending to bring my lips to his. "Thanks, baby."

His hand gripped the back of my leg, slowly sliding up and down, the tips of his fingers teasing just shy of the apex of my thighs. "Let me see what you plan to wear first, then decide if you want to thank me."

It was my turn to raise a challenging brow. Being courteous about checking with him before I made plans was one thing, but this modern woman would wear whatever the hell she wanted. In fact, I suddenly felt an intense need to wear my most revealing, most salacious dress. Not that I even owned anything all that risqué, but I was about to dig around and see what I could uncover.

I hmphed haughtily and withdrew from the room.

An hour later, I was back in Conner's office, approaching his desk in a sage green dress that stopped just short of my ass, clinging to every curve I possessed. It wasn't particularly revealing otherwise—the scoop neck didn't descend too low, and it even had long sleeves, but that didn't detract one bit from the sex appeal. I looked smoking hot, from the dress to the sculpted waves in my hair to my winged eyeliner.

Soaking up every bit of confidence my outfit provided, I sauntered up to Conner and leaned my hip against the side of his desk. "All ready," I said coyly, reveling in the way his entire body stiffened at the sight of me and his eyes dilated to jet black.

He'd gone from civil to savage in the blink of his sapphire eyes.

He eased up from his chair, pushing it back to make room for me. "Come here." The dark command wrapped like black silk around my throat, tugging me toward him. I slipped into the space between him and the desk, the cleft of my ass resting on the hard wood behind me.

In a matter of a second, he'd pulled his laptop out from behind me and lifted me onto the desk. Then his hand was on my chest, pressing me down flat, my knees raising involuntarily to follow my body. Conner slipped off my heels and set my feet on the edge of the desk. I was open wide to him, the thin fabric of my thong the only thing shielding my slick center from his view.

"Fuck if I'm sending you out like that." His fingers glided beneath my panties, then swiftly ripped away the crotch. Before I could argue, his mouth was on me.

I gasped and writhed. He licked and sucked and nipped until I was totally mindless. I was so lost in the sensation that I didn't notice until too late that he'd sucked what had to be a remarkable hickey on my inner thigh. I couldn't even complain, not when he had me seeing stars seconds later. My orgasm ricocheted out from my pussy, barreling through my body until it filled every nook and cranny with euphoric bliss.

"You gave me a hickey," I said weekly, my brain frazzled.

He kissed the spot tenderly before helping me back upright. "Go put some panties on. It's time to leave."

I was going to argue that he'd ignored my comment when I suddenly realized the thong I'd been wearing was the only clean one I had left. "Dammit, the only thing left in my drawer is period panties."

Wait, wasn't the laundry done two days ago? I should have more than enough clean thongs.

"I suppose you'll have to make do," he said, patting my ass to hurry me along, but I wasn't going anywhere.

"Did you do this on purpose? Are you holding my thongs captive?"

The most salacious, shit-eating grin I'd ever seen spread

across his face. "You can have them back tomorrow. Now, you better hurry, or you'll be late."

It was so brutish and ridiculous that I couldn't help the hint of a smile when I rolled my eyes and walked away.

"This is exactly what I needed," Pip called over the pulsing music. "And Shae is really great. I'm glad Conner sent her along, even though it was unnecessary."

We both looked toward the dance floor, where Shae had the eye of every man and woman in the place.

"And, with her here, we didn't even need our fake IDs," I added, lifting my glass in a toast.

"Hell yeah!" Pip cheered, clinking her martini into mine before we both drank.

We'd started our night with yummy Mexican and margaritas before heading to the club and kicking things off with a Patrón shot. We were on our second martini, and I felt it.

"You have got to be fucking kidding me."

My brows drew together in confusion at Pippa's sudden outburst. I followed her scathing stare to find Bishop across the room, glaring at Pip with an equal degree of fury. I'd never seen the normally playful man look so serious. So savage.

"Why do I get the sense you two know each other?" Sure, they'd met at my wedding, but their reaction to one another went well beyond acquaintances.

She took a deep breath and brought her eyes back to me. "Remember when we were drinking at your place and Conner showed up? He had Bishop take me home that day."

I'd completely forgotten.

"Aaand?" I prompted, knowing there had to be more to

that story. You didn't have a staring match like that with someone you barely knew.

"We kind of … got to know each other." Pippa, queen of no regrets and feminist extraordinaire, dropped her gaze to the table in an uncharacteristic show of bashfulness.

"Uh, you do realize you're going to have to give me more than that," I balked at her.

She shook her head, exasperated, and grabbed my hand. "Okay, but not here. Let's get out there and dance. We can dish later."

Oh, man. This is going to be good.

I let her lead me to the dance floor, knowing I would corner her for information later. A Lady Gaga dance mix reverberated from the speakers and into my body, where it electrified the alcohol already buzzing in my veins. I felt amazing. We joined Shae, the three of us forming a small circle. It didn't last long, though. Shae pulled the woman she'd been dancing with against her, leaving Pip and me together. We moved closer to one another, but that didn't stop a guy from coming up behind her and joining our duo.

Having been in this situation before, I gave her the *you want help*? eyebrow lift. I could easily pull her away and give this guy the slip, but Pip waved me off. Not only was she okay with the intrusion but she also leaned back into him, making a show of it. The move was, again, out of character, and I knew the motivation seconds later when Bishop plowed through the crowd and yanked the two of us off the dance floor.

"Noemi, call your husband to come get you. We're leaving." He let out a sharp, short whistle that instantly had Shae's attention. He motioned to me, then began to tow my cousin toward the exit.

Both wide-eyed, we gaped at one another as she disappeared into the crowd.

What the hell just happened?

Maybe it was the alcohol, but I doubled over in a fit of giggles. I should have been outraged for my poor cousin, yet all I could do was laugh. Someone had met her match.

I explained to Shae what had happened when she joined me. She wasn't ready to call it a night and suggested we stay, but I was ready to go home. We went out front so I could call Conner, then she waited with me until he arrived.

"I can't believe he fucking left you there," Conner grumbled once we were headed home.

"I assume you sent him to keep an eye on us?" It seemed unnecessary since he'd already sent Shae with us, but I wasn't totally shocked.

"No, I didn't," he bit out.

"Really," I mused. That was interesting. "Did you know something was going on with them?"

"No. Makes me think there isn't anything. He's not the type to keep secrets."

"Neither is Pip, but there was *definitely* something going on. And don't be too upset, he didn't leave me alone. You said yourself that Shae kicks ass."

He grunted, not taking his eyes from the road.

I watched as he shifted gears. "I just realized how freaking hot it is to watch you drive a stick," I said dazedly, reaching my hand across the console to ride up his muscular thigh.

"Fuck, woman." That was all he said before the car surged forward.

He had me home and naked in record time, erasing all thoughts of my cousin.

♠

Conner had warned me not to drink too much, so I did my best to hide my headache the next morning. He must have known, though, because I found two painkillers and a bottle of water sitting on the bathroom vanity after I showered. By the time we left the house for Nana's party, I was much better.

The Byrne family matriarch was turning eighty-five. She and Paddy made a rare departure from their house, conditioning their appearance on holding the party at a pub. The family had found the largest Irish bar they could and bought it out for the afternoon. The place was decorated floor to ceiling in shades of lavender, Nana's favorite color, and filled to the brim with family.

We wove our way back to the birthday girl first. She fussed that we'd all made too much commotion over her, but it was plain to see that she was delighted. I'd quickly come to adore Conner's grandmother and was so happy to be a part of her special day. We talked for a bit, then made way for the newest arrivals to get their chance with her.

Settling in, Conner got himself a Guinness while I stuck to soda. My stomach wasn't ready to tackle alcohol yet so soon after my night out.

"I didn't realize Mia had been invited," I said to my husband after spotting his birth mother and her husband across the room.

"I guess Mom invited her. The two have gotten together twice over the last couple of weeks. Apparently, they're really hitting it off. Feels a little strange, but I'm getting used to it."

"That's really great. Your mom could easily have felt threatened by her. The whole family has handled it so well. Mostly."

Conner had told his parents first about Brody being his biological father. Then he'd sat down with Brody's widow and her three kids. Shae had laughed until she turned blue. According to Conner, her older brother, Cael, had seemed unfazed, but the eldest, Oran, had been openly wary. Poised to take over his father's role in the organization and challenge Keir for leadership, he wasn't thrilled with Conner gaining more clout in the family.

"Eh, there's always gonna be at least one heckler in the crowd," Conner murmured. "Once he sees I'm not a threat, he'll calm down."

"I'm glad you're not gunning to take over. I don't want that kind of target on your back."

He put his arm around me and tucked me into his side. "I have everything I want right here," he said, lips ghosting over my ear.

I warmed at his words, realizing as he removed his arm to shake hands with a distant relative that I felt the same. After Mom died, I'd told myself I could never be happy marrying a man who led the sort of life my father had. But now I knew that a man was more than his lifestyle. A person could live by a different moral code than society and still be honorable. He could steal all my thongs and still be thoughtful—order me onto my knees and still worship me like a goddess.

And if I was honest with myself, I didn't want some of his parts without the others. Conner was who he was because of his dark complexities, and I adored every enigmatic piece of him.

Six Weeks Later

"WE'RE GOING TO HAVE TO MAKE THIS AN ANNUAL THING," I told Conner after our pilot informed us that we'd be landing in a half hour. "I'm ready to be home, but also, I can't wait to go back."

We'd spent a magical honeymoon week in Turks and Caicos snorkeling on Smith's Reef right off the shore and soaking in the sun. It was lazy and lavish and perfect. I had a new golden tan heading into the rainy season back home and a blossoming appreciation for travel. I'd known my father took private jets when he traveled, but the rest of us had rarely left the city, and when we did, we'd flown commercial.

Conner didn't do commercial. After a luxury flight in his family's private jet, I could understand why.

"That can be arranged. There's a lot of Caribbean to explore, and next time, we hopefully won't have to fly on your actual birthday."

"This isn't exactly a hardship," I teased, my arms lifted to indicate the gleaming cherry wood and leather cabin around us. He and I sat in two cushy chairs facing one another, my feet propped up on his lap.

"Yeah, but this is your twenty-first. You should be out celebrating like every other twenty-one-year-old does on their birthday."

I grinned. "There's still time."

"Hmm," he mused, his azure eyes reminding me of the waters we'd just left behind. "I'd thought I'd wait until we were home to give you your present, but I think I'd rather do it now." He reached down into his laptop bag beside his chair and presented a small black box wrapped in a white satin bow.

My feet dropped to the floor as I sat tall with surprise. "We just took an amazing vacation; you didn't have to do anything else."

"Just open it," he said softly.

I untied the bow and lifted the lid to unveil a set of stud white gold bell earrings—a perfect match to my mother's necklace. "Oh, Conner," I breathed, my hand flying to the pendant around my neck. I'd worn it almost every day since first putting it on months ago and had told him the significance of the necklace when he'd asked. It never occurred to me he'd do something so incredibly sweet as having a jeweler craft a matching set of earrings.

I closed the lid and rushed from my seat to climb onto his lap, straddling him in the leather chair. "Thank you, baby. They're perfect." I pressed my lips to his. Conner's hands kneaded the modest globes of my ass, deepening our kiss just as the pilot announced that we'd be landing in fifteen minutes.

We both stilled, eyes locked in silent communication.

"Plenty of time," he growled, lifting me in his arms and walking us to the small bedroom in the back of the plane.

I laughed until the door shut behind us, and the room suddenly filled with Conner's domineering presence. He lay me on the bed, gingerly sliding my panties down my hips. The weather back home would be cool, but I'd stubbornly worn one of the sundresses I'd taken on the trip, hanging on to every last vestige of my tropical paradise.

In a matter of seconds, Conner was pushing inside me.

We'd had all kinds of sex in the days since our wedding. Playful, rough, dirty, and even gentle. Every time with Conner seemed a little different, as dynamic as his multifaceted personality. I adored every version, but this was more than sex. Our eyes remained locked on one another, every barrier tossed aside, and nothing but raw devotion pouring between us.

I'd debated telling him how I felt a couple of times. Admitting to the depths of my emotions for him. I'd talked myself out of it each time, but now the words came unbidden to my tongue.

"I love you, Conner Reid."

His movements, already measured and deliberate, stilled. He lowered his lips to graze over mine before locking eyes with me again.

"I love you so goddamn much." The raw emotion in his voice filled my chest with elation. He must have felt the same because it only took a matter of minutes before we were both shattering in a shared orgasm.

The experience was overwhelming and transcending.

I had to order myself to let go of him, and he seemed just

as reluctant to tear himself away from me. We hardly had time to get back to our seats before the wheels of the plane hit the runway.

I peered out the cabin window, hoping to calm the heat blazing in my cheeks. I had to be positively glowing. As we turned toward the hangar where the plane was kept, I spotted Keir standing next to a black SUV.

"Is Keir giving us a ride home?" I asked, surprised to see him.

"No, he called earlier today and said he needed the jet. He'll head out as soon as they re-fuel."

I grimaced. "Please tell me they'll change the sheets, too." I didn't think he'd be able to smell sex on the bed, but still. It just seemed icky.

Conner shrugged, completely unconcerned. Men.

Once the plane was stopped and the stairs were lowered, we stepped out onto the tarmac and froze. Keir was now holding an unconscious woman in his arms. She was young and beautiful, her long auburn hair hanging in loose waves over his arm.

"That the governor's daughter?" Conner asked casually.

"Yup." Keir eyed me briefly before pushing past and taking the woman up into the plane. No other pleasantries. No explanations.

I was the only one left to hear my husband's muttered curse.

"Well, fuck."

You got that right.

Thank you so much for reading *Silent Vows*!
The Byrne Brothers is a series of interconnected standalone novels—there are three directions you can go from here:

1. *Silent Vows Bonus Epilogue*
2. *Secret Sin* (Pippa and Bishop's story)
3. *Corrupted Union* (Keir and Rowan's story)

Read more about each option below.

Silent Vows Bonus Epilogue

Before you move on to the next book, make sure you grab your FREE extended bonus epilogue for Silent Vows. Five more chapters of Noemi and Conner that will leave you swooning!

To download your free copy of the *Silent Vows Bonus Epilogue* scan the QR code below or head to my website at www.jillramsower.com/bonus-content/

Secret Sin (The Byrne Brothers #1.5 Novella)

Pippa wanted a one-time fling with the charming bad boy Bishop Bohanan. But when he realizes he was her first, the possessive Irish mobster demands to be her one and only...

🔥

Corrupted Union (The Byrne Brothers #2)

Keir Byrne wasn't looking for a wife, but the governor's daughter is in danger, and a marriage would benefit both of them. The only problem? Rowan is already in a relationship with someone else. Fortunately, Keir isn't the type to let an unwilling bride get in the way of his plans…

🔥

Stay in touch!!!

Make sure to join my newsletter and be the first to hear about new releases, sales, and other exciting book news!
Head to www.jillramsower.com or scan the code below.

ACKNOWLEDGMENTS

If asked, I would say that my books in the past have been good, but *Silent Vows* marks the arrival of something truly special. There are several women who were instrumental in bringing about that change, even if in a somewhat roundabout fashion.

First, I'd like to recognize Skye Warren for organizing her Romance Author Mastermind conference. I can't imagine a more incredible learning experience—both in the realm of content and networking. The 2021 virtual conference started me on a journey of learning that led to this book.

Second, I'd like to give a huge thank you to Heather Hildenbrand for agreeing to let someone she hardly knew crash her RAM workshop weekend. Her wealth of positivity and generosity enabled me to get the very most from the conference. In addition, she was the one who encouraged me to read a book written by my next mention.

Last, but by no means least, I want to recognize the incomparable Theodora Taylor and her book, *Seven Figure Fiction.* With the explanation of a fairly simple concept, she completely changed how I looked at writing. It was a truly "mind blown" moment. I was even more delighted to learn after attending a retreat with her that she's not only insightful but also a delightful human being. Thank you Theodora!

My learning journey isn't complete, but my work progresses with each book, and I can't wait to see what comes next because with each improvement, I bring more joy to my readers, and that's what it's all about.

ABOUT THE AUTHOR

Jill Ramsower is a life-long Texan—born in Houston, raised in Austin, and currently residing in West Texas. She attended Baylor University and subsequently Baylor Law School to obtain her BA and JD degrees. She spent the next fourteen years practicing law and raising her three children until one fateful day, she strayed from the well-trod path she had been walking and sat down to write a book. An addict with a pen, she set to writing like a woman possessed and discovered that telling stories is her passion in life.

SOCIAL MEDIA & WEBSITE

Release Day Alerts, Sneak Peak, and Newsletter
To be the first to know about upcoming releases, please join Jill's Newsletter. (No spam or frequent pointless emails.)
Jill's Newsletter

Official Website: www.jillramsower.com
Jill's Facebook Page: www.facebook.com/jillramsowerauthor
Reader Group: Jill's Ravenous Readers
Follow Jill on Instagram: @jillramsowerauthor
Follow Jill on TikTok: @JillRamsowerauthor

Made in United States
North Haven, CT
08 June 2024

53389099R00200